PRAISE FOR LIA MATERA AND
STAR WITNESS

"You simply have to keep reading, just to see how it comes out."
—The Washington Post Book World

"Matera'a latest mystery is a hoot. . . . Peppered with eccentric characters, snappy dialogue, and a creative plot."
—San Francisco Examiner

"Lia Matera writes brilliantly."
—Cleveland Plain Dealer

"Matera gives her client—and readers—their money's worth. . . ."
—Chicago Tribune

"One needn't believe in aliens or flying saucers to admire Matera's gift of weaving her by-now incredible knowledge of the field into a tight, alien-dunit mystery."
—San Francisco Chronicle

"Santa Cruz writer Lia Matera has proved more than once that she is the master when it comes to dabbling in Northern California flakiness for her mystery plots. . . . She cleverly walks the line here between milking the material for humor and taking it . . . seriously. She teases. . . . Mystery fans . . . can't fail to be entertained. . . ."
—San Jose Mercury News

"I'm in love with Willa!"
—John Leonard of Fresh Air

"Say this for Willa Jansson: She doesn't shrink from the big cases."
—Kirkus Reviews

LAST CHANTS
Featuring super-sleuth Willa Jansson

"It's a treat to watch the normally levelheaded Willa crawling around in the woods, searching for naked gods."
—The New York Times Book Review

"The real pleasure is Willa, who alternates between humor and annoyance at her predicament—and whose love-hate relationship with men strikes a chord with many female fans."
—Entertainment Weekly

"Learning to tell the difference between the evil killers and the good weirdos is half the fun of this . . . enchanted mystery."
—San Francisco Chronicle

"Readers will find *Last Chants* an unexpected gift that will stay with them a long time after they finish reading it."
—Ed's Internet Book Review

"An intriguing plot, well developed with interesting characters in a picturesque location. *Last Chants* rewards a read."
—Washington Times

"Fortunately, Willa is back in fine form in her fifth adventure. . . . Matera has produced a first-rate mystery, exhibiting her usual hallmarks of excellent plotting, solid characterizations, and brisk pacing. A sure thing for fans and a great way to introduce new readers to an outstanding mystery series."
—Booklist

"Few writers possess Lia Matera's wry humor, especially when it comes to putting down lawyers. . . ."
—San Jose Mercury News

Books by Lia Matera

Havana Twist*
Star Witness*
Last Chants*
Designer Crimes
Face Value
A Hard Bargain
Prior Convictions*
The Good Fight
Hidden Agenda*
The Smart Money
A Radical Departure*
Where Lawyers Fear to Tread*

A Willa Jansson Mystery

HAVANA
Twist

A WILLA JANSSON MYSTERY

LIA MATERA

POCKET STAR BOOKS

New York   London   Toronto   Sydney   Tokyo   Singapore

This book is a work of fiction. Names, characters, places and incidents are products of the author's imagination or are used fictitiously. Any resemblance to actual events or locales or persons, living or dead, is entirely coincidental.

A Pocket Star Book published by
POCKET BOOKS, a division of Simon & Schuster Inc.
1230 Avenue of the Americas, New York, NY 10020

Copyright © 1998 by Lia Matera

Originally published in hardcover in 1998 by Simon & Schuster Inc.

ISBN: 1-4165-0173-8

This Pocket Books paperback printing May 2004

10 9 8 7 6 5 4 3 2 1

POCKET STAR BOOKS and colophon are registered trademarks of Simon & Schuster Inc.

Cover design by Michael Accordino

Printed in the U.S.A.

TRADING WITH THE ENEMY ACT
(50 United States Code App. 16)

Section 16(1) Whoever shall willfully violate any of the provisions of this Act . . . shall, upon conviction . . . be fined not more than $100,000 or imprisoned for not more than 10 years, or both. . . .

HAVANA
Twist

I often hear people complain about their mothers. But I'd celebrate if all my mother did was skewer me with advice and bore me with anecdotes. I think anyone who hasn't had to bail her mother out of jail cells full of demonstrators is lucky. Anyone who can guiltlessly utter a cynicism or consort with an occasional Republican is lucky. My mother once organized a petition drive to oust the man of my dreams from office. (Needless to say, that cooled the romance.) And she'd objected to every job I'd held since graduating from law school—except the ones that didn't pay enough to live on. Even now that I'm a sole practitioner there's no convincing her I'm not "holding up the capitalist structure." But the capper, as far as I'm concerned, was last year, when my mother flew to Cuba with a bevy of gray-haired *brigadistas,* then failed to return with them.

When fourteen sweet and unpretentious women dedicated to not hugging their children with nuclear arms filed off the plane, I could tell by their faces that something was wrong. Global Exchange and the Women's International League for Peace and Freedom had, by natural selection, assembled an ecstatic group prepared to bliss out on revolution. The women should have been flushed with the rapture of *connection,* they should have had that noble Dances with Revolutionaries look. Instead, they looked worried and confused. And members of WILPF rarely look confused. They are the Jewish mothers of politics, ready to chicken-soup the whole third world. So I knew something had gone wrong. But, foolishly, I thought maybe they'd been disillusioned. I thought maybe something had cracked their rose-colored lenses.

I should have known better. I'd accompanied Mother to an itinerary meeting filled with women who couldn't stop exclaiming about Cuba's excellent schools and health care, the warmth of its people, and the fact that no racial inequality existed there. My mild question about political prisoners provoked a temper tantrum about our CIA-backed press and the hypocrisy of blockading Cuba while maintaining relations with governments of torturers. I followed up—at considerable risk to my mother's reputation—with some particulars about a recently jailed poet. Until her sudden fall from favor, she'd been relentlessly trotted forth as an epitome of the Cuban spirit. Could a repressive regime produce a world-class poet? Castro argued.

"A perfect example of distortion by a biased press," one of the Fidelistas sniffed. "When we asked our Cuban hosts about that, they explained that since the U.S. is waging war on Cuba, certain things the poet did were tantamount to treason."

I let the war on Cuba slide. "What things?"

"Well, she was talking to foreign journalists." The woman's voice was hushed with disapproval. "She was leafleting."

Leafleting. Any woman in the room would run into a burning house to save her stash of WILPF pamphlets. Most would sacrifice family photos before they'd let their leaflets burn.

My mother poked me in the ribs. "You have to understand their context, Baby—their whole economy is being ruined by our government! They have a right to try and stop that."

Leaflets were powerful weapons, all right: look how WILPF's tracts had brought the Republicans to their knees.

Since that evening, I'd been inundated with alternative-press articles on Cuba. Mother's friends couldn't bear to have me think bad thoughts about the place. The regular press, on the other hand, was gleefully monitoring the collapse of the Cuban economy. See, it said, socialism doesn't work. Never mind that Castro's "final hour" had dragged on for a decade.

Anyway, the WILPF women did not look righteous as they deplaned—not a good sign. They huddled together, stopping short when they saw me. Also not a good sign.

"We had to leave," one of them blurted. "Because of visas and other commitments and things. I'm so sorry."

My first thought was they were apologizing for

not having defected. "Of course," I murmured. "Where's my mother?"

"We wanted to wait for her, we really did."

By now they stood close enough for me to smell their cheek powder.

"She's still there? Why? What's she doing?"

I was suddenly flanked, motherly hands on my back.

"We don't know. Last night she went off on her own and didn't come back to the hotel. We looked everywhere we could think of this morning."

Sarah Swann, the alpha granny, added, "Our Cuban hosts were so upset. They've made finding her their top priority."

I'll bet. My mother was not a cannon you'd want loose in a controlled society.

"I know you have some funny views about Cuba from the Western media," Sarah continued, "but, honestly, it's such an open society. The one thing you can count on is that there's no monkey business from the government. It's not like other countries— ones our government supports—where people get disappeared."

I sat on a hard plastic airport lounge chair. I was quickly going numb. My mother had "disappeared" from my life many times, getting arrested for pouring blood on draft files, attacking missile nose cones, blocking access to nuclear power plants, and, more recently, driving chainsaw-demolishing spikes into old-growth redwoods. My government was committed to arresting her, usually at her insistence. I didn't see why a foreign government should be more charitable.

I looked up at the concerned faces of women who resembled my mother: spry seniors with uncolored hair and intelligent eyes. I took comfort. Like them, my mother believed in the Cuban revolution. She'd see their militarism—anything they did, including jailing of dissidents and polluting of their coastline—as a pitiable result of U.S. policies. She would save her civil disobedience for her return to this country.

"No," I said finally. "I can't think of any reason for the Cuban government to bother her."

"Oh no! They're wonderful there, you can't imagine."

Unless you're a homosexual. Unless you leaflet.

But Mother would have agreed with these women. She would—for once!—have made no ideological waves. So where was she?

"The crime rate is very, very low there," Sarah consoled me. "If you're thinking she might have been . . . attacked."

The thought had certainly crossed my mind.

On the other hand, I could imagine Mother meandering off with newfound friends and missing her plane. In which case, maybe she'd already turned up.

At worst, how difficult would it be to find a pale-skinned blond American in Cuba?

Famous last words.

$\mathcal{A}$ll the airplane needed was a few chickens and goats—God knew it smelled just like a rural Mexican bus. It had less leg room, though; when I squirmed, the woman in front of me cried out. Or maybe she'd noticed the flickering light fixtures dangling from wires, the doorless overhead shelves unburdened with oxygen masks, the cardboard showing through thin seat fabric. Looking out the window at the plane's chipped paint and loosely connected wings, I considered getting up and walking off. I'd been considering it for three sweltering hours punctuated by the squeal of an engine that failed to engage.

Now and then, a man with a wrench wandered down the aisle. In the distance, to one side of the runway, another Cubana de Aviación plane lay strewn in fire-blackened bits. That fact that it had been left there troubled me. I was flying out of Mexico City; were crashes so frequent here that no one bothered clearing them away? Was it

Cuba's way of needling soft capitalists? If so, it was working.

Getting to Cuba (assuming the plane made it) was complicated enough, thanks to the U.S. State Department. Only those going for "research" purposes could fly from Miami; presumably academics could withstand Castro's mesmerization. And they had to be lengthily screened and vetted. Though a number of tours handled this aspect of the paperwork, none happened to be departing soon. I heard about a group leaving from Mexico City and hastily made arrangements to go with them. This had involved frantic Federal Expressing and faxing, and a horrifyingly expensive no-advance-notice flight that almost didn't get me to Mexico City in time to board (and then spend three hours in) this Cubana sweatbox. So I'd already done as much flying as I could stand.

Plus, my sojourn in the airport reminded me my Spanish ranged from rusty to embarrassing. I was born in Mexico because Mother had wanted me to be bilingual. And sometimes I was. But I hadn't been back here since college. Today, I'd been snickered at without being fluent enough to know why. Feeling inadequate rarely improves my mood.

Add to this the frustration of not having reached my father—with my mother away, he'd decided to sneak off to the San Juan Islands in Washington state. He and a flotilla of nerdy acolytes were working on a computer project with a physicist guru of whom my mother disapproved. Unfortunately "Brother Mike"—gurus, like rock stars, apparently can't use normal names—lived on an island so remote its phone lines there were currently, and frequently, down. An answering service on the main island literally had to ferry messages there in the interim. I hated to break the news in a terse note, but I'd tried without success to access voice mail and e-mail, so I'd had no choice but to explain the situation to an astonished-sounding operator. I would try to get through to my father from Cuba—I prayed with good news—before he panicked.

But as the Cubana engine engaged on perhaps the twentieth try, I wondered whether I'd even survive the flight. I looked around, gauging whether other fliers prepared to run screaming off the plane. In the seats beside me, a tall couple ignored each other as they scribbled in notebooks. They seemed to be about my age—mid-thirties—she with short brown hair anchored behind her ears, he with longer graying hair similarly anchored. They looked rumpled but sophisticated in khaki and cotton, and they weren't bolting. They weren't scanning the plane to see if any parts were about to fall off.

My other fellow travelers (so to speak) looked equally unconcerned. They were without exception too old to be cane cutters or graduate students. Some were Mexican, others might have been American or Canadian or European, somewhat tan, but not primped. They didn't look especially earnest, nor did they have the traveling-to-Graceland look of young socialists.

I just hoped I hadn't hooked up with the Hemlock Society, looking to Cubana to save them some trouble.

When we finally landed, I nearly burst into tears, I was so relieved.

The Havana airport was a low-ceilinged building

in the architectural style of campground bathrooms. While we waited in the customs line, the notebook-toting couple chatted to me about the trip. A small film festival had drawn the group here. They looked forward to seeing new films from a dozen Latin American countries.

So when the customs officer said to me, in English, "Films?" I nodded vaguely. He stamped a piece of paper and handed it to me—no mark in my passport to get me sidelined by U.S. customs. They were clearly used to Americans trooping through, embargo or not.

Luckily, the group's chartered bus was going to a popular hotel, the same one Mother's WILPF brigade had used. I saw no taxis outside, and was grateful to hitch a ride.

As the grimy old bus rattled over potholed roads, I could make out palm trees and low buildings that had seen better days. We passed billboards with smiling faces touting Full Equality and Social Security and Power to the People. Writing on building walls—far too even and artistic to be real graffiti—brightly advocated Socialism or Death. Occasionally, I saw the outlines of light paint over what must have been real, if cryptic, graffiti; 8A, it read.

By the time we reached Havana, I was sweltering in the sticky night heat. But it seemed appropriate to the scenery. The buildings were porticoed and hung with flowering vines, a vision of colonial splendor—except for a total lack of fresh paint. Even at night, huge pocks, blisters, and gashes of bare stucco were visible beneath old layers of faded colors.

And though there were no cars on the road, parking spaces around hotels were showcases of perfectly maintained American cars from the forties and fifties. I expected to find the Godfather sitting poolside with Meyer Lansky.

Others on the bus seemed used to the sights. They chattered in Spanish about hoping to find enough hot water this time.

The hotel, despite the busload of folks with reservations, had room for me. It asked to be paid in dollars, but the U.S. Treasury Department considered spending dollars in Cuba "trading with the enemy." That could get me arrested (ten years maximum sentence), fined $100,000, and disbarred, so I persuaded them to take Mexican pesos instead.

I asked the desk clerk, a young black woman in a cheap polyester uniform, if she'd seen the person I was here to meet. I showed her a picture of my mother, squinting crankily into the sun, her flyaway hair blown in wisps across her face by the ubiquitous San Francisco wind, her stretched-out sweater billowing.

The clerk flashed me a big smile. She leaned close to me. "She tries to give us soap! From her room, you see, extra soaps she has saved. We cannot accept." She glanced over to see a stern-faced older clerk watching her. "We have everything we need. She was mistaken. But nice, a nice lady."

Trust my mother to be offensively obvious in her attempts at equitable redistribution of toiletries.

Refusing a bellhop's offer of help (since I couldn't tip in dollars), I hauled my bag upstairs. My room was small, it stank of mold, and the furniture was decrepit. The sink was stained and the water was tepid. My mother had probably gone into socialist ecstasy, assuming the lack of luxury proved goods were fairly apportioned here. Myself, I'd have preferred a scalding shower and cheerier surroundings. But then, I always did disgrace her with my bourgeois longings.

There was no phone in the room, so I went back down to the lobby to call my father. I was told that the international phone lines were not currently available. Yes, there were pay phones nearby, but outside the hotel an international call often took eight or ten hours of constant redialing. I tried to look on the bright side—perhaps Mother had been trying to call home.

Feeling jittery and frustrated, with nothing useful to do at this time of night, I decided to take a stroll. I didn't make it out of the lobby before a man in a light blue shirt and dark pants stepped in front of me. He wore a badge that translated to "Tourism Police."

He flashed me a big, toothy smile. "If you should wish directions or suggestions at any time, or if—we hope not!—you are bothered in some way by anybody, you have only to find someone wearing this." He fingered his badge.

I supposed most tourists would appreciate this level of service. Trust an old hippie like me to get nervous at the sight of a uniform.

"We are here especially to help you, señorita." Behind him, potted palms cast shadows on oiled wood walls, giving the impression of an old movie set, *Our Hippie in Havana*.

I mumbled my thanks, then bolted. I walked a few palm-lined blocks to sea, passing other colonial-style hotels. I could smell the ocean—not the bracing air of the Pacific coast, but an almost fetid smell, the perfume of slime on rocks, of salt spray on unwashed streets, of fish in humid air.

A winding street was bordered by a thick, waist-high wall. Young Cubans, their clothes old and ill-fitting, sat or leaned there, talking, embracing, giggling. Groups of boys from early to late teens watched the street. A few were turned the other way, fishing.

I looked over the sea wall at the ocean, lapping against rocks ten or fifteen feet below. A voice beside me startled me.

"You are American!"

I hesitated. Unlike the desk clerk and tourist police, this young man was speaking Spanish, a very rapid Spanish with most of the n's and m's mumbled and the s's dropped. I tried to shift to the little-used portion of my brain that stored the language.

The boy moved farther from me. "They will pick me up if they see me talking to you. Do not look at me, look ahead."

"Who will pick you up?"

"Tourist police. They will not let us talk to Americans—very strict. They do not want us bothering Americans. Do you have any dollars? For my family? I will exchange pesos for dollars."

"I only have pesos."

He snorted. "Pesos are worthless. Cuban pesos? How did you get Cuban pesos? They do not let Americans have Cuban pesos. They have special tourist money for Americans. Is that what you have? Tourist pesos?"

"Mexican pesos."

"Too bad. Only dollars can buy you anything here now. Everything we have is in the tourist stores, and those will take only dollars. We Cubans can buy nothing with pesos. Dollar apartheid." He stepped a little farther away when headlights lit the street. "Only the police drive cars. No gas. All reserved for foreigners to rent cars and go to Varadero Beach to spend dollars."

I was surprised he'd launch straight into a lament. He had no idea who I was, after all.

"Tell me about America," he continued. "From this spot, it is only a hundred and forty-eight kilometers to Florida. If I would launch a raft, I would reach America in only days."

It sounded like a surer bet than Cubana airlines.

"I have a cousin in Miami," he continued. "If I could go to him! But the water is like prison bars. All of us at the Malecón"—he swept his arm to indicate the young people lingering along the sea wall—"we would be gone in a moment! What is there to do here? We are educated, yes, but there is nothing to do with it. We cut cane to pay back the state for our college, and then? Myself I am a most excellent guitar player, but you cannot play in a rock and roll band unless you have a license, and only salsa bands can get a license—the old men hate us *roqueros*."

"Could you slow your speaking down a little?" And put some of the consonants back.

But he seemed too excited to vary his pace. "In La Habana we have nothing. No entertainment, no books. Everything we produce is exported—sugar, fish, pork. And we are left hungry, with no electricity, no gasoline or buses, no computers. But the worst is that there is no soap. In this climate to go without soap—I tell you, if there is a riot, it will not be over food. Cubans are accustomed to be hungry. We make the coffee stronger and we try not to notice. But we will never grow accustomed to having no soap. If we riot, *compañera,* it will be because we are all sticky and cannot bear to smell ourselves!"

No wonder my mother had tried to donate some to the hotel staff. I was about to shift the conversation around to her, when he continued, still at mumbling double speed.

"Girls are lucky. They can go to tourists, old fat men from Venezuela and Canada, and trade for a bottle of shampoo and a night in the tourist clubs, where we are not permitted. They can have drinks and hear music, and come home with bags from the *diplotiendas,* the big dollar stores. But what can the men do? Stand at the Malecón and try to catch fish. Try to change pesos for dollars, and watch our lives pass by."

"You haven't seen an older blond woman down here, have you?" My mother would certainly have emptied her wallet of dollars, though she might have been troubled that the glorious and ongoing Revolution hadn't obviated the need.

"Many old American ladies here last week," he offered, in a helpful tone.

"Let me show you her picture."

The flash of headlights made him step farther away. "Tourist police. If you will put it on the wall and walk away, I will look at it and leave it for you. We can take our spots again after."

I pulled my mother's picture out of my wallet. Twice in an hour—that was probably as often as I'd done it in the previous twenty years. One thing about living near your parents, you didn't get much of a chance to miss them.

I sauntered off, attracting the curious gaze of neckers. They waited for the tourist police car to cruise past. Then one whispered to me, "American lady, you have dollars? You want a date? Go hear real Afro-Cuban jazz?"

A bicyclist zipped by, reaching out a hand as if—I feared—to yank away the handbag I hadn't brought with me.

I returned to my previous spot along the sea wall, and slipped the photo back into my pocket. The young man was a little farther away and to my other side now. Despite the fact that the tourist police had passed, he seemed reluctant to stand beside me again.

"Perhaps I have seen her," he said. "There are many friends here I can ask. But," he shrugged, "we are very desperate for dollars."

"I'll pay for information about her—if it turns out to be accurate."

"Then I will ask. I will ask everybody!" He flashed a broad smile, looking almost unbearably young and sweet in his sagging T-shirt and too-large shorts.

My first spy in place, I returned to the hotel. At the door, the tourist police stopped me again.

"You were not molested by the children at the Malecón?" His smile was pleasant and his eyes were like steel. "The youngsters here, they are happy to spend the nights strolling and talking among themselves, falling in love like young people will do. But in their happiness they can be, how do you call them, chatterbugs."

"No, I didn't meet any chatterbugs," I assured him.

Mother's WILPF companions had made a point of telling me they'd been free to walk wherever they wanted without restriction. ("Fidel wants people to enjoy his city!") But none of them, it turned out, had gone anywhere but the Malecón or the tourist zone of shops, museums, and restaurants.

Tomorrow, I'd try to slip out a side door to avoid the bossy tourist police, just in case.

I rode an elevator that smelled like a cat box and lurched fitfully up several floors. A grim-looking woman in a maid's uniform was just coming out of my room. I was taken aback—housekeeping service at 10 P.M.?

She stood looking at me. Then she held up a plastic bag of hotel-sized soaps and shook it.

Late night soap replenishment—oh sure, they had so much to spare.

But whatever in my room had been rummaged, it had been left roughly in place. There was a dead moth and a huge dust ball in the middle of my bedspread, though. I didn't think it had been there before. I looked above it. On the ceiling, a light fixture was slightly askew.

If this weren't the land of magical socialism, I'd have guessed a bugging device had just been inserted there. No matter. El Comandante himself was welcome to hear me snore the night away.

3

$\mathcal{I}$ couldn't face the complimentary breakfast, a buffet of old meats in congealed sauces. Luckily, a couple of cups of coffee as thick as black syrup took away my appetite. After trying without success to make an overseas call, I left the hotel by way of a door near a pool filled with shrieking Canadian kids. Tour buses resembling depression era Greyhounds were lined up in front of the hotel, loading people in for (I assumed) day one of the film festival. Only the rumpled yet elegant couple who'd been seated in front of me on the plane had a car, an odd, plasticky sedan I'd never seen before.

I kept my eye on the tourism police—several of them were present this morning, as the tourists were being herded. I slipped away, turning as soon as possible down a side street.

I imagined Mother strolling these neighborhoods swapping anecdotes with people on their porches, handing dollar bills to teenagers, kissing babies in their buggies. Surely someone would remember a motormouthed American woman bursting with goodwill—and with cash.

Within minutes, I was far enough from the hotel that no trace of tourism remained. The houses were crumbling old mansions, windows broken and doors unhinged. Peering into their gloom, I could see mattresses and bedding covering much of the floor space.

Passersby were thin, clothed in worn pants and shirts from the sixties and seventies. Not only did they show no willingness to chat with me, most crossed the street to avoid me.

I couldn't figure it out. Wasn't it natural to be curious about strangers? And with my blond hair and pale skin, I was clearly no Cuban. So why did everyone keep their eyes averted? Why were they so obvious about keeping their distance?

They were afraid to be seen interacting with an American. No other explanation made sense.

The farther I walked, the more palatable the hotel's congealed breakfast meats seemed. But I didn't find any restaurants. And the few stores I spotted were closed and empty, with blackboards listing names and marking rations. When I finally spotted an open store, the line outside wrapped around the block. People stood there stoically, looking too bored to talk. Signs read, "Flour tomorrow," or "Oranges, one per family."

I began fantasizing about cafés. I was fooled a few times by windows plastered with colorful posters. But they were invariably political slogans—Viva Cuba Libre! or Viva Nuestra Revolución Socialista! The initials CDR—Comité de Defensa de la Revolución, Committee for the Defense of the Revolution—and revolutionary posters appeared as often as ads in a U.S. business district. Which might explain why no one wanted to stop and talk to an American stranger.

I returned to the hotel utterly demoralized. Obviously I'd get no leads wandering the 'hoods in search of Cubans who'd befriended my mother.

I'd have to begin retracing her steps. The ever-energetic WILPF group had toured a hospital, a school, and a women's prison; they'd visited nearby beaches and resorts; they'd been fêted by the writers union and the film department of the university; they'd gone to a nightclub; they'd toured a cane field.

I would try those places, hoping Mother had mentioned additional plans to someone there. Perhaps she'd made a date or been given some suggestion.

If that proved useless, I'd be forced to begin contacting bureaucrats, both Cuban and American. The fewer political types on alert, the slimmer the chances of Mother's ending up under arrest. Given the maximum penalty of ten years and $100,000, I'd delay as long as I could. But eventually, I'd do whatever I had to, to find her.

4

$\mathcal{O}$n the hotel veranda, I encountered the couple with the natural-fibers traveling clothes.

The woman said, "Would you like to join us for lunch? We're on our way to La Habana Vieja, Old Havana."

"Yes," her companion added, "please join us."

"You've been to Havana before," I remarked non-committally.

"Oh yes." The man's tone was dry. In fact, everything about him looked dry. In the sticky noonday heat, I was wiping my cheeks. But his long face looked cool, and his clothes, though wrinkled, were unstained with perspiration. "This is our fourth visit."

"You're Americans?" I knew this from our brief conversation in the customs line.

"Journalists. With Associated Press. I'm Dennis, this is Cindy."

"Willa. Sure, I'd love to have lunch with you." Though I wondered why they'd offered, I could use a few pointers about getting around this town.

Cindy, her freckled face showing no particular emotion, said, "We're waiting for the car. We gave it to someone to park for us . . . trying to spread a few dollars around."

"Where are you from?"

"Mexico City for the last two years. We're off to Russia in a few months."

Dennis said something to her in Russian. When she frowned, he said, "We've been working on the language, but it's not easy."

A young man trotted up. The couple gave him a five-dollar bill. He looked ecstatic.

As we piled into the car, I tapped the body.

"Yes, plastic," Dennis said. "A Moskvich. It's Russian. They imported thousands of them in the good old days before the USSR collapsed."

"You're here for the film festival?" I shaded my eyes from the intense silver light of the midday sun.

"In theory. But the Cubans rarely give journalists permits to visit—in fact, we've never been able to get one. So we attach ourselves to groups like this whenever we can. We come in as Mexican tourists rather than American reporters." He frowned as he tried to shift a stuck gear. "Every year or so, unfortunately, we have occasion to write another story about how much bleaker the economic picture has become. Even last year there were a few cars on the road. This year, there's no gas at all for Cubans, only for us foreigners and our rental cars. Most neighborhoods have electrical power less than two hours a day. See the layer of black grime on the buildings? They're cooking with wood and coal now—dirty stuff."

Bicycles zipped by us.

"Chinese," Cindy commented. "Flying Pigeons. They've imported probably a million Chinese bicycles on credit. In return, there are Chinese military officials everywhere. We hope they aren't going to export their prison labor economy."

"Mm," the man agreed.

He pulled into a parking spot beside a stone plaza. We were surrounded by castlelike buildings with archways and pillars and porticoes and wrought-iron balcony rails. It looked like old Spain.

We walked through narrow cobblestone streets, alongside well-dressed tourist families. Shops sported signs in English, patio tables were spread with white cloths.

We sat at one of them. My companions ordered mojitos and lobster. Without knowing what a mojito was, I ordered the same. We were brought minty, sugary rum drinks splashed with lime. The air smelled of hot stones and trellis flowers.

"So," Dennis said, "what brings you to Havana?"

Cindy sipped her drink daintily, but her eyes were intent on my face.

I could trust them with the truth and try to enlist them as allies in my search. Or I could be wary of this couple who'd picked me up in a Havana hotel lobby. I was in no position to decide which was the better option.

"My mother was just here," I hedged. "She was very impressed with it."

"Did she come with a group?"

"Yes." Again I hedged, "ElderHostel, you know, old ladies on the go."

We were brought lobster so succulent and firm we temporarily lost ourselves in an orgy of enjoyment. With a second mojito in my hand, and a pile of lobster shells in front of me, I leaned back and surveyed the undercrowded plaza. The air was sultry and perfumed. Passing tourists looked prosperous and happy.

"Well," Dennis said. "We've got an appointment with the Yum King."

"Young urban Marxist," Cindy explained. "The foreign press calls them Yummies—party members with plenty of perks. He's an official of the Interior Ministry and soon to be a member of Cuba's politburo. He's got quite an air, a fascinating character." She watched me. "We're posing as movie buffs with a message from a mutual friend in Mexico City. I wouldn't miss meeting him for anything."

I felt myself stiffen. Was she inviting me along?

Instinct warned me to return to the hotel. But an Interior minister, soon to be a politburo member . . . maybe he'd be amenable to questions—general ones, of course—about missing tourists. Maybe, after some mutual-friends chatter, he'd be in a friendly mood. Maybe he could offer a shortcut.

"I don't suppose . . ." Danger, Will Robinson, danger. "I'd love to go with you."

"Well, having you along *would* make us seem more touristy." Cindy looked at Dennis.

And he shrugged, almost nonchalantly enough.

5

*W*e drove through a neighborhood of plain high-rises, fifties style, to a building that resembled a suburban grade school, low and L-shaped. "They never meet with you in their own offices," Cindy explained. "They always say they have business somewhere else, and have you join them there."

We were greeted in the nearly empty parking lot by a Cuban writer—a bestseller in the days when paper was available, he explained. He showed us into a meeting room with rows of rusty metal folding chairs facing a larger wooden chair. He seated us in the first row and offered us pineapple juice in demitasse cups. Dennis gave him a half-dozen pens and traded addresses with him.

Then the man Cindy and Dennis called the Yum King entered.

He had long curls that spilled over both shoulders like a Louis XIV wig. He was tall and pale-skinned, with an arrogant mouth and impatient brows. He wore a guayabera shirt, the four-pocket style often seen in photographs. His was starched and pressed, impressive for its blinding whiteness and seeming newness. And he wore a wristwatch and a pinkie ring, the first pieces of jewelry I'd seen on any Cuban.

He shook our hands, looking very sour.

"I'm so glad you could see us, Señor Emilio," Cindy all but gushed. "Martin sends his regards. He was so glad we'd be able to take home news to him. And this is our friend from the film festival." She didn't offer my name. "Martin was anxious to let you know his wife is having a child. And he wanted us to be sure to find out what's new in your life."

The Yum King nodded, as if Martin's interest could only be expected. "All is very well, tell Martin. The politburo has taken my advice regarding preserving our cultural traditions. And our literary community deeply appreciates Martin's support."

Cindy blinked innocently. "He does love literary people! We've been hearing rumors, you know. I know Martin will be glad there's no basis for them."

"Rumors?" He smiled ironically. "When are there not rumors about Cuba? What are we said to be doing now? Stifling speech—that's a laugh, isn't it? You have seen our brilliant and internationally acclaimed movies at the festival. The only impediment to speech here is the lack of goods occasioned by your government's embargo."

Cindy nodded. "So true. But you know how Americans misunderstand. The government gets so much mileage out of reports like the one about Lidia Gomez."

Emilio scowled. "What reports?"

"That she was attacked by a mob outside her home—a mob incited by the Interior Ministry to stage a repudiation act. That they forced her to burn all her poetry and that they dragged her through the streets and beat her. That you have her under house arrest now."

His eyes narrowed. "Where have you heard these rumors? Certainly not from Martin?"

"Oh no," she assured him. "Just at large."

Señor Emilio waved an impatient hand. "They are only rumors."

Cindy's smile was looking a little strained. "How do you suppose these rumors get started? I assume Gomez has been publicly complaining?"

"I suspect that foreign journalists have embellished and misreported for the sensationalistic conglomerates that run your so-called news agencies." He rose abruptly. "I regret that I have another appointment. Please tell Martin I shall expect him to name his new child after me." He smiled graciously. "Tell him I have not found the right woman yet, but that one condition of marriage will be that she like the name Martin."

Offering the top of his hand as if we were to kiss his ring, he gave us limp handshakes and departed.

Cindy and Dennis were all smiles and cheery, "What a lovely person," "What a nice place," kinds of comments—until we reached the car.

Then Dennis said, "Jesus, what an ass."

Cindy looked troubled. "It's worse than I thought. I wonder how bad off she is."

"The poet?" I asked.

Dennis explained, "If she were okay, he'd have

denied everything and told us to feel free to go speak to her. Of course, he would have had her spirited away so we couldn't talk to her, but he'd have given us the impression we could. And that we'd be satisfied by what she had to say."

"I wonder how badly she was beaten." Cindy sounded shaken. "I wonder if they've got her at home or in prison."

"Either way," Dennis mused, "it's odd he didn't go with complete denial. If we were really harmless friends of Martin's, we'd have no way of tracking her down. No way of checking up." He started down the palm-lined street.

"It's almost as if someone else asked about it recently," Cindy mused. "Maybe got the usual denial, then went and checked it out anyway. Like he was afraid the boilerplate would be useless."

I sat forward. I'd made a fuss about this very poet in front of Mother's friends. Had she inquired about it when she got here? Had she gone in search of Lidia Gomez, determined, as usual, to prove me wrong?

Dennis took a left into a neighborhood of unpainted houses, their plaster walls showing ghosts of former colors. "Let's see what they've got in front of her house right now." He glanced over his shoulder at me. "Do you mind a detour?"

"Not at all."

Cindy shifted in her seat to get a look at me. As if reading my mind, she said, "I should just tell you: We know about your mother."

I sat there, the humid breeze from her open window whipping my hair back.

"The boys down at the Malecón were excited about a missing American woman. They think there's a hundred dollar reward if they find her." She smiled. "You talked to one of them and showed him a blond woman's picture. That is, we assumed it was you. You're blond. And you mentioned your mother having come here."

I didn't know whether or not to admit it.

"Here," she said, digging in her handbag. She handed me her wallet. "Take a look—driver's license, AP card. I'm not a Cuban spy or anything. Just a reporter."

Her driver's license read Cindy Corlett, with an address in Houston.

Dennis said, "We're really here to try to get a look inside the tunnels."

"Tunnels?"

"Our last two visits, our contacts kept telling us about underground explosions, even an occasional sink hole. We did some snooping around, saw guards at an entrance on the outskirts of town."

Cindy looked excited. "The word is that they're building a labyrinth beneath Havana. The Cuban version of Vietcong tunnels, we assume. They're gearing up for an attack by America, either by the government, the Mafia—they want their casinos back—or the Cuban expatriates."

"You think if Cuba's invaded, Castro will go underground?"

"We think he's preparing to fight another guerrilla war," Dennis confirmed. "Vietnam style. Because we just don't have a track record of winning that kind of war."

"Slow down," Cindy said. "Better turn here so they don't see us."

She was looking through binoculars now.

Dennis turned the corner and pulled over.

"Chinese soldiers out front," Cindy said. "She's still at home."

"That's good, right? Versus prison?" I hazarded a guess.

"It might be good. Or it might mean she's in bad shape and they don't want her seen. Castro rarely has anyone taken away by soldiers—it looks too banana republic. Instead the CDRs—the neighborhood committees—round up mobs for 'repudiation acts.' That's supposed to make it look more grass roots. Of course, if you refuse to take part, they mark it down. It's not illegal, just like attending church isn't illegal. But you won't get a job if you do it."

"You said Lidia Gomez was dragged through the streets and beaten?"

"We heard the repudiation acts lasted three days, that she was kicked and beaten with rocks and sticks, and that her poetry was stuffed down her throat."

"If my mother went there to check"—Cindy turned, looking startled—"if she did something like that for some reason, what would happen to her?"

"Why would your mother do that? Who are you?" Cindy's tone was sharp.

"It's not who I am, it's who she is. She's a lifelong activist, she came here with the Women's International League for Peace and Freedom. But I . . ." I ran my hands over my face, wiping away sweat. "I was trying to inject a note of realism into her revolutionary fervor. I'd just read an article about this poet and so I asked her WILPF group about it. They got very hot denying it. And I guess I'm wondering whether my mother wanted to prove I'd been taken in by capitalist propaganda."

"How long has she been missing?"

"The rest of her group got home day before yesterday. She wasn't on the plane."

"You haven't asked any Cuban officials about her?"

"No."

Cindy nodded. "Just as well. You wouldn't get any information, and you could cause a lot of trouble."

Even Dennis was looking sweaty now. The afternoon heat was as wet as a steam bath. The streets were virtually empty. Our cheap Russian car smelled of inferior vinyl and encrusted dirt.

"Just as well," she repeated. "Cuba modeled its security forces on the very best, the USSR's, so you can bet they already know about this. But if you approach them, you make it official, you make it public. And you can't be sure what they'll do with it then. Relations between the U.S. and Cuba being what they are, it might suit them to accuse her of spying." Cindy must have seen the horror on my face. "That's if they have to come out into the open—I'm sure they'd just as soon not. I would really avoid discussing this with anyone else. That includes phone calls to the U.S.—they're always monitored by both governments."

So much for trying to reach my father. "What if my mother did go see the poet? Would she have been arrested?"

"More likely she'd have been turned away. Unless she really got into their hair."

My mother had racked up seventeen arrests for getting in American cops' hair. I hoped her regard for her foreign hosts meant she'd be more respectful here.

"Lidia Gomez might know," Dennis mused. "We're determined to try and see her—journalists are absolutely panting to turn her into another Aung San Suu Kyi." Burma's famous political heroine, under house arrest for many years. "But the car's going to attract attention. I think we'd better take it back to the hotel—the tourist police are probably keeping an eye on it. We'll have to set out on foot. Quite a trek, unfortunately."

"How about that Trader Vic's–looking restaurant by the water, the one where we saw Fidel last year?" Cindy offered. "Let's park there tonight—it's closer. They'll assume we're taking an after-dinner stroll on the beach. We'll see how near the back of Gomez's house we can get."

Dennis glanced at me.

"Sounds like a plan," I agreed. And God knew, I needed one.

6

The restaurant was a tourist fantasy of thatched roofs and plank tables, more like a theme-based mall chain than a slice of the tropics. But twilight did its best to fill the air with magical colors, and the ocean whispered over the sand. An Afro-Cuban jazz troupe drummed and danced its heart out, ruffled taffeta swirling.

They were the only Cubans in the place, since it was "dollars only." Every diner was pale, and every accent European.

After dinner, Cindy, Dennis, and I strolled along the beach until we were certain of being out of the public eye. Then we commenced something more akin to a power walk. Dennis was so fast that, at times, in the sticky night heat, it seemed more like a death march.

We cut through neighborhoods filled with dark houses, their doors open. There was no electricity right now. Nor did we see much candlelight—apparently candles were scarce. Occasionally we saw the glow of coal or wood burning in stoves. And here and there, bonfires were ringed with people talking and laughing, taking shots of rum.

Judging from the sounds emanating from many a dark household, there were plenty of babies being made, and also quite a few arguments in progress, especially among children.

Long after I'd had my fill of walking, Dennis motioned to us to stop. A light was visible in a corner building whose windows were plastered with "Socialism or Death" posters.

"*La vigilancia,* revolutionary watch committee," Dennis whispered. Inside, a man with a T-shirt and Fidel beard gesticulated to a Chinese man in an olive People's Republic uniform. "Her house is around the corner. Looks like they're keeping an eye on things."

He motioned us down an alleyway. Garbage was piled high on either end.

We walked along, trying to be silent, listening to snippets of conversations through unshuttered windows: *Were you able to get milk today? Did the school find a soccer ball for the kids? Did the doctor say the cut would heal without a scar?*

Finally, Cindy whispered, "That one. Over there."

The house was a modest two-story colonial, with bas-relief flourishes crumbling off its unpainted walls. There was no one stirring inside, no sound through window frames that were empty of glass but covered with chain-link mesh. Though there might be soldiers on the front porch or inside the house, none were apparent in the back. But the entrance was nailed over with boards.

While I gazed through chain link into what

appeared to be a storage room piled with broken furniture and picture frames, Cindy and Dennis conferred in some kind of couples shorthand.

"I'm lighter, but are you tall enough?" she whispered.

"We can always try the Brementown Musicians bit," Dennis replied.

The next thing I knew, Cindy was hoisting herself onto Dennis's shoulders. It can't have been easy or comfortable, but I was impressed by how noiseless they were. Did AP reporters routinely do circus stunts to get stories?

A moment later, Cindy slid down Dennis as if he were a fence post. She motioned me over. "Dennis is going down on all fours and I'm going to stand on his back. You're the smallest. I need you to climb on Dennis's back right behind me and get up on my shoulders. We're just a foot shy of seeing into the window. Can you do it?"

I wanted to tell her no, I am the least athletic person I have ever met, of course I can't do it. But Dennis dropped to his knees, and Cindy gingerly climbed aboard. Talk about peer group pressure.

Poor Dennis. I could feel the sharp bones of his hips. And poor Cindy, I almost strangled her as I hoisted myself up, using her cupped hands as footholds.

When I reached the point that I could look inside, I knew we were too precarious for me to spend more than a minute or two in this position. I tried to grab the chain-link window covering and steady myself.

The room was dark and quiet. There was a bed and little else inside. At first I thought the bed was empty and that the blankets were rumpled. Then I realized that a very small person lay there.

"She's here," I murmured to Cindy.

"Ask her if she's okay."

I stage-whispered the question in my best Spanish.

The person in the bed stirred.

I repeated my question.

The person sat partially up. I could see loose bandages around her head covering one eye.

"Are you okay?" I repeated. "We're friends. Are you okay?"

"Getting better," she said. Her speech was slurred, she sounded drugged. She seemed to struggle with the blankets as if too weak to push them aside. "Can you come inside?"

"We can't, I'm sorry. Have you had a visit from an American lady, gray-blond, very pale?"

"No. No one has been upstairs to see me. I think there must be soldiers below."

I could feel Cindy collapsing under my weight. "Tunnels," she whispered.

"What about the tunnels?" I asked quickly.

I heard her breathing grow agitated. "I don't know about any tunnels." But she sounded scared.

"Ask her about Myra Wilson," Cindy said urgently. "In the women's prison."

I did. But there was no reply. I repeated the question.

Cindy tugged me, letting me know collapse was imminent. When I got down on the ground, she had a whispered conference with Dennis while he held his back.

He lurched down the alley, still slightly bent, while Cindy held his arm and motioned me to hurry. We dashed the rest of the way down the alley, turning the corner. For several blocks, we walked as fast as we could, ignoring groups lounging on dark porches. I described what I'd seen inside.

We were several blocks away when, suddenly, lights came on in most of the houses. The din of televisions and radios filled the humid night air. From a dozen houses, I could hear a cooking show describe how to make tomato jam.

We picked up our pace, feeling spotlighted. But everyone had moved indoors to watch television and listen to radio. We could see children writing under dim lamps with stubs of pencils. Adults were reading so intensely they seemed to be vacuuming words off pages. Men and women jockeyed for burners of vintage stoves.

If anything, the electricity had made us less conspicuous. Still, we rushed.

"Who's Myra Wilson?" I asked them. "Why did you bring her up?"

"We've been trying to get someone to talk about her, someone disaffected enough to tell us something," Cindy explained. "Wilson's an American woman, recently arrested and sentenced to seven years for smuggling drugs. Whenever foreign journalists ask to see her, they get a tour of a model prison and a ten-second glimpse of her, long enough for her to tell them she's being well treated."

Dennis said, "Look, maybe we can help each

other. We've got the Moskvich, we know the island—we'll help you look for your mother, okay? And you can go see Myra Wilson for us."

"Me? How can I do that?"

"They're very intent on demonstrating they have nothing to hide. If you ask for it, they'll offer you a tour. But we're here on false pretenses, supposedly as tourists at the film festival. It won't take them long to find out we're journalists, and then it'll be no dice. They'll glue a minder to us."

"A minder?"

"Every group that comes here is assigned some smiling young man or woman from the Foreign Relations Ministry to guide the tour bus and take care of them. Minders—to make sure they see only what they're supposed to see—Old Havana, Morro Castle, Varadero Beach—and to keep them out of the neighborhoods and away from the prostitutes that supposedly disappeared after the revolution. And journalists, well, we can hardly take a leak without a minder beside us."

"Tomorrow we'll have to start going to film festival events." Cindy didn't sound happy about it. "A day of nontour sightseeing is one thing—we've been careful to keep up the right kind of chatter in our room. You do know all the rooms are bugged? But we can't do this again without attracting attention."

Though it was my sincerest wish never to set eyes on the inside of a Cuban—or any other—prison, Mother's group had gone there, too. It was as good a place as any to begin retracing her steps.

"If you'd just go to the women's prison for us,

just try to talk to Myra Wilson . . ." Cindy put her hand on my forearm. "If we find your mother, we can try to get her back as part of our film festival group, you know."

"That's right," Dennis agreed. "Scoot her through customs with the rest of the crowd."

Wow, they really knew how to dangle a carrot. But did they also carry a stick?

could hardly sleep for worrying, despite the fact that my muscles ached from the long hike. I tossed and turned, finally sliding into fitful sleep. I dreamed I was trying to get my mother out of a Cuban prison that resembled the San Bruno jail, where I'd spent two horrible and traumatic months in my protest-era youth.

I awakened with relief to intense daylight streaming through a gap in my mildewed curtains.

I went downstairs and lingered over a breakfast of syrupy coffee—for which I was developing a penchant—and a strange array of tomato dishes. A poster on the dining room wall extolled the tomato, *A special food for a special time*. I assumed this meant, the only food we have plenty of right now.

Knowing Cindy and Dennis were putting in an appearance at the film festival, I decided to hit some of the other places on last week's WILPF itinerary, starting with the hospital and the school.

It was a spectacular day. The sky was pale blue

and the sun cast a light so silver it looked like super-bright moonlight. I'd apparently slept through a cloudburst. The wet sidewalks glared, and vintage American cars gleamed like props on a movie set.

At the end of the block, I saw the boy I'd encountered night before last, the one who'd promised to ask around about my mother. He motioned to me, then walked off toward the Malecón. I followed.

Teenagers sat on the sea wall fishing with poles made of sticks. As I passed, they stared at my clothes.

The boy's eyes widened as I approached. "I waited for you yesterday!" he exclaimed. But he turned his back as if ignoring me.

I glanced over my shoulder and saw the ubiquitous tourist police approaching. I leaned against the wall as if ignoring the boy.

"You told the American couple about me," I complained.

"But they are your friends!" he protested, keeping his face turned away.

"Don't assume anyone is my friend, okay?"

I could hear him chuckling. "Ah, you are becoming a Cuban already. Isn't it very beautiful?"

"The ocean?"

"All of Cuba, it is very beautiful. If only the tourists would come back. We need the tourists—without them there are no nightclubs, there is no fun. We need the dollars. Without dollars we have only what the island can produce, and all of that, we export. Except when the boats are late to pick it up. Like now—I am so tired of tomatoes!" He sighed. "Straight ahead and so close—Miami. I have relatives in Miami. We all have relatives in Miami. The sharks know this, and they wait for us. Only the sharks in Cuba have enough to eat. And if the patrol boats get you, well, there is a jail in the east, *combinado del este,* they call it *bota la llave.*" Throw away the key. "If you go there, you do not return."

"I was thinking of touring a jail."

"No, no, they will take you to a model jail, not a real jail, not a serious jail."

No doubt in my mind which I'd rather see. "Did you learn anything about my mother?"

"There is a part of La Habana where the tourists do not go—it is not on the maps, only the tourist areas and the beaches are on the maps. There is a neighborhood where my friend lives. He has most definitely and absolutely seen an American lady there, on the very edge of the city, an old lady like your mother."

"When was this?"

"Monday."

The day Mother should have returned with her tour group. I tried not to get my hopes up. There must be a lot of "old lady" tourists in Havana.

"Can I speak to your friend? Can we go to where he saw this woman?"

"Yes, yes, I will take you to him." I could hear the happiness in his voice. "But we must meet someplace else. And can you perhaps cover your hair and wear something . . . not so fine?"

I was wearing jeans, a blue cotton shirt, and moccasins. I wasn't sure how much less grand I could look.

"Do you perhaps have plastic sandals? And a shirt without buttons?" he suggested.

"Okay. Where do you want to meet?"

"From your hotel go two blocks from the ocean and left for another three. There is a house with a broken pillar. I will wait for you there." He was smiling. It lifted the part of his cheek that I could see, though his face was turned away. "But I must have ten American dollars to rent bicycles from my *compañero*. Can you give me ten dollars?"

The real question was, would I see him again if I did? And was it worth risking ten years in jail and a $100,000 fine?

"The person who saw the woman . . . did he say anything else?"

"That she is very wrinkled. And she is wearing a shirt that says Computers for Cuban Children."

Mother's pet project. I tried not to get my hopes up. Any of the WILPF women might have worn that T-shirt.

"What else did your friend say?" I tried to sound calm. "Was the woman all right? Would she be safe in that neighborhood?"

"No, no, never worry. Perhaps she is robbed, but Cubans are not assassins. We have the greatest hearts in all of Latin America! Your country, it should welcome us. We get along with everybody. Well, perhaps not with the Bolos, the Russians. They will not learn Spanish, even the ones who are here thirty years. And they are very ugly when they drink. They build Soviet-Cuban Friendship Clubs but they do not permit Cubans inside. Good riddance to them." He turned to face me. "Is it really so hard in America for a mulatto like me?"

I was distracted, worrying about Mother, worrying about "trading with the enemy." "Sometimes, some places."

"They tell us ninety-five percent of the million Cubans in America are white. Here, sixty percent are black. They say the white Cubans want to come from Miami and turn back the clock, take away our rights."

I was out of my depth. "I don't know any Cuban immigrants. I've never been to Miami. Won't your friend take Mexican pesos?"

"His mother is diabetic. Only dollars will buy her medicine. I swear to you, you would be glad to help him. It is only for medicine for his mama that he would rent his prize bicycles."

A half hour later, after buying thongs, a T-shirt, and a scarf in the hotel gift shop, I stood in front of a decaying colonial house with a broken pillar. Though my clothes were arguably less "fine," passersby still looked startled by their newness. They averted their eyes, worrying, apparently, that an American could be trouble.

I stood there wondering what made the boy at the sea wall different. Why was he willing to talk, to meet, to help, when everywhere else his compatriots played it safe by crossing the street?

I grew increasingly nervous, sweating in the humid air, shading my eyes against the sunlight glaring on cracked and crumbling palaces, their porticoes sagging, their yards overgrown, their windows long since broken.

"Ha, you look much better!" The boy's voice startled me. "But still, your clothes are very new and your skin is very white. Only the Canadians and Germans are as white as you. You are like a nice fresh fish!"

A nice fresh fish or a lifelong San Franciscan.

I turned to look at him. I'd spoken to him only at night or from a distance of several feet. This was my first good look at him.

He was skinny and dark-skinned, his curls tight and glinting with reddish highlights in the sun. His eyes were huge and almond-shaped, a moss green. His nose was small and upturned and his lips were thick and sweetly grinning. He looked just out of his teens, with hands and feet so big he reminded me of a puppy destined to grow into an enormous dog.

In each hand he gripped the steering column of a black Flying Pigeon, walking between them. "You can ride, yes?"

"It's been a long time, but I suppose so."

"Then come, let us hurry. Somebody will go to the *vigilancia* if they see us together." As he swung onto his bicycle seat, he said, "Do not follow too close. And if I get too far, call for me. Shout, 'Ernesto, slow down,' and I will wait for you."

There were more than a few times I had my doubts about the endeavor. The bicycle was heavy and clumsy, with only two working gears.

In the part of town not shown on maps, where tourists never ventured, the streets hadn't been resurfaced in a long time. And the Flying Pigeon didn't steer well to begin with.

There were no cars on the road, though, so my wobbling progress didn't put me in danger of getting hit. We passed a few old models along the curb, highly waxed classics that looked as if they hadn't been driven for years. There were other bicyclists on the road, as well, but not many of them. Mostly, people sat on crumbling porches, their yards overgrown with vines and exotic flowers. Though I covered miles of ground, I saw only two small stores with very long lines outside. Those emerging from them carried only tiny bundles.

But even here, billboards with revolutionary slogans loomed over street corners. Political posters covered walls and windows as ubiquitously as advertisements in America. Socialismo o Muerte! Securidad Social! It got to be as numbing as Read People Magazine! or Breakfast of Champions!

I noticed a few hasty scrawls of graffiti: 8A. I made a mental note to ask Ernesto about it.

By the time we'd been bicycling for three quarters of an hour, I was no longer sure we weren't traveling in circles. Ernesto seemed, toward the end, to take my presence behind him for granted. I had to bicycle increasingly faster—no easy chore in toe-torturing thongs on a heavy bike prone to wobbling—just to keep him in sight.

And then he rounded a corner too soon. By the time I turned, he was nowhere in sight. I began shouting his name, as instructed. I pedaled to the next intersection, looking all four ways. All I saw were quiet streets with plants poking through broken concrete in front of the usual dilapidated houses.

All four showed empty patches overrun with bountiful, colorful weeds. They were strewn with cement blocks, empty barrels, and rusted machine parts. Were we approaching the city's edge? I bicycled to the end of each of the streets comprising the corner, straining for a glimpse of Ernesto, happily bicycling along, one arm dangling, like a big, happy kid.

I circled each of the blocks, searching for him. I returned to the spot where I'd last seen him, and I waited there, trying to attract less attention than a purple elephant. I examined the blisters the thongs had put between my toes. People passed me, but didn't speak to me. A couple of kids ran up and looked at my bicycle. Their mother, down the block, called them back.

It got to the point where I wouldn't have minded seeing the tourist police.

Finally, I climbed back on the bike and started exploring the neighborhood, going in the direction Ernesto had been leading me. Houses were clustered between empty lots piled with detritus and overrun with vines, as if houses had collapsed there years before and every usable portion had been hauled away.

That's when I saw it. I veered off the road as quickly as I could, struggling to steer the recalcitrant bike behind a jumble of flowering shrubs. I peered through the leaves. A few hundred feet ahead, machinery lay idle around some kind of construction site. There were no workers to be seen, but judging from the number of backhoes and trucks, something major was in progress.

A huge mountain of dirt had begun to sprout grasses and tiny wildflowers. A few broken beams, maybe eight inches square, littered the ground near a mound of rocks. Tin sheets were wedged tight beneath a backhoe.

Moved earth and makeshift walls . . . a tunnel? Cindy and Dennis had mentioned coming here to look for a tunnel system. Maybe this was an entrance.

I waited until I calmed down. I watched for signs of activity—the movement of vehicles, the flash of colored clothing or sweaty skin, the sound of voices. But all remained quiet and still.

I left the bicycle in the bushes and approached cautiously. But for a couple of encrusted coffee cups buzzing with bumblebees, some dirt-streaked hard-hats, and an olive People's Republic jacket, there was no sign of life. There was just a gigantic, beam-reinforced hole.

I peered inside. The afternoon sun reflected off a tin wall. Through swirls of airborne dirt that stuck to my damp face, I could see that the hole descended perhaps ten feet, its sides reinforced with stacked rocks, tin sheets, and wooden beams. Then it doubled back under the road toward the more populated areas of the city.

A tunnel under Havana. Maybe a maze of them. I stood there marveling, trying to see things from Castro's point of view—the assassination attempts, the Bay of Pigs attack, the periodic small-plane assaults, the relentless embargo, renewed media attacks and sanctions, the constant spying and threats. To build a network of tunnels, Castro must fear an irrational foe, an America crazy enough to invade outright after all these years.

Mother's WILPF friends might be taking a rose-colored view of Cuba, but seeing this tunnel made me want to sit down and cry. While its people starved, Cuba prepared to hide from us in case we attacked. It squandered scant resources trying to second-guess us.

If my mother had found this tunnel, it must have torn her heart out. And chances were, if she'd come to this neighborhood, it had been to get a look at the tunnel. I certainly hadn't noticed any other roadside attractions.

I wondered whether to go down. Mother would have, I knew that. But she had the fearlessness of a true ideologue. She'd have descended like some proselytizing Persephone, ready to sympathize and offer donations. Ready to discuss teach-ins and petition drives at home, to plan picket lines and letter-writing campaigns.

But who'd led her here? And why hadn't she made it back to the hotel in time to catch her plane?

Had something happened to her down there? Had she gotten hurt? Gotten lost in the maze?

Beams staked into compacted dirt created a toe-hold ladder for climbing into and out of the tunnel entrance. I didn't want to go down, I really didn't. Part of me was shrieking in dread: a secret tunnel in Cuba, no! Don't do it!

Perversely, I could also hear the lullaby my mother used to sing me as a child when I got frightened. No other memory would have been inducement enough. My mother had a real knack, even in absentia.

8

$\mathcal{B}$eing underground made me so phobic that I shut my mind to it. I would have nightmares for months afterward, but now I followed the tunnel as if it were just another tourist experience. And indeed, it was so quiet and uneventful it might as well have been. It was gloomy down there, but pipe shafts to the surface kept the air breathable and offered dim light throughout. Comparing the size of the pipes with the pinpoints of daylight overhead, I supposed I was about ten or fifteen feet underground. It smelled like moldy roots, the air was thick with dirt particles, and I kept imagining crawly creatures running over my toes. But I could stand with arms outstretched and not touch the ceiling or either wall, so it wasn't cramped. It might even have been large enough to drive a vehicle through.

I was especially reassured to see that the tunnel walls were reinforced with boards, corrugated tin, and heavy cross beams. I tried not to look closely enough to notice insects, rats, or other critters.

Frequently, wooden crates were piled beneath the

air and light holes. I assumed they were rations, perhaps weapons. But without a crowbar, I had little hope of opening them. Probably just as well—if I was caught, I didn't want to be accused of theft as well as spying.

On the other hand, I was growing so parched I might have tried to claw my way into any box labeled Agua. It was cooler underground than above, but it was more humid and close. I was walking in the dim light, fantasizing about San Francisco's bracing summer fog when I saw, up ahead at some distance, a wide shaft of light. It was too big to be coming through a pipe.

The good news was that I was at last approaching an exit. The bad news was that I hadn't stumbled across my mother.

As I walked closer, I could see the tunnel was less rustic here. Tin sheets covered most of the wall, there were twice as many supports, and it had widened into a chamber.

It looked like a place for people to enter and wait for . . . what? American bombs to fall? Expatriates from Miami to swarm the streets firing American weapons at uppity mulattoes?

I continued cautiously forward. The tunnel chamber widened to a kind of hub. Two more tunnels opened into it. Going to other such hubs? Leading eventually out of the city?

There were stacks of crates along every inch of the wall now. I could see the People's Republic stars on some of them. Directly above me, a shaft rose upward. Metal rungs formed a ladder leading, I presumed, out of the tunnel.

I considered looking into the other tunnels. But I was weary and frightened and my feet were bleeding from blisters between the toes. All I wanted (besides finding my mother and getting her home) was to be safely back in the open air.

I started cautiously up the metal rungs. The shaft wasn't leading outdoors—I was becoming increasingly certain of it. The quality of light was wrong. It was too dim, as if filtered through curtained windows in a room above.

I stopped, hearing voices. A man was laughing as another tried, it seemed, to imitate a doorbell. He kept saying, "*Dong, dong*" at different pitches, starting over several times. The other man repeated the dongs. But with the tone and accent perfect, it no longer sounded like a doorbell. It sounded like a Chinese language lesson.

I leaned my forehead against a metal rung, wondering what to do. Dozens of magazine and news stories raced through my head: Chinese prison camps, political prisoners, public beatings, Tiananmen Square, slave labor—I didn't want to deliver myself into the hands of Chinese soldiers.

What could I say to them? That I'd once had People's Republic posters on my wall—healthy-looking girls with thick braids happily picking corn for Chairman Mao? That I'd purchased the little red book from the Black Panthers just like everybody else? That I'd had as many naive misconceptions about the Cultural Revolution as everyone around me? The problem was, I knew better now.

I knew enough to be scared as hell.

"*Dong, dong. Dong, dong.*" The Chinese man laughed as the Cuban practiced the tones.

Then I heard the Cuban say, "*Que es?*" What's that?

I was sure, despite the fact that I hadn't made a move in minutes, that they'd heard me.

Footsteps sounded like drumbeats overhead. Suddenly there was a great deal more light in the shaft. More footsteps. I still couldn't see the opening. I had no idea what was above me.

"Time to get to work," the Cuban man said.

I thought he was referring to me. I thought he was about to yank me out of the shaft. Instead, I heard an engine engage. The Chinese man called out, "*Dong dong, dong dong,*" as the Cuban told him to do something vulgar to himself.

The engine revved for a few moments, then there was a scraping sound as of a door opening. It became lighter in the shaft. The vehicle rumbled directly over me—it felt like an earthquake—then drove away.

I waited a while longer, but I heard no footsteps, no words, nothing. I began to hope I might be safe, that the Cuban had driven out of a garage, and that the Chinese man had followed on foot. I climbed closer to the top. I could now see a thick mesh covering the opening, letting in air and light but leaving no hole gaping.

I was close enough to touch the metal mesh, close enough to taste a fantasy of climbing free. Then, suddenly, the covering was yanked off. I gasped, finding myself face to face with an astonished-looking Chinese man in a People's Republic uniform. He was square-faced and middle-aged. He barked out something in Spanish so tortured I had no idea what he was saying. Then he got a terrifying look on his face—his nostrils flared, his lips drew back into a snarl, his scowl was as exaggerated as a cartoon's. Worse, he was reaching for me with one hand and reaching into his jacket—for a weapon, I was sure—with the other.

I didn't have a chance to think. Nor was I in any position to bargain or to make excuses. I was an American woman in a secret Cuban tunnel. The Cubans weren't likely to be pleased. And I certainly didn't want to see the inside of a Cuban jail except, perhaps, on a guided tour. And if I appealed to my government to help me, they would probably revoke my passport and fine me, possibly even jail or disbar me.

All of that was in the back of my mind. More urgently, I was afraid of a frighteningly angry man in a uniform I'd come to associate with repression, imprisonment, and forced labor. My gut took over.

The man was reaching for me, and I couldn't let him get me: It was that simple. I grabbed a handful of his uniform. I don't know if I was trying to pull myself out or yank him off balance. I was just doing what I could.

Because he was after his gun (I think), he wasn't braced against the tunnel entrance. He had one hand down the hole reaching for me and the other in his jacket. When I clutched his coat, he lost his balance. He fell headfirst toward me. He knocked me off the rungs and we both went painfully through the shaft, clunking the rungs and sides all the way down.

I was lucky. I ended up on top of him. But he landed hard, taking his own weight and mine. He landed on his head.

I scrabbled off him. I could see that he was out cold, blood trickling from his nostrils and shallow gashes on his face.

I backed away. Had I killed him? Had I killed a Chinese soldier in Cuba?

I broke into a cold sweat. What would the State Department say? What would WILPF do to me at the next rally?

That got me moving. I went up the rungs so fast Spiderman would have been jealous.

I went up too fast to listen for the Chinese soldier, to decide if he was following me, to worry about whether he was stunned or dead. I climbed to save my skin.

I reached the top and pulled myself out. I was on an oily floor in a basement garage. Beside the opening was a metal grille, the kind that fits over crawlspaces and heating vents. I left it off. If the soldier was dead, perhaps his Cuban companion would assume he'd fallen.

The garage showed a row of small sedans with antennae sticking out the fronts and backs. There were also a few military trucks resembling jeeps. And there were shelves of radios, walkie-talkies, and flashlights. Gasoline jugs, jacks, tools, and other pieces of hardware lay in organized piles on the concrete floor.

I quickly walked through the dark room to a rolled-up corrugated door leading to another garage level. There were a few cars parked there, too, most of them up on blocks, with one or more tires off.

That room led to a huge opening flanked by a yawning metal grate. There were four Mercedes sports cars parked beside it.

I slipped through the open grate and dashed off. I was in some kind of business district. Wide boulevards curved past modest monuments and short office buildings. Palm trees lined the streets. The humid air seemed cool and wonderfully fragrant after my hour underground.

I saw a group of preteen children in school uniforms, and I asked them what these buildings were. One of the girls said, "Are you looking for the theater? You are looking for the film festival?"

I said yes, and she gave me directions.

It took me less than ten minutes to reach the theater, a low building with an abstract mosaic embedded in its stucco.

The tour bus was still parked in front. I waited in the building's shadow perhaps half an hour before I started hearing American, Mexican, and German voices in the lobby. Someone was exclaiming that the director got better every year. Someone else was saying the films were just a rehash of *Death of a Bureaucrat,* a shallow attack on didacticism instead of a genuine exploration of artistic vision.

I pulled off my head scarf and wiped my face with it, shaking my damp hair free. I rounded the corner as people began filing out of the lobby toward the bus. I recognized some as passengers on my Cubana Airlines flight.

A moment later, the tour's "minder" spotted me. She was a tiny Cuban woman in a print dress and low-heeled wooden mules.

She motioned to me, saying, "No, no, this way. We have just enough time for the farm. Come, come."

I asked her where the rest room was, and she directed me inside, telling me I must hurry. By the time I returned to the bus, I hoped I wasn't so smeared with dirt and perspiration that I'd cause comment.

A couple of people on the bus smiled at me, recognizing me from the plane. A couple more looked puzzled, obviously realizing I hadn't been with them on the bus earlier.

Toward the back, heads bowed together, talking intently, were Cindy and Dennis. Cindy stopped mid-word when she saw me. Dennis frowned and followed her gaze.

They were again unrumpled and cool-looking in natural undyed fibers. I dropped into the seat in front of them and said, "There's a problem."

Cindy said, "The minder will do a head count before we leave." She stood. "I can find my way back. Meet you there."

She walked up the bus aisle, scooting past incoming passengers. With her head bowed, she ducked off the bus right past the minder.

Dennis called out, "*Compañera!*"

The minder looked at him, startled, while Cindy dashed back into the theater.

"*Compañera,*" he said again, "is there time for a bathroom stop?" As he said this, he rose and took a step forward, disconcerting the people trying to get to the back of the bus.

The minder looked all too patient. "There is a bathroom on the bus, señor." She emphasized the word *señor* as if the Spanish version of "comrade" had fallen out of favor. "I think we should go now if we are to have time to tour the citrus plantation."

"Oh, right," Dennis said. He dropped into the seat beside me.

As people continued filing past, he pressed a handkerchief into my hand, murmuring, "You've got a bit of a scratch on your chin."

Bending as if to tie my shoe, I mopped my face.

"Luckily this is the first outing we've taken with the group," he said quietly. "Perhaps no one will notice you've gotten shorter and blonder. But after our visit to the farm, you may imprint to the point where you're forced to go to the rest of these things with me instead of Cindy." He grinned. "Which would please her no end."

"The farm?"

"We're going to a citrus plantation. Fruit for dinner, a little rum. To distract us from the fact that one of Cuba's greatest directors can't be with us this evening because he's under arrest."

"What for?"

The bus engine was revving now. Everyone was in their seats. The minder was counting heads.

"Last year it was still all right to poke a little fun. This year, with the tightening of the embargo, with the restlessness over no food or medicine coming in, well . . ." He shrugged. "This year El Comandante doesn't have much of a sense of humor."

All around me, I could hear happy chatter about the movies *du jour*. A slight breeze through the lowered top halves of the windows cooled my damp scalp.

I hadn't learned any more about my mother's whereabouts, but I wasn't in custody, either. I wasn't being interrogated. I wasn't looking at a choice between Cuban prison and American censure. Not yet.

I put my hand over my heart, watching the street, half-expecting a bleeding and infuriated Chinese soldier to rush toward the bus brandishing a gun.

Finally, thank God, the bus pulled out.

9

*H*ours later, when the bus dropped us off at the hotel, I saw Ernesto pacing back and forth across the street, all but wringing his hands. He seemed to be watching for me.

I stood conspicuously on the well-lighted hotel veranda for a couple of minutes, until I saw him retreat into the shadows of the neighborhood.

A voice behind me said, "Hi. I've got the car."

I turned to find Cindy giving me a can't-wait-to-hear look. She slipped past and headed toward the curb. I supposed she didn't want lingering tour members, and especially the minder, to get a look at us together and realize there had been a midday switch.

Dennis angled closer, saying, "Come on, we'll go get some lobster. Fruit may be all the locals get for dinner, but I'm still starved."

"Fifteen minutes." My toes were bleeding, my hair dusty and oily, and my clothes—well, I could only be glad I hadn't spoiled my "fine" ones. "Meet you down at the car."

But when I finished taking a tepid, low-pressure shower—a trickle splashing into a rust-ringed tub—their car was no longer parked out front.

I sat on the hotel veranda, enjoying the sight of palm trees swaying above streetlights. More than ever, I appreciated the magic of outdoor lighting. I inhaled the perfume of a muggy night and trellis-trained jasmine. I kicked off my moccasins and wiggled my blistered toes. I molded myself to the chair back, and I dozed like the middle-aged woman I was becoming.

I was startled out of a slack-jawed nap by a tap on the arm. A young man with a gnomish face and a ponytail had pulled a chair around to face mine. On his blue-jeaned knee was a tape recorder. He was hunched forward, apparently trying to charm me with a crooked-toothed smile.

"Hello," he said in English. "I am from *La Prensa Mexicana*. I am doing an article on the film festival. They say you are of the party. May I ask your opinion? Miss . . . ?"

"Don't use my name," I said, blinking myself awake. "And I'll be honest about the films."

In my postnap stupor, I was relieved to hear English. But then, I'd have been relieved to hear Mexican Spanish, every letter and syllable pronounced, and at a speed the human ear could process. I wondered if this man spoke English because I'd recognize his speech as Cuban.

"I may tape-record you?" Again he flashed me the big smile.

"Sure." I thought it would attract more attention to say no. When he clicked on the recorder, I said,

"Nothing I've seen so far has measured up to *Death of a Bureaucrat.*" I spoke confidently, parroting comments I'd heard on the tour bus. If this man was really with a Mexican newspaper, he'd throw specifics in my face, talking about directors and actors, quibbling with my opinion. No Mexican I've ever met has been able to resist quibbling.

On the other hand, if the film festival was a pretext, he wouldn't have a hell of a lot to say. And I would have established today's alibi.

"Can you elaborate on that?" he tried again.

"Another time," I said. I stood, stretching. Then I hightailed it back into the lobby.

I'd been stupid to fall asleep outside where anyone could jump me with a tape recorder and a trick question. It had been my fault. But what the hell had become of Dennis and Cindy?

I crawled into bed and tried not to think about it. I tried not to visualize the Chinese soldier lying beneath me in the tunnel, his mouth gaping and blood smeared across his forehead. I tried to ignore my rumbling stomach—I wasn't used to grapefruit and rum for dinner. And I tried to ignore the cramps in my legs from the lengthy bike ride.

Most of all, I tried not to worry about my mother. Nothing had changed, I reminded myself. She had left America a Cuba booster, and wherever she was, she was probably as sold on Fidel as ever. The Cubans wouldn't be harsh with someone whose cynicism and mistrust was reserved for her own government, not theirs. Wherever she was (I prayed!), she must be there by choice.

I felt like one of those parents you see wandering

the neighborhood at dusk searching for an hours-late child. My face must have borne the same expression—anticipation of gratitude at finding the miscreant mingled with determination to administer a hell of a spanking shortly thereafter.

As tired as I was, it took me a long time to get to sleep. I worried about my father's reaction to the message I'd left him. I longed to talk to him, to find some comfort in his voice. But Cindy was probably right: Overseas calls were most likely monitored by both Cuba and the U.S. Until I was ready to talk to government officials, I'd better play it safe.

I hoped I was doing the right thing. I fretted. I tossed and turned. It seemed I'd just nodded off when there was a knock at my door. I was going to ignore it—whoever it was could come back in the morning. But as the knocking continued, I opened my eyes to find that it *was* morning. The sun was streaming through gaps in the curtains, and huge dust motes were dancing in the light.

I climbed out of bed and opened my door wide enough to peek out.

Cindy stood before me in her cool natural fibers, her chin-length hair shiny and unfussed-with. She put her finger to her lips to warn me not to say anything. Then she beckoned me to come out.

I nodded, closing the door.

I was down in the lobby within fifteen minutes. I'd spent five of those minutes in the breakfast room drinking syrup-thick Cuban coffee, the perfect morning jolt. Espresso would seem watery to me now by comparison. If only Starbuck's knew about this stuff.

Cindy was sitting at a lobby table opposite a woman in a hotel uniform. Behind the woman was a poster of scuba divers in tropical waters dense with colorful fish. Brochures were fanned across the tabletop. Cindy was looking through them, saying, "Too bad I forgot my prescription diving mask."

When she caught sight of me, she motioned me over. "I don't think we have time to do a snorkeling trip today. Plus they don't have prescription masks there, she doesn't think." Cindy nodded toward the woman behind the table. "Weren't you saying you wanted to tour a hospital or something like that?" She turned so the woman couldn't see her face, and she mouthed the word *jail*.

"A hospital would be interesting," I agreed. "But I ran into someone last night who was telling me they have a model prison system. He said he'd toured a women's prison on the west side of the island. He said it was worth a trip."

If the woman behind the table found my request odd, she didn't show it. Instead she said, "Very regularly, people wish to tour our hospitals and our prisons. Our hospital supplies are limited by the embargo, of course, but we have distributed everything to take the best care of our sick and to offer the most humane rehabilitation to those in prison. We do not have the problem of people who make mistakes being turned into hard criminals like it is true in other countries." She smiled. "I am certain I can arrange a tour for you. But you will need a car. Unless your tour group wishes to go as well."

"We have a free day," Cindy said. "But I'd rather beach-comb or something. How about if we drop

you at the prison, and meet you back there later
with the car?"

"You would enjoy it, too, señorita," the woman
said to her.

"No, I don't want to spoil anyone's plans," I said,
"just book the tour for me alone. If you can."

"Of course." The woman showed a bright smile
and white teeth.

While she made phone calls, I whispered, "What
happened to you last night?"

"Interior Ministry people all over the lobby. We
thought we'd better decamp rather than have them
associate you with us. Something's definitely up."

"The Chinese soldier?" I assumed Dennis had
filled her in.

"Maybe. But I wouldn't worry—it doesn't sound
like he could identify you, not if you were wearing a
scarf." But she didn't look entirely convinced.

Within ten minutes, we'd gotten approval to visit
the women's prison. The woman drew us a map and
told us to enjoy ourselves.

We walked out of the hotel and turned right, away
from the ocean and the sea wall. We passed groups
of Cubans standing at a bus stop. They looked bored
and patient as if they'd been there a very long time
already.

"That was awfully easy," I commented.

"The credibility of the revolution rests on the
appearance of having an open society. But nothing
could be farther from the truth—the level of censor-
ship, the total management of the news, the restric-
tions on travel . . . So instead they've got model versions of everything—a model school with extra

supplies, a model hospital with their most innovative features, a model prison with well-coached, quiet inmates." She wiped perspiration from her forehead. It was muggier and hotter today. "For years, they secretly sold tons of seafood through Panama, exchanging the profits for under-the-table food shipments for the *diplotiendas,* the dollar stores. In essence, those were Cuba's model stores. The shelves were crowded with Cheerios and Tide so the tourists would think, *How bad off can they be?* Noriega's arrest was almost as big a blow to Cuba as the USSR's collapse."

The air was buzzing with bees as we passed tangles of vines overrunning a wrought iron fence. A group of girls in school uniforms screeched and giggled, brushing bees off one another.

Dennis pulled up beside us.

With a sigh, I climbed into the back seat of the Moskvich. I wished the tour were already over. I hated prisons, "model" or otherwise.

Miles of lush countryside lay between us and Women's Prison West. Dennis pulled over before the building came into view.

"Better if you approach alone," he explained. "Just meet us back here when you're ready."

"But—"

"We can't have our names reported to the Interior Ministry too often—it raises too many flags. We went to see the Yum King. Now we have to be circumspect."

I watched them climb out of the car. Dennis opened my door. I sat there a minute, not wanting to do this.

Finally, I climbed behind the wheel. The plastic-bodied car was the least responsive, crankiest vehicle I'd ever driven.

A few minutes later, I entered an area fenced with fifteen-foot chain link topped with razor ribbon and barbed wire. It was crawling with men and women in military fatigues, machine guns slung across their backs. Camouflage-painted trucks intercepted me. I felt trapped in a Costa-Gavras movie about a Latin American guerrilla war.

I talked to a uniformed woman flanked by Chinese soldiers. I explained that someone from my hotel had phoned ahead and arranged for me to tour the prison. In the distance, I could see a convoy of trucks driving away.

"We were told to expect two women. You have identification?"

"The person arranging the tour must have made a mistake." I handed over my passport.

She took it and left.

A few minutes later, she returned, handing me back my passport, and motioning me to walk with her. She looked about nineteen, with a thick ponytail and a bouncy walk bespeaking perfect muscle tone. We hustled through the fenced area, then crossed a parking lot with very few cars in it. They were like the small sedans I'd seen in the garage above the tunnel. Their emblems read Lada. Russian, I thought.

Outside the building, a woman in a more formal, light brown uniform waited to greet us. Her jacket had epaulets and ribbons, her skirt was tailored, and she wore heavy stockings despite the heat. She was round-faced and middle-aged, and she looked more than a little confused.

"I am the chief of the prison," she said in Spanish. "I am sorry I do not speak English better."

Beside her, smiling hugely and insincerely, was a short, dark-haired older woman in a plain civilian dress and grandma-style leather shoes, probably the best shoes I'd seen on nonmilitary personnel in Cuba. The warden didn't introduce her.

The warden began an obviously canned rap. "The prison holds nine hundred inmates, but we are fortunate never to be full. Just now, we have not even four hundred, the majority convicted of economic crimes which carry sentences usually of a few years' time."

We walked into a drab box of a building and up a corridor with a locked grille at one end. As she unlocked the door, she continued, "Over there are the conjugal visit rooms." The walls had vented slats six feet up so sounds from inside could be heard in the corridor.

She continued walking me down the hall. "And here is the infirmary." A room with four cots, all empty. "And the nursery for babies up to one year old." Another empty room, this one with a few cribs and play pens.

The warden sighed as if this weren't going nearly quickly enough. I knew the feeling. God, I hate prisons.

She walked me to another locked door with yet another Chinese soldier standing guard. While she unlocked it, her civilian companion continued smiling.

The door opened onto a corridor whose outside wall was made of cinder blocks with flower-shaped cutouts. The sun beat in, making bouquet shadows in the prison cells across the corridor.

"The women are working now. Sewing. That is why the cells are empty."

Each had three cots, a curtainless shower, and a hole-in-the-ground toilet.

It took all my strength of will not to visualize myself in there.

We rounded a corner and entered a big room that smelled of steam irons and hot fabric. "This is the workroom," the warden said.

At the back of the room, two guards, one Cuban and one Chinese, stood impassively watching.

The room was about fifty feet long, with several rows of old-fashioned sewing machines. Perhaps forty inmates were sewing dolls or purses or dirndl pants. A few cast listless glances at us.

I was surprised. Surely the sight of someone new would arouse curiosity in an environment of sameness and dull stitchery?

In the San Bruno Jail, where an antiwar protest had landed me for two long months, the warden had forced us to sew curtains, endless blue curtains, for some purpose I never learned. With every stitch, frustration had wound me tighter. I'd been a slave, and I'd hated it. And I'm sure I'd never looked as passive and incurious as these women.

They were drugged, I was sure of it. And God knew what life was like for the hundreds of prisoners not on display today. And for the prisoners not in showcase jails.

Standing beside the sewing machine closest to me, one young woman was doing virtually nothing. She wasn't cutting anything out, she was just handing another woman fabric. She looked flushed, upset, and embarrassed. Her skin was European pale, and her hair, once bleached, had an inch of dark root showing. She was clearly on display and just as clearly hated it.

It had to be Myra Wilson. The prison must have assumed I'd come here to check on the American. I supposed American journalists trooped through regularly to make sure she was all right.

She glanced at me with a glint of tears in her eyes. She continued handing fabric to the other woman.

The warden stopped in front of her. "Are you well today, Myra?"

The woman nodded. Then, because she seemed to know it was expected of her, she lifted her chin and said to me, "I have six and three quarters years left in my sentence. I tried to smuggle cocaine, which isn't tolerated. Drug use isn't tolerated here." Her voice was high-pitched and girlish.

"Where are you from?" I asked her.

A slight frown. "Jersey City."

"Great town," I said. The warden was motioning me to come along, but I persisted. "You ever eat at June's Diner? A relative of mine owns it, a blond woman in her sixties."

"No." She kept her eyes averted, smiling slightly. "But I used to cook for Ernest Hemingway."

A Chinese soldier stalked up, glowering at her.

The warden said, "There is no conversation during work hours." Her companion smiled and nodded. "Or no work would get done. With four hundred women, you understand that gossip can be an enemy of productivity."

The smiling woman moved to my other side to block my view of Myra Wilson. I heard Wilson sigh when I walked away. Ernest Hemingway? What could she have meant by that?

We continued through the sewing room, where more young women worked listlessly without looking up. The warden was saying, "It is true that Cuba has no tolerance for drugs. We have refused to become a stopping place between Colombia and Florida!"

The warden took me downstairs to her office, which opened into a courtyard ringed with thriving schefflera plants three stories tall, their broad leaves glistening in the sun.

She offered me coffee, which I drank quickly and gratefully, pretending to admire the plants while I took stock. The building was four stories and built to house nine hundred.

I'd seen ten cells and a workroom containing no more than forty women. Where were the rest of the inmates?

It was all I could do to suppress a shudder. It was all I could do, recalling my two months behind a sewing machine, not to cry.

I was hot and cross and tired. And what had I really learned?

I was relieved, when we walked through the fenced area, to see the Moskvich right where I'd left it.

Five minutes down the road, I was even more relieved to find Dennis and Cindy waiting.

"Any luck?" Cindy asked.

I climbed into the back, gratefully relinquishing

the wheel to Dennis. "Myra Wilson looks miserable. She gave me a set speech, obviously memorized."

"About how Cuba doesn't tolerate drugs?"

"That's right. I mentioned my mother's name to her. I said it was the name of a restaurant in her hometown. I asked if she'd ever eaten there."

Dennis grinned, looking at me. It hardly mattered if his eyes left the road. Ours was the only car in sight. "Did they give her a chance to say anything?"

"The guards were on her right away. But she did say, 'I used to cook for Ernest Hemingway.' "

They exchanged glances.

"Do you know what she meant?"

"Ernest Hemingway's house is here on the island," Dennis offered. "He lived here in the forties and fifties. The place is a museum now."

"I wonder if that's what she meant." But Cindy didn't sound as if she wondered. "Association of ideas or something."

Dennis mused, "I wonder if it's an Ochoa situation?"

"That's what I was just thinking," Cindy agreed.

"What's Ochoa?" It sounded more like a plant than a predicament.

"He was a member of Castro's original revolutionary cadre. He led Cuba's army all around the world, Nicaragua, Zaire, Angola, you name it. He was wildly popular with his troops. Castro leaves it to his generals to finance his foreign wars—he can't be bothered with details. So Ochoa used to export natural resources, ivory and diamonds in Angola, for instance, to maintain and supply his troops. After Angola, Ochoa came back to Havana and started pushing for better treatment of veterans—fifty thousand of them hit the streets with no jobs waiting, no pensions, nothing—Angola was Cuba's Vietnam. People wanted to believe Ochoa could do for all of Cuba what he'd always done for his soldiers— namely, get them food and fuel and basic amenities."

The air was cooling down, and lush roadside plants caught the evening sun, their exotic fronds and blooms glowing. Above fields of six-foot grasses and shrubs, tiny insects sparkled like sequins.

"So?" I prompted.

"So meanwhile high-ranking officers in the Interior Ministry had been doing exactly that: making drug deals to pull in enough money to keep Cuba afloat. Remember, the USSR had been subsidizing Cuba to the tune of about four billion dollars a year. When that dried up, well, they had to do *something*. But when the U.S. got wind of it, Castro had to choose between loyalty to his ministers and a reputation for being antidrug. He had to choose between the Revolutionary Idea and the cash to make it work."

"I gather he remained ideologically pure?" It didn't look to me as though there'd been an infusion of money here recently.

"When Castro arrested the Interior Ministry people, he pulled in Ochoa, too. But Ochoa was old guard, what they call an *histórico*. He wasn't one of the Rolex-wearing, drug-trafficking, world-traveling Yummies from Interior. He didn't line his own pockets like they did. And Castro knew it. He was afraid of Ochoa's popularity and charisma. Ochoa supported perestroika and glasnost, a loosening of the communist chokehold, which the people favored but Fidel absolutely opposed. So Fidel had him put before a firing squad on trumped-up drug charges. After his execution, there was a moment when we thought there might be riots here. Even after all these years, you still see the graffiti."

Graffiti? I'd only seen 8A. "Eight is *ocho* in Spanish," I realized. "*Ocho*-A, Ochoa."

"You've seen it, then. The people are bitter—they think Fidel didn't want them to have the freedom and goods Ochoa would have brought them. That Fidel couldn't bear anyone to be more popular than he was. He executed a Hero of the Revolution, someone who'd fought beside him like a brother, like Abel beside Cain."

"Why does this remind you of Myra Wilson?"

"Virtually everything that goes on here is authorized—not always legal, but authorized," Cindy offered. "So how would an American go about smuggling drugs in a fishbowl like this? She'd have to be working with someone in Interior. Either that or the drug charge was a pretext."

"And like Ochoa," Dennis finished her thought, "Wilson's being punished for something else entirely."

10

Cindy and Dennis dropped me off at the sea wall so I could return to the hotel on foot, as if returning from a solitary walk. They had to hustle off to a film-festival event—an evening of what they described as the Cuban version of lounge singing. The whole group would be there drinking rum and singing "Guantanamera," so they felt they should show their faces.

That was fine with me. As usual, I wanted to be alone. In fact, I was in no hurry to return to the hotel. I moseyed along the Malecón, watching young Cuban couples kiss and grope in the darkness.

All of a sudden, I heard Ernesto's voice, "I was insane with fear for you, *señora!*"

I turned to see him standing at a distance of about ten feet, leaning against the wall as if looking out to sea.

"You lost me on purpose," I snapped. "You sped up without any reason."

"No, no, I swear to you! I became distracted only for a few moments, and then I could not find you. My *compañero* is ready to tear away my skin because his bicycle is lost. For his sake, you will tell me where you left the bicycle? Please?"

"I have no idea where I was." I dug in my pocket, pulling out a twenty. From what I'd seen, that would be a huge sum here. "Tell your *compañero* to buy himself a new bicycle. And bring your friend, the one who saw the American woman, bring him here. Have him meet me at the Malecón."

I walked away, wondering whether he would. Wondering whether, instead, he'd take the twenty and stay away.

Before I reached the hotel, I paused. My mother would have been a sucker for a kid like this. She'd have emptied her pocketbook and wandered anywhere with him.

I was still feeling disturbed and mistrustful—part of the Cuban tourism experience—when I wandered into the hotel lobby and was immediately confronted by last night's "reporter" with the tape recorder. He stood before me, full attention on my face. His hair was pulled into a tight ponytail, so curly it looked like a rabbit's tail. His skin was grainy, with a grayish cast. He stank of tobacco.

When he smiled, he looked like he was going to try to take a bite out of me. "I was hoping to escort you to the evening of *boleros*."

"I'm not feeling well. I'm going to skip it."

He stepped closer. It was all I could do not to recoil. "Oh no, you must not miss it!" Then, in a more conversational tone, he added, "These are the finest singers in all of Cuba." There was a coy lilt to his voice.

I noticed his tape recorder hanging by his side. Was it turned on?

He tried again. "There will be many reporters there anxious to hear your opinion of the films." As if he thought that would be a turn-on.

"I'm sorry, I'm just too tired."

"There will be in particular one from Radio Havana. His English is very excellent, much more than mine."

Did he really think I'd change my mind in order to hear excellent English? It wasn't like I'd been away from home a long time.

I smiled pleasantly, no easy feat, and tried to step around him.

"You must meet the reporter from Radio Havana," the man insisted. "He is very good with Americans."

"Look, I'm just—"

"With American women. Blond women of more advanced years."

For a second, I took offense. Thirty-seven is hardly "advanced years." Then his words sank in.

"Like members of the Women's International League for Peace and Freedom? Women like that?"

He nodded. "His English is very excellent to speak with women like that, yes. I think you would be very happy to meet him. His English is most excellent."

I looked at him, my skin literally crawling with mistrust. But he was making it as plain as he could in this crowded lobby. The Radio Havana reporter wanted to talk to me about my mother.

I said, "Let me go upstairs and change my clothes. I'll meet you back here in fifteen minutes."

He nodded, turning away and walking out.

I hurriedly washed up and changed into clean clothes. But when I went downstairs, the reporter—or whoever he was—was nowhere in sight. I waited in the lobby for a while. I considered going back up to my room.

Finally, I asked the desk clerk if she knew where the film festival group had gone.

She looked almost wistful, as if she would happily take my place at the event. She gave me directions to a nearby hotel. "Very deluxe," she assured me.

The very deluxe hotel was, luckily, within walking distance. It looked like a cement box. Its lobby was only a little too clean to pass for an American flophouse. A man at a podium asked what my business was.

When I told him, he handed me a piece of paper with a prestamped floor number. I thought it was odd he didn't just tell me, but I took it around the corner to the elevator.

I punched the button and almost leaped with fear to hear the loud creaking and grinding in the shaft. When the door jerked open, an elevator operator in an organ-grinder's monkey suit held out his hand. I wondered whether he wanted a tip.

In rather labored English, he asked for my elevator pass. I handed him the slip of paper I'd been given. Jeez, an elevator pass. To keep out Cubans trying to sneak into a tourists-only nightclub?

The minute I stepped off the elevator, I knew I was going to have a rotten time. I was tired, unsociable, unwilling to elbow through the crowd spilling through the nightclub doors. And the music, though enthusiastically received by a roomful of people singing happily along, was not very hip. Through the doors, I could see a long U-shaped bar with a small stage at the center. Under colored lights, a heavy woman with a bubble hairstyle and two guitar-playing older men were crooning a sentimental ballad.

The U-shaped bar was crowded, every stool was occupied, and people were standing between them. There were small tables all around, equally crowded. Where there was room, people danced. I noticed several scantily dressed Cuban girls with older tourists.

I didn't want to go inside. If I could endure the cigarette smoke out here, perhaps the Havana Radio guy would spot me. If he really was here.

Almost immediately, I became aware of a light-haired man with an Andy Gibb haircut making his way toward me. In his white sportcoat and new blue jeans, he looked like a trendy European ready for a disco evening.

He said, "May I ask five minutes of your time?"

"Radio Havana?"

He nodded, taking my elbow and steering me through knots of people to a corner near the elevator. Inside, people were cheering and stomping and whistling out their appreciation. The club obviously didn't water the rum.

He leaned close to my ear. "Let me speak plainly. We have a very bad situation, you see. A situation in which a certain . . . involving the return to you of something you have been most desirous of finding."

I instinctively grabbed the sleeve of his jacket to ensure he'd stay with me until he finished his thought.

"It is to no one's advantage for this . . . to remain

lost. But we would be most interested in your assurance that further discussion could be accomplished in strictest confidence. And that this confidence would continue to be maintained indefinitely, for the equal benefit of all parties."

I wondered if this guy was a Cuban lawyer.

"My only agenda is to find what I've been looking for," I assured him. "Period. I have absolutely no desire to talk to anyone at all about it, ever. I just want to make this as short a trip as possible."

His frown made it clear he didn't think it would be quite so simple. It suddenly occurred to me that the problem might be my mother. Maybe the Cubans didn't trust her to shut up about something. Maybe they didn't want to let her go without some guarantee.

"I have enough influence," I lied, "to make my wishes prevail." Like hell.

But I'd worry about that later. With our passports and my law degree at stake, I'd lock Mother in a soundproof room if I had to.

"Really," I said. "I just want to make our mutual problems go away." I stressed the last two words. People often responded favorably to the notion of my mother going away.

I wanted to ask a hundred questions, make a thousand promises, jump through hoops, shower him with American dollars—anything to get this done.

I forced myself to calm down and slow down. No use being tricked into confessing some crime. I didn't want to find myself sitting at a sewing machine beside Myra Wilson, wondering how my statements had been misconstrued.

With an uncertain glance at me, he said, "Come."

He took my elbow and guided me into the elevator, just now disgorging a giggling group.

It wouldn't be the first time I'd left a bar with a guy with a bad haircut. I just wished I could remember a time I hadn't regretted it.

When we got off at the ground floor, he looked around the lobby, his eyes large and, I thought, fearful. He put a hand between my shoulder blades, barely touching me. But the gesture was so proprietary I almost bridled.

We left the hotel. He looked over his shoulder. "Just around the corner, please, we can talk."

We walked quickly into a well-lighted town square with lots of trees and benches. It was bordered by tourist hotels and dollar stores.

Even at night, the ice-cream stand in the middle of the square had a line blocks long.

My companion scanned the square, apparently reassured we hadn't been followed. "Let me speak more plainly. We would like to conclude this matter without incident." He looked like he was choosing his words carefully. "But there is a slight problem requiring discussion."

I waited.

"Your companions."

"Which companions?"

"Mr. Jamieson and Mrs. Travolta. From your seeya."

"Who? My what?" I was starting to feel stoned. My surroundings were strange, and he wasn't making any sense.

"Your seeya. C.I.A. Cia." He pronounced it as a word, not as letters in an acronym.

I backed up a step. "No, trust me, I don't know anybody in the CIA. I really don't."

He pulled photographs from his pocket. "Garrett Jamieson and Angela Travolta," he said.

He handed me small color photos of Dennis and Cindy.

I looked back up at him, mystified. "You have their names wrong. And they're just . . ." I didn't want to say, journalists. "Film reviewers, here for the film festival. And they're not my companions, I just met them. They're Americans with a car. I've gotten a couple of rides with them, that's all."

Oh Jesus, what if he was right? What if Dennis and Cindy were CIA agents?

I handed him back the photos. "They can't be CIA agents—you'd never have let them into the country if they were. Would you?"

"Oh yes." He nodded emphatically. "For various reasons. Not every tourist is who he seems. We are aware of this. But we are an open society," he said, raising my hackles. "Willing to open our doors too wide rather than not wide enough. You have found this to be true, have you not? You have wished to see a prison, and it was no problem, you were not denied access nor were excuses made to keep you away."

I had toured selected areas of a model facility. I'd hardly call that opening the doors wide. But I said, "Yes, and thank you. But—"

"Even known Cia agents, perhaps they will learn to respect our openness, this is our goal. We wish only to survive as your neighbor without interference and sabotage. But of course we keep track of where the Cia goes and what it does. We cannot take foolish risks."

Oh Jesus, I'd hooked up with a couple who, CIA or not, had been watched and followed every minute. Unless this disco-haircut stranger was lying to me.

"What do you want?" I knew I sounded hostile—hell, I felt hostile. "I thought you had . . ." I didn't want to say "my mother." I was losing hope very damn fast.

"We wish to help you, as you no doubt wish to help us." He sounded anything but convinced of this. "But we have certain pressures. You must understand our history, how many attacks we have suffered and how much adversity has been unfairly thrust upon us." He leaned closer. I could smell rum on his breath. "It is difficult to deal fairly with another when that person will not deal fairly in return."

I felt like I was trapped in a bad movie, *The Endless Preface.* "So what are you saying?"

"We propose an arrangement to trade information, in exchange for the information you wish to receive from us."

"And that would be?" But I was afraid I knew.

"We would like to know what Mr. Jamieson and Mrs. Travolta are doing here. Not their excuse, but their objective."

"First of all, you've misidentified them. But even if you hadn't, why would they tell me anything? I just met them." God, if they were CIA agents, I might as well kiss my passport good-bye right now. "Can't you just bug their rooms or something?" Like they hadn't thought of it.

But he didn't seem to be listening. He was looking over my shoulder. Without another word, he walked past me, hurrying across the square.

"What the—" I started after him.

Then I heard someone calling my name.

It was Cindy. She and Dennis were trotting toward me.

No wonder Andy Gibb had fled.

I wasn't sure whether to chase after him—did he really know where my mother was? But as Cindy and Dennis drew closer, I realized he wouldn't say any more now, not with "CIA agents" close at hand.

But it was hard to stand still, hard to watch my best potential source of information get lost in the ice-cream-eating crowd.

"Are you all right?" Dennis looked alarmed. "Do you know who that was?"

I shook my head. No use volunteering anything.

"He acts as a liaison between the Interior Ministry crowd, like the Yum King, and MINFAR, the Ministry of Revolutionary Armed Forces. You know, the old generals who fought with Fidel, the *históricos*." Dennis looked surprised I'd been talking to him. "What did he want?"

A political honcho. That explained the new jeans and white jacket with shiny buttons. But did Dennis learn this as a reporter or as a spy?

"He went into a riff about the ice cream here," I hedged. "I couldn't figure him out. He looks European. But he drops his s's like a Cuban."

Dennis put his arm around me, giving me a quick

squeeze as if I'd barely avoided some calamity. "Did he ask you any questions?"

"Where was I from, what had I seen here. What you'd ask a tourist."

Cindy and Dennis exchanged glances. Cindy said, "This is not good."

Whatever their true identities, I heartily agreed with that.

"What brought you out here?" Dennis asked me.

"They told me at the hotel to try the ice cream."

Cindy laughed. "And we're fleeing 'Guantanamera.'" She looked at me expectantly.

Had they spotted me at the nightclub? Seen me leave with White Jacket, then followed us here? I had the feeling they were waiting for me to admit something.

I reviewed my conversation with Mr. Radio Havana. As short as it had been, I'd gathered one thing: I'd have to give the Cubans something in exchange for my mother. (Did they really know anything about her? Or were they just guessing I'd lost her, based on my behavior?) But could I offer information about Cindy and Dennis, even innocuous information, without getting them arrested for spying?

God knew I wanted my mother back, but I didn't want to trade anyone for her.

I changed the subject. "Have you already gotten ice cream?"

Dennis raised his brows. "I wish. Tonight, it's taking hours to get the ice-cream tickets, and then hours more to stand in the ice-cream line. We're told it's averaging about five hours right now."

"It is wonderful ice cream," Cindy sighed. "Worth it, if you can get it in less than an hour or two. But almost none of the food lines are that quick, not these days."

No wonder the people I'd seen lined up in the neighborhoods had looked so bored.

"On the other hand," Dennis smiled, "they've been able to get out of neighborhood meetings because of the food lines. They used to have to go to four or five CDR meetings a week—usually featuring the biggest busybodies in the neighborhood poking mercilessly into everybody else's business. Now they can say they were stuck in a food line. Even El Comandante had to cut them a little slack and reduce the number of mandatory meetings!"

A society that welcomed food lines as the better alternative to mandatory meetings had my deepest sympathy.

The next morning, I was determined not to get sidetracked. I'd check the other places Mother had gone with her WILPF group. And if nothing came of it, I'd begin contacting officials, Cindy's warning notwithstanding.

By the time I went down for coffee, I'd decided one more thing: I had to tell Cindy and Dennis what Mr. Radio Havana had said about them. If they were CIA agents, which I doubted, maybe they already knew where my mother was. And if they were just reporters, as I believed, they should know what was up. They might be in danger.

After breakfast I wandered around the hotel looking for them. The rest of the film festival group was lingering in the breakfast room or the lobby, idly waiting for their tour bus. But Cindy and Dennis didn't board it when it came.

Feeling stressed and impatient, I asked the desk to ring their room. The smiling clerk said, "Oh, I'm so sorry you did not know. The lady's mother sent a message that she is ill, and they have left very early this morning to catch an airplane home."

I stood there gaping at her. "They checked out of the hotel? They left Cuba?"

"Yes, I am so sorry. Perhaps if it was not an urgent matter, they would think to leave you a note," she suggested kindly. "I'm sure they would."

I braced both palms against the desk, staring at her. She was wearing a collar necklace that looked like a fabric-covered piece of PVC pipe. I stared at it, thinking it was a very odd adornment. Just big enough to hold a microphone.

I walked away as nonchalantly as I could manage.

I asked the tourist police to call me a cab. I rode around all day, cramming a week-long WILPF itinerary into several hot, wearying hours. I saw an understocked hospital, a pencilless school, a gorgeous beach that stank of pollutants from waterfront hotels, a nightclub full of cranky dancers halfheartedly rehearsing, several museums, the writers' union office, and the film department of the university. Everyone I talked to was friendly—at times, extravagantly so—and seemed to be expecting me.

I didn't tell anyone my mother was missing, but I brought her up often enough to rival Norman Bates. No one had a single useful thing to say about her. She was just one of fifteen umprimped older women quick with supportive comments and warm smiles.

By the time evening fell and the film festival group returned for dinner, I knew I was out of options. I could wait indefinitely, hoping my mother would turn up or that someone would approach me with information about her. Or I could contact the U.S.

officials here and the State Department back home, and let them figure out what had happened to her.

Mother would lose her passport. Criminal charges might be brought against her. If so, her history of activism and symbolic gestures meant she already had more than enough convictions to ensure jail time. But maybe with the best lawyer . . .

What a day. Finally, I returned to my room.

I opened my door and found an envelope on my bed. I crossed to it at warp speed.

But there was no note inside. It was an empty envelope. A perfect metaphor for this trip, in fact.

I sat on the bed staring at it. It was a hotel envelope with the preprinted address of the hotel I'd visited last night, the one with the penthouse bar.

I wondered how long the envelope had been here. With my luck, whatever I might have seen or whomever I might have met was long gone.

I hustled through the hotel district. Even the dollar stores were empty. A fabric store had barely enough bolts for a card-table display. A shoe store showed a few boxes stacked against a wall. A clothing store had bare mannequins in the window.

I slowed down as I neared the hotel, looking to see if I recognized anyone milling in front.

I stopped, noticing a flash of white through a lobby window. In a country bereft of new clothes and without the electricity to run loads of hot wash, bright whites were rare. Even the hotel bedsheets were dingy. The only startling white I'd seen so far was Mr. Radio Havana's jacket.

The envelope had come from him. I wasn't surprised.

I took a deep breath, starting across the street to

the hotel entrance, keeping my eye on the white jacket through the hotel window. That's when I saw the drab green fabric beside the white. Another step closer and I saw an unmistakable blob of red—the Chinese star on a People's Republic cap.

I stopped, backing up. A Ministry honcho (if Cindy and Dennis could be believed) had arranged for me to come to this hotel. He was waiting for me with Chinese soldiers beside him.

I backed up and turned around, walking swiftly away. The scenario suggested I was about to be detained, and that the Cubans wanted it to happen quietly, in a hotel where no one knew me.

Were they planning to take me somewhere to question me? Did they have my mother? Did they have Cindy and Dennis?

I hurried back to my hotel, entering through a side door near the swimming pool. I was scared to death skulking to the elevator and going upstairs. I stayed in my room just long enough to grab my passport and my money. I left my clothes and suit-case—I didn't want it to look like I'd decamped.

But I was afraid I had no choice. I wouldn't deliver myself to Mr. Havana Radio—I'd seen nothing on this trip, absolutely nothing to engender trust in Cuba's commitment to personal freedom.

When I left the hotel, again through the pool door, I caught a glimpse of Chinese soldiers in the lobby, walking slowly as if looking for someone.

I crossed the street into the neighborhoods. With my "fine" jeans and T-shirt, I stood out like a pea-cock on a chicken farm. I was scared. I was hot. And I'd never felt so alone in my life.

I wandered in an aimless and paranoid heat until nightfall. Then I ventured to the sea wall, hoping to encounter Ernesto. I wanted to believe I'd misjudged him, that his losing me near the city's edge had been an accident, just as he claimed.

Perhaps he could help me get to the airport, so I could try to get on a flight out of here. As much as I wanted to find my mother, I was getting nowhere. And I was too scared and bewildered to keep looking.

I mostly kept my back to the sea wall and my eyes on the road. I tried to stay in shadows, especially when the tourist police cruised by.

I finally heard Ernesto's voice. "Señora! I have been searching for you! My friend is not able to come tonight but tomorrow—Señora? You are still angry?"

Angry? I could have hugged him, I was so glad to see him.

"How can I convince you I did not leave you on purpose? I am sorry! Truly!" he continued. "And my *compañero* thanks you for the dollars."

"Let's go somewhere," I said hastily. "Can we go somewhere where we don't have to stand ten feet apart? I want to talk to you."

"Yes, follow me." He sounded happy again, like a puppy who'd been forgiven for chewing on the furniture.

I kept a distance of twenty feet or so as I followed him past huge houses that had once been mansions. The neighborhood's hours of electricity hadn't started yet, so there were no television or radio sounds. Few candles or lanterns burned. A trash can fire lit a street corner. Young people stood around it laughing and teasing and embracing.

Ernesto waited so we could walk together. "Not so long ago we still had electricity much of the night. Now everybody is inside making babies. We have so many in each room already that it is ridiculous, and now all the new babies—many girls are secret Catholics. You can be a Catholic here, but you will get no work if it is known. The revolutionaries get abortions—even twenty is not uncommon. There are no pills! You want to take girls walking and be romantic, but it is hard when every one has a baby on her breast." He sighed.

"AIDS isn't a problem?"

"Those who are infected are taken away when they are diagnosed positive, many years before they will have symptoms. They are taken to a colony on the eastern shore and imprisoned there until they die. But they say it does not look like a jail. And they are given plenty of food. Some people, desperate because there is nothing left, inject themselves with tainted blood. To live less long but with more to eat."

I fought a major case of the creeps. A good time to change the subject: "The two people I've been spending time with, the Americans, you know them, right?"

"They ask me questions, and they give me dollars. I have found out for them the address of a certain poet." There was something odd about his tone. I wished I could see his face, but the trash can fire was too distant.

"Do you know who they work for?"

"American newspapers."

"You're sure they don't work for the American government?"

"No." His voice grew paranoid. "No, that would be extremely bad trouble. Contact with someone who works for the American government, that would be very wrong in the eyes of my government, very hard to explain. It is for crimes like this that people are sent to the men's prison *combinado del este. Bota la llave* . . ." Throw away the key.

"The reporters, what names did they give you?"

"Dennis and Cindy." He pronounced the latter Seendy.

"Have you seen them today?"

"Oh yes. They have asked for two bicycles. Do you wish to see them? We can wait at the house of my friend with the bicycles."

I was glad he couldn't see my face. I was close to tears, I was so relieved to think I'd see Dennis and Cindy again.

"Yes, let's go wait for them. But, Ernesto . . . if they don't show up soon, can you get me to the airport? I need to get home."

"Your flight is tonight?" He sounded distressed.

"I thought I'd catch the next plane out, wherever it's going, and make connections."

"But, señora, you have just gotten here."

Whereas to me, it seemed I'd been here way too long.

He mused, "Perhaps Dennis and Cindy will cheer you up and you will stay longer, after all." We rounded a corner. "It's very close, the house of my friend."

"When did Cindy and Dennis pick up the bicycles?"

"Not so long ago, perhaps five o'clock, when the tour bus returned."

"The tour bus?" I tried to keep my tone normal. "You mean from the film festival?"

"Yes." He sounded confident. "They came off the bus and walked to me at the sea wall."

"They didn't go into the hotel and freshen up?"

He hesitated a moment. "Did you see them at the hotel?"

"No, I haven't seen them since last night."

"Perhaps they freshened up. The tour bus was still unloading, but if they went in quickly, I don't know." There was a question in his voice as if he weren't sure which way this story should play out. "The bus was still there." He'd probably seen the tour bus pull up, all right. "And then they came to me. I think they will be back with the bicycles very soon."

I walked beside Ernesto wondering what to do now. He was lying to me. Should I turn and run? Or would he just chase me down?

Worse yet, how close were we to whatever trap he was leading me into? Was he working for the man with the white coat? Was he going to turn me over to the Cuban government at its request?

Or was he just taking me somewhere to rob me of my dollars?

I stopped. "My hair's so light it's conspicuous," I said. "Will you ask that girl over there to sell you her scarf?" I pulled a dollar out of my pocket. "I'll feel more comfortable if my hair's covered."

He hesitated. "She will see you here. And getting the dollar . . . she will maybe talk about it."

"How about if I give you the dollar and I go around the corner where she can't see me."

"For a Cuban to spend a dollar on such a stupidity . . ."

"Maybe you can act like it's a way to try to get a date with her. Please, just think of something."

He remained very reluctant.

But I pressed the dollar into his hand. "Hurry. Before my hair screams out at somebody. I'll be right around the corner."

"If you are stopped? If someone approaches you?"

"I'll act like a dumb tourist. Just go. Hurry up."

Our relationship had been such that he was pretty much obliged, I thought, to go fetch, to continue doing my bidding. I rounded the corner, waiting a minute to make sure he wasn't following.

Then I took off running.

I was afraid to return to my hotel, afraid to go near the hotel with the bar, and now, I was afraid to approach the sea wall.

So I headed for the one area I could be sure was full of tourists. At least there, my hair wouldn't call out, "Look at me, I'm different."

Twenty minutes later, I ducked into a colorful little bar gleaming with hardwoods and cozy with potted plants. Ernest Hemingway's photo was up on the wall—I supposed he'd helped keep a few bars here afloat in his day. I sat in a corner behind a group of laughing Germans, and I ordered seafood and a mojito. The latter went down so easily I quickly ordered another. And because it went well with dinner, I had a third.

I'm not used to rum. I wonder how many excuses, plea bargains, and divorces have begun with those words. In my case, what started as an attempt to hide, eat, and think things through, ended with me very much in my cups, all but blowing kisses to the portrait of Papa Hemingway. Except for the fact that I didn't trust a soul I'd met here, Cuba (the Cuba of historic restaurants with ceiling fans and palms in brass pots) seemed like a great place.

Anyway, I reasoned, it was no use running off to the airport. There probably weren't any flights tonight. And the ticket clerks were undoubtedly required to phone some ministry or other when drunken Americans demanded immediate exit.

This must be what it was like to be a Cuban. (Well, except for the good meal, the hotel room full of clothes, the passport, and the pocket stuffed with dollars.) There was just no way to get the hell out of here. Short of grabbing an inner tube and floating to Miami, I was stuck.

I returned to my hotel, almost too belligerent to care who might be waiting there. But no one stopped me on my way up to my room. And when I opened the door, no one was waiting behind it.

I looked up at the light fixture with the hidden bug. "*Fiat lux,*" I said. "Let there be light." Fiat Lux, wouldn't that be a great name for a model of Fiat? But I guessed they didn't get many Fiats here. "And at these prices, you won't get many more!"

When you're drunk, the old jokes are the best. I lay down and giggled myself to sleep.

12

$\mathcal{A}$ nightmare couldn't have been more frightening. I was startled out of a deep, rummy sleep by a pounding at my door. I sat up, thinking I'd overslept, that housekeeping needed to get in—a problem I've had in many a hotel. But the room was still dark. I groped for my wristwatch on the night table. It was one in the morning.

I sat up in a cold sweat. I was in Cuba. I'd gone places I shouldn't. I'd harmed, maybe killed, a Chinese soldier. I'd consorted with people who might be CIA agents.

The pounding on my door stopped. I clicked on a bedside lamp just in time to see the bolt turn as the door was unlocked from the outside.

I jumped out of bed, and climbed quickly into my sweatpants. Not quite quickly enough—Mr. Radio Havana and two Cubans in military fatigues saw more of my legs than any recent dates had. But I was too scared for mere indignation. Was I about to be arrested? Was there bad news about my mother?

I stood there in my T-shirt and sweats, clammy with fear, staring at them.

Strangely enough, they looked equally surprised to see me. It was a moment before Mr. Radio Havana cleared his throat. "We were informed that no one has seen you at the hotel for many hours. We did not expect to find you here."

I shook my head, still mystified.

"We are sorry to burst in on you in this fashion, but . . . You did not answer our repeated announcements through the door."

I stammered out the word "Mojitos."

One of the soldiers grinned.

"We are afraid that a situation has arisen. We will need to question you. We can go to my office or we can remain here. As you wish."

I motioned him to take a seat. If I could avoid leaving the hotel for some scary elsewhere, I might yet avert a heart attack.

He motioned the soldiers outside and closed the door so it didn't quite latch.

He took the room's one flimsy chair. I sat on the bed, finger-combing my hair as if tidiness would enhance my sobriety. I was so dehydrated, my mouth felt fur-lined. Judging from the taste, skunk fur.

He reached into his pocket and extracted more photographs. I braced myself for more questions about Mr. Jamieson and Mrs. Travolta, the CIA's own Avengers.

But the people in the small color photos looked like pale-skinned Cubans. The woman was thin and dark-haired, without makeup. The man was curly-haired and slightly swarthier. There was something vaguely familiar about them.

I said, "Who are they?"

"You tell me."

I scowled down at the photos. They looked so hopeful. I hadn't seen this expression on many faces here.

"I don't know." And I didn't want to know, not unless it helped me find Mother. The last thing I wanted to do here was get some Cubans thrown into jail.

"Take your time."

"I really don't know. I mean, maybe I've seen them somewhere. But I have no idea who they . . ." What was it about them? Something was setting off alarm bells, making me very damned uncomfortable.

"You have no idea?" he prompted.

"I'm sure I haven't talked to them. But there is something familiar about them." Despite my disquiet, I was glad not to be looking at a photo of a dead Chinese soldier.

"Could it be the clothing?" Mr. Radio Havana asked.

"Oh my God!" I felt tears spring to my eyes. "Oh God, it's Cindy's blouse. Dennis's shirt." How many Cubans had access to natural-fiber, button-down clothes? "What happened? Did something happen to them? Did these people rob them?"

"These people," he said, taking back the photos, "attempted to purchase airline tickets departing Cuba using the passports of the Americans you call Cindy and Dennis."

I shook my head. "But they don't look like Cindy and Dennis."

"The passport photographs had been replaced by the photographs before you. They were adequately, but not perfectly, substituted."

"Where are Cindy and Dennis?"

"We do not know."

"These people have their clothes."

"Yes, it would appear that Mr. Jamieson and Mrs. Travolta have cooperated in this charade."

"No," I disagreed. "No, come on. If the CIA were involved, wouldn't the passports look—how did you put it?—perfect. I think Cindy and Dennis got robbed. You haven't found them?"

"No!" He looked angry enough to take it out on me. "Perhaps a boat has come to return them to your country. Or to Gitmo."

I scooted backward on the bed. Cindy and Dennis were gone, and their clothes were on the backs of Cubans trying to sneak out with their passports. "Wouldn't you know if a boat came for them?"

"We cannot patrol everywhere at once. We have six thousand kilometers of coastline in Cuba."

"But if they left on a boat, why bother altering the passports? Why not just take this couple with them?"

He said nothing. Perhaps this logical flaw had kept him from bursting in and arresting me for consorting with the CIA.

"Where's Gitmo?" I wondered.

"Your illegal naval base in Guantánamo."

I slumped, thinking over what Ernesto had told me. He said Cindy and Dennis had come to him for bicycles. I hadn't believed him because I'd been told they'd left Cuba. There were two possibilities: Either

Cindy and Dennis had turned over their passports in an altruistic attempt to smuggle some Cubans to America, later renting bicycles to go . . . where? To a pickup point along the coast? Or Ernesto had led them off this morning and stolen their passports. If so, I shuddered to think what might have happened if I'd stayed with him tonight.

"Could they have driven or bicycled to Guantánamo?" What I really wanted to know was whether my mother might have gone there. She'd hassled military men in bases up and down California and the eastern seaboard. Perhaps she'd hoped to shout some sense into the soldiers here. Perhaps they'd detained her.

"No, no. There is no entrance by land, only mine fields and fences, guarded on both sides. One must fly from Havana to Miami, and then fly back with the approval of your military to Gitmo."

"Could a person swim over from the Cuban side?" My mother was no Esther Williams, but it couldn't be far to paddle.

"The sea there is thick with jellyfish, very deadly. No sane person would attempt this." He sat straighter, as if exasperated. "But it is irrelevant. Clearly there are accomplices with a boat."

I had to assume even Mother wouldn't swim through schools of deadly jellyfish to proselytize.

"You must tell us what you know about your Cindy and Dennis." He spoke the names as if only a fool would believe them to be correct.

"They told me they were reporters from Associated Press based in Houston and living in Mexico City. They said their next assignment was in Moscow, and that they were learning Russian. They said it's impossible to get reporters' visas, so they attach themselves to tour groups and come in as tourists as often as they can."

"Why?"

"To get news."

"Did they tell you what news they get?"

It didn't take a genius to figure out he'd be more, not less, unhappy with me if I told the truth. So I said, "No, not really. They went to see someone who's a friend of a friend of theirs. They were glad to hear that rumors about some poet weren't true." If Cindy and Dennis were still on the island, maybe a few white lies would help them. "The only negative thing they said was that some Cubans were bitter about a general who was executed. But they didn't seem to agree with those people. They just seemed . . . interested without being judgmental. Like reporters."

I hoped that's all they were. Even more, I hoped they were all right. I hoped Ernesto hadn't led them off somewhere and killed them for their passports.

"What about their bags?" I asked. "Did these people have Cindy and Dennis's luggage?"

"Yes."

"So they were able to get into their hotel room."

"Not necessarily. The luggage might have been given to them."

"The desk clerk, she'd know whether Cindy and Dennis checked out and took their bags."

He watched me impassively.

"Right? Did you ask the desk clerk?"

"The woman in the photograph," he said finally, "she is the nighttime clerk here."

"Oh." I thought about it. "But doesn't that settle it? She lied to the incoming shift. She had their passports and bags."

"This does not answer the question of whether Mr. Jamieson and Mrs. Travolta conspired with them."

I supposed he was right about that.

"In the usual course of such matters," he continued, "the impostors might have managed to board this morning's flight to Mexico City. However, given our suspicions of Jamieson and Travolta . . ." He shrugged.

Of all the luck: The Cuban couple had doctored the passports of suspected CIA agents. I felt the profound empathy of a chronic screwup.

"Look," I said, "if someone is stealing tourists' passports . . . do you know if it happens often? Do you know if someone used my mother's? Do you know where my mother is?"

He glanced at the hotel door. He sighed.

I wanted to grab him by his startlingly white lapels and shake an answer out of him. "Can't you just tell me if you know my mother's okay?"

He leaned forward. "I should not speak of this. But I sympathize with your feelings."

I sat very still, not wanting to do anything to change his mind.

"We believe you should look for your mother . . . elsewhere."

"Elsewhere?" That didn't narrow things down much. "Do you know she's not in Cuba?"

I hadn't asked anyone in government yet. I'd asked a boy at the Malecón and two reporters who might be CIA agents. I'd asked a poet under house arrest and a drug smuggler under actual arrest. As long as a bureaucrat was offering answers, I wanted to be quick with questions. "Does your ministry have information that my mother left?"

He shrugged. "It is not up to us to monitor these matters."

"But do you know?" I imagined the Ministry of Revolutionary Armed Forces knew a great many things it wasn't "up to" them to know.

"I have said all that I will on this matter. I am here to question you about Jamieson and Travolta."

"Is this a problem you've been having for a while? Passports being stolen and altered, Cubans sneaking out?" Was there any way my mother might be involved in some aspect of this?

"We have a word here for Cubans who turn their backs on the revolution for their own personal narrow interests, their own selfish fantasies." His eyes flicked again to the door. "*Gusanos,* worms. Every society has its small portion of *gusanos.* And so, yes, we have the rafts and occasionally the theft of passports."

Small portion? When Castro got fed up in 1980 and offered to let the *gusanos* go, over a hundred thousand fled the island. There were almost a million in Miami alone.

"Have you ever found the people whose passports are taken? What happens to them? How are the passports stolen?"

"They are not stolen. In every instance where we have discovered the true owner of a passport, that person has been not a victim, but an accomplice." His brows were raised. He watched me carefully.

Were we talking about Cindy and Dennis or my mother? I was tired and intoxicated, but I'd have been confused regardless.

I said, "My mother believes in Cuba. She agrees with Castro and admires your revolution. She would treat her hosts with more respect than to turn her passport over to a *gusano,* as you put it." But Mother's bleeding heart was sometimes at cross-purposes with her ideologue's mind. "If you know where she is, you've got to tell me!"

It was all I could do not to lie back down. I felt shaky from the stress, the mojitos, the lack of sleep.

"I am afraid that I cannot help you," he concluded, rising. "And, since you will not assist us on the matter of Mr. Jamieson and Mrs. Travolta, our government must request that you leave Cuba. We have lost confidence in your willingness to uphold our laws. We have tried to make you welcome, but we now feel that you are no longer welcome in Cuba."

I blinked up at him. If I didn't give him information I didn't have, he wouldn't give me information he did have? Or was he bluffing?

He answered that question quickly enough. "We have come to escort you to the airport, Miss Jansson."

"You're kicking me out of Cuba? But my mother? Where is she?"

"Perhaps you will find her already waiting for you at home."

"Cindy and Dennis—I think you're wrong about them. I'm worried about them." Should I tell him about Ernesto? Express my fear that he'd been luring me someplace to steal my passport? Suggest that he find the boy and question him about Cindy and Dennis, about my mother?

But what if I was wrong? Would Ernesto end up in the prison he called Throw Away the Key?

Mr. Radio Havana said, "We will wait outside for only twenty minutes. Then we will reenter and escort you onto the next airplane to Mexico City, which leaves at dawn."

Kicked out of Cuba. That would look terrible on my lefty résumé.

13

$\mathcal{M}$exico City seemed fabulously opulent after my three days in Havana. The outdoor markets with their tottering stacks of toys, clothes, and souvenirs, everything so bright and gaudy and useless, trinkets in staggering profusion—it was beautiful to my eyes. The sight of food carts on virtually every corner, their griddles frying meats and tamales and tacos, their cooks and vendors splendid in eye-popping floral prints, it seemed so luxurious, so sensual. I stuffed myself with fried foods. I drank neon-colored pops. I wandered through mercados, rejoicing in the overkill of ugly T-shirts and cheap wristwatches.

I used pay phones, happy to be able to call my father, even though I didn't reach him. At least here, I could try as often as I pleased. I could leave him messages. I could talk to Mother's friends, though they had no news. It was good to feel connected again, to feel comfortable.

I sat in the main square, the Zócalo, and admired

the perfectly maintained old stone of the Palacio Nacional, the Catedral Metropolitana, and the supreme court building. I wandered the alleys, appreciating the paint on stucco houses, the windowboxes in bloom, the plumpness of small children.

And people spoke the Spanish I was used to hearing. They didn't lose their s's and n's, they didn't mumble like speed freaks on a rush.

I would have been happy to be here but for the fact that I hadn't accomplished anything. I'd just found a couple more people to worry about.

I'd taken a room rather than going on to San Francisco because I wanted to know if Cindy and Dennis really were Associated Press reporters living here. I didn't dare hope I'd find them at home, but I wanted to know whether they'd lied to me.

In a way, I hoped they had. I hoped they were CIA agents, after all, in Guantánamo or back on U.S. soil, filing secret reports as busily as Boris and Natasha. I hoped they weren't in a Cuban prison. I hoped they weren't lying in some field on the outskirts of Havana. Whoever they were, I hoped they were safe. (My respect for safety had grown fervent, almost devotional.)

And if they were in any position to do it, I hoped they would help my mother.

I started at one of the city's biggest newspapers. It was a vast suite of offices in a building that seemed more impressive than convenient. The ceilings were high and ornate, and the air was chilly and still. The furniture was heavy and the floors were worn alabaster.

I asked the woman at the front desk if I could talk

to someone about two Associated Press reporters living here in Mexico City. I didn't know Dennis's last name. Cindy's name was Corlett—I remembered it because it sounded like a kind of bird.

The names got her attention, but she seemed determined not to offer any comment or information. She suggested I ask the editor in charge of receiving AP stories for the newspaper. But she didn't think he would want to be disturbed now. Perhaps I wished to leave a note?

We haggled for a few minutes, me insisting this was very important, and she reassuring me that the note would be delivered.

Finally, I sighed, taking the sheet of paper and the pen she pushed toward me. When I asked the name of the person I should address, she said, "Martin Marules."

Martin, as in the mutual friend of Cindy, Dennis, and the Cuban Yum King? I tried not to get excited.

"Mr. Marules, he's the short, corpulent man with the gray hair?" I asked her.

"No, no, his hair is very black and thick." She blushed as if she liked that in a man. "And he is more distinguished than corpulent."

"But very tall," I said with certainty.

"Under six feet."

I turned my attention to the note. I wrote, "Cindy Corlett and her companion, Dennis, mentioned your name to me in Cuba just two days ago. Now they are missing and accused of working for the CIA. Their passports were stolen and they are being sought as accomplices. It is urgent that you call me." I added my hotel phone number.

Then I left the building, and walked around back to see if there was an exit. When I saw there was, I found a side street from which, with minimum walking, I could frequently check both the front and back doors.

I got very sick of the cobblestones on that narrow street. They were six-inch squares of gray stone, and I learned too much about their spacing and arrangement. It seemed as if hours ticked away, but my wristwatch insisted I'd been pacing only twenty minutes.

A man of above-average height with thick black hair and a pot belly under a sweater-vest and brown suit exited the back way. He clipped along quickly. With a sigh, I followed him. An awful lot of Mexican men fit the description I'd been given of Martin Marules. I could only hope.

I trailed at what I prayed was a discreet distance. The entire time, I marveled at the beauty of this well-maintained city. I kept thinking of my long bike ride behind Ernesto, comparing these stone palaces and freshly painted buildings, the colorfully overdressed people, the kids with tacos in each hand, to what I'd seen in Havana.

Most of Mexico lived in rural poverty—I knew better than to think its capital was typical. But as poor as the country might be, no one was actively keeping out medicine and food. It might not filter equally to the middle classes and the poor, but it existed, it was here. Cuba didn't stand a chance.

The man strode purposefully down alleys full of hookers, waving them aside as they tried to interest him. He blitzed through mercados hung with cheap clothes and stacked with Kmart-reject toys. He dashed across streets and cut through narrow alleys. Just when I began to worry that I was tailing the Marathon Man, he stopped in front of a pink stucco building with grillwork balconies and an intercom out front. He pressed a bell repeatedly.

When no one answered, he stepped back, craning his neck to look up at a second story balcony. He returned to the intercom, and, I thought, rang a different bell. He had a short, intense conversation into the speaker, then he waited.

A man in slippers, slacks, and an unbuttoned shirt over a sleeveless T opened the door to him. When they went inside, I kept my eyes on the second-floor balcony. Soon, I could see Martin Marules's brown suit near the sliding glass balcony doors.

I crossed the street and looked at the door buzzer. The nameplate read "G. Jamieson." I heard myself murmur, "Oh no." But I pressed the buzzer anyway.

A hesitant voice, very deep, said, "Yes?"

"Señor Marules?"

There was a pause. Another voice came through the tinny speaker. "This is he. Who is there, please?"

"Willa Jansson. I left you a note this morning. I just saw you go up there. Please let me in. I need to talk to you."

A second later, he buzzed me in.

The lobby was cool and quiet, with marble floor tiles and faux silk wallpaper. I climbed steps carpeted with an anchored runner.

At the first landing, Martin Marules waited in the

frame of an open door. He was scowling as if he would gladly shoot the messenger.

I didn't think, at first, that he was going to back up to let me in.

Behind him, the other man finished buttoning his shirt. He carried a bunch of keys and had the look of an inconvenienced concierge.

Marules said to him, "We will leave the front door open so you can check on us at any moment. But you have seen me here many times. Please allow me a private conversation at the home of my friends."

The concierge seemed relieved to go.

I looked around Dennis and Cindy's apartment. It was immaculately clean. A television was the living room's focal point—CNN junkies? There were bookcases stacked with magazines and papers, but very few books. At regular intervals along the floor, brightly painted carved cats faced the center of the room.

Marules had his back to the sliding balcony doors. Despite the silhouette, I could see he was fiftyish and close-shaven with an excellent haircut.

"Your letter struck a very serious note," he said. "What can you tell me about my friends?"

I sat on a soft couch, relieved to be off my feet after a great deal of pacing and a very fast hike. "They aren't back, are they?"

"To my knowledge, no. I see no luggage, no fruit, no garbage in the waste bins. I can only assume they have not yet returned from the film festival." With a sigh, he crossed to the couch and sat three cushions away, angled toward me.

"Are they really reporters? For AP?"

He nodded.

"The Cuban government thinks they work for the CIA."

He made an impatient gesture, as if to say, No, they don't.

"I was taken aside and shown their photographs. I was told their real names were Garrett Jamieson and Angela Travolta. I was told they worked for the CIA."

Marules shook his head. "No, no, perhaps you misunderstood. They are merely subletting this apartment from the Jamiesons, an American couple currently in Belgium."

"Are the Jamiesons CIA agents?" I felt silly even uttering such a question. But presumably there were real CIA agents in the world.

"Of course not. They are a retired couple with children abroad. They do little more than travel." But his brows pinched. "I believe, however, that she uses her own name, Travolta, rather than her husband's. But enough about them. How and with whom did you come to discuss Dennis and Cindy? And you—do you have identification?"

I handed him my passport. "You'll notice I left Mexico four days ago and returned yesterday. I went to Cuba to look for my mother. She was there with a tour group and she didn't come back with the rest of them. Cindy and Dennis were staying at my hotel. In fact, I went with them to meet a ministry official who's a friend of yours. They told him your wife's expecting a baby."

He flushed. Apparently it was true.

"They didn't tell him they were journalists, though. And their real agenda seemed to be to ask him about a poet named Lidia Gomez."

For a moment he froze. Then, with a *pshaw* wave of the hand, he said, "There has been a great deal too much ink wasted already on this minor poet."

"Well, I saw her with my own eyes. She's been beaten badly enough to have her head and one eye bandaged. She's under house arrest guarded by Chinese soldiers."

He looked more than a little reluctant to accept this on a stranger's say-so.

"Dennis and Cindy also asked me to visit an American who's being held prisoner there, a woman named Myra Wilson."

"The cocaine smuggler?"

"Cindy and Dennis don't think so. Or they think she's taking the rap for someone higher up. They brought up General Ochoa."

"Ochoa?" He sounded surprised. He slipped his hand into his suit jacket pocket, jiggling something in there. Change? Rosary beads?

"I went to see Myra Wilson. They'd bused most of the prisoners away. There were only a handful left, and they were drugged, you could tell. Wilson was trotted out so I could see her. I tried to ask her, in a veiled way, about my mother." I sighed. Too much detail. I wanted to know what he knew, not blither on about my trip. "Anyway, that night when Cindy and Dennis were occupied, I was approached by a man who never did tell me his name. A small man with lots of light brown hair. He accused them of being CIA agents and said if I'd spy on them, he'd give me information about my mother. The next morning, they disappeared from the hotel. A Cuban couple tried to use their passports to board a flight to here. And because I'd spent time with them, I was escorted onto the first plane out."

Marules rewarded me with a dropped jaw. He shook his head slightly.

"It's true," I assured him. "Dennis and Cindy are somewhere in Cuba without passports—I assume, anyway—and the government thinks they're CIA agents." I ran my hands through my hair. "And I guess . . . I'm afraid my mother might be in the same boat. So if you've got any influence or any ideas . . . ? Can you intercede with your friend in the Interior Ministry?"

His shoulders rounded, and he hugged himself, straining the seams of his elegant jacket. He looked over the apartment as if seeing it for the first time: the television around which the furniture was grouped, the carvings on the floor, library tables pushed against windows as if Dennis and Cindy liked to stare outside when researching or writing. The place was clean, spare, nothing on the walls but almost enough windows for it not to matter. It didn't seem to say any more about the couple than their tasteful, serviceable clothes had.

Finally Marules rose. He scowled at me for a moment, then walked to a telephone on a library table. He picked up the receiver and ran his finger down what seemed to be an autodial list. He hit a key, then waited. A moment later he said, "Agosto." His voice was tremulous. "There is someone I need for you to see." A pause. "Yes, right now!"

He cast me a confused glance, as if wishing I would disappear and take this problem with me. Then he told Agosto (whoever he was) to come to

Dennis and Cindy's. "Yes, yes, I know they are in Cuba! That's the problem. Hurry, *chico*."

He returned to his spot on the couch, sighing as he turned to me. "Please wait. Agosto Diaz is one of our fact-checkers. He works frequently with Dennis and Cindy. He is a close personal friend. Perhaps he will have an idea."

"Okay." God knew I didn't.

We mostly avoided each other's gaze for the next ten minutes or so. The concierge popped his head in a couple of times, but didn't seem concerned to see us sitting there in uncomfortable silence.

I was lost in thought when I heard the bell sound. I jumped up, startled. Marules gave me an odd look as he went to buzz Agosto Diaz in.

Diaz appeared at the door looking like a tennis star who'd survived a hurricane. He was big and handsome, with wildly disheveled hair, sports slacks and tennis shoes, and a white sweater that had at some point been tied around his neck but now dangled one sleeve on the floor. He was panting slightly, looking at Martin Marules as if ready to shake some words out of him.

"There she is," Marules said, gesturing toward me. "She says she has been in Cuba with Dennis and Cindy. That they have vanished there. Someone else attempted to use their passports."

Diaz all but pushed him aside to get to me. He dropped onto one knee in front of me. Under any other circumstances, it would have been a bit of a thrill. With his big dark eyes, cleft chin, and strong nose, he looked like a cologne ad—Mexican Love Match.

He said, "Yes?"

I told him about it.

He listened, motionless on one knee, a testament to his well-disciplined muscles.

A few times, he prompted me for details. His voice was deep and refined, a college-educated and urbane voice.

When I was through, he commented, "Your Spanish is very fluent."

"I was born in Mexico." More to the point, I'd been speaking it for the last four days.

Diaz crossed to the couch and sat beside Marules. "First thing, we had better search this apartment. Then, we will go try to find out if anyone has used the passport of this lady's mother or of Myra Wilson to enter this country."

"Wilson?" Marules's tone was sharp. "Why Wilson?"

"Dennis and Cindy are accused of giving their passports to impostors. The day before, they are doubting the reason for Myra Wilson's arrest and detention. Perhaps there is a connection." He raised his arms in a huge shrug.

"How can you find out?" I wondered.

"Customs records, airline records. Regarding your mother, the dates are obvious. For Myra Wilson, we will first determine when she was arrested. That would be within a few days of her passport being used by another."

"*If* it was used by another," Marules said. "This is mere word association, Agosto."

"But because Cindy and Dennis's passports were stolen, I think we should seek a pattern. It could fit with the *norteamericana*'s mother not returning."

"But surely not with Myra Wilson," Marules insisted.

"Cindy and Dennis did not believe the charges against Wilson are true. So who knows?"

I wasn't sure I followed. "If Wilson was arrested for turning her passport over to someone else, why wouldn't the Cubans just say so? That's as much a crime as drug smuggling."

"Ah, but drugs may be blamed on the decadence of capitalist societies. The desire of ordinary Cubans to flee their homeland, that is more embarrassing."

Marules made a pooh-poohing noise.

I had to agree—embarrassing or not, *gusanos* were no secret. "And why would Wilson confess to drug smuggling?"

"We begin by checking what we can." Diaz grinned. "Eh, Marules? So you always tell us." He ran a hand over his dark waves. "Perhaps Myra Wilson is trying to protect the person to whom she has given her passport. If we can find that person, we will know more about this passport scheme. Perhaps it will point us toward this lady's mother. Perhaps it will tell us something about the fate of Cindy and Dennis."

Marules looked distressed. "If we are to go through their things, we had better do so quickly. I would not want to try to explain to the concierge."

Diaz jumped to his feet, going straight for the library tables against the windows. Marules followed his lead, going to the other desk.

I felt strange about joining them. I rose reluctantly. Unlike these two men, I didn't know Cindy and Dennis well enough to invade their privacy. I walked slowly into their kitchen, looking at the tidy tile counters, the clean appliances, the rust rings in the porcelain sink. There was a note taped to the fifties-era refrigerator. It listed things someone named Consuelo should do in their absence. Judging from the items on the list, Consuelo was their maid.

I wandered through the rest of the apartment. The bedroom was tidy, the closets were clean and understocked. The couple definitely stuck to beiges and wheats and light browns, very mix and match, very practical. The walls were bare, but as in the living room, there were almost enough windows to disguise the starkness.

I tried to imagine the life of an Associated Press reporter. There would be little incentive to accumulate souvenirs, especially large wall hangings, when they'd have to be packed up for frequent moves. It wouldn't be like living in a military family, piling everything into a truck every year or so. No, moving from Mexico City to Russia, dealing with customs on both ends, bribes to various officials, the inevitable damage and theft that must occur along the way . . . it would be much easier not to accumulate anything, to keep a minimal wardrobe and not much else.

Diaz joined me in the bedroom. He went through the pockets of every article of clothing in the closet. He looked inside shoes. He checked the closet walls and ceiling, presumably for crawl-space panels. He went through the drawers in a plain wood dresser. He pulled back the bedding, felt the sheets, stuck his arm between the mattress and the box spring, running it along the full perimeter. He looked under the bed. He examined corners. He tapped at floor-boards.

When he was through, we both returned to the living room. Marules stood near a window, looking at a sheet of paper, creased as if recently unfolded. He looked troubled.

Diaz crossed the room in a few long-legged strides. He took the paper from Marules, who was saying, "Just the señorita's note to me."

Diaz looked at me. "Come with me, Señorita Jansson. We may be able to help each other."

The concierge appeared at the door. "I'm thinking that perhaps I have waited long enough, Mr. Marules? Shall I lock up now?" When Diaz turned, the concierge flashed him a friendly smile. Apparently he'd seen him before.

Marules seemed on the verge of asking the concierge something—strange comings and goings, perhaps? But he must have thought better of it. Instead, he shook the man's hand.

As we left, I watched the concierge pocket the currency Marules had pressed into his palm.

$\mathcal{M}$arules and Diaz walked straight over to a Volkswagen Beetle, of which there seemed to be thousands, maybe hundreds of thousands, in Mexico City. Diaz held the passenger seat forward for me, and I climbed in back. Marules took the front seat, as any Latin male would. Crammed behind the two men, I felt little nostalgia for the Beetle's demise in the United States. As we rode the narrow streets back toward the Zócalo, I tried to ignore the loudness of the engine and the stink of exhaust coming up through the floorboards. I tried to enjoy the scenery through a back window the size of my hand.

Diaz parked near the newspaper office. Marules went straight inside, while Diaz took a moment to help unwedge me from the back.

"If you will just wait with the car a moment . . ." He pulled some bills from his pocket, handing them to me. "If the police ask you to move, give them this *mordida* and tell them the car belongs to Marules."

He trotted off, leaving me standing there open-mouthed.

But I didn't have to bribe any policemen during the twenty minutes or so that I waited. I'm not sure I would have, in any case. This part of the culture, like haggling over prices, made me uncomfortable. If I was too capitalistic for Cuba, I wasn't enough of a free-marketeer to be comfortable in Mexico.

When Diaz returned, he looked grim. He motioned me into the passenger seat. "Unfortunately, I have no news of your mother—I am sorry. But on the other matter, I have had better luck." He put the car into gear. "It was a simple matter to learn when Myra Wilson was arrested in Cuba. As to her passport, some money will have to change hands, naturally, before details will be forthcoming. But I have been given the hint that someone used the passport of Myra Wilson to come to Mexico City."

"You found out so quickly?"

He looked a little surprised. "Of course. It is my job to find out things, to check details. It is not for nothing that I have apprenticed myself to a famous *chilango* lawyer." Mexico City natives called themselves *chilangos*. But the rest of his statement made no sense to me. He noticed my bewilderment: "It is most crucial to pay exactly the correct *mordida* for the occasion. To give less is an insult, to give too much shows a naïveté that is suspect. Therefore lawyers and sometimes reporters apprentice themselves to those with experience, those who know to the peso the appropriate *mordida*. And I have, on this occasion, made exactly the correct offer."

It couldn't be any more inconvenient than my

having to learn conflicting rules for county, state, and federal courts, not to mention individual judges' prejudices. And it was certainly more direct.

"I have requested a search of customs records for the week before and the week after Myra Wilson's arrest," he continued. "The newspaper has excellent contacts at customs. Do you know how many stories we write about illegal immigration?" A half smile. " 'The grass is greener when it is fenced,' " he said in English. "Isn't that the adage?"

"Close enough."

We blasted down Reforma, a boulevard built to showcase the giant statues and monuments of which Mexicans are very fond. I expected to go to some old building with dark hallways and little rooms with nervous immigrants filling out paperwork. So I was surprised when we got on the freeway, heading toward the airport.

A person could grow very sick of Mexico City's airport. For one thing, it's about five times as crowded as any U.S. airport. For another thing, it has spooky charred aircraft lying around its tarmacs.

We rushed through the international flights terminal at the speed of lifelong *chilangos*. I caught up to Diaz as he was knocking on one of several closed doors in the customs and duty area. To our right, bedraggled travelers stood waiting for lights to flash green or red, letting them know whether to step aside and have their bags searched.

A cranky-looking man opened the door to us. Diaz greeted him warmly, clasping his hand in a long handshake. The customs agent slipped his hand into his pocket afterward, making it clear to me that a peso-perfect *mordida* had changed hands in the process.

The office was a hovel of paperwork. A one-way mirror allowed us to look out at block-long lines behind red and green lights.

"Look," he said, "this will go no farther, and you did not hear it from me."

"That's understood, Pirí," Diaz assured him. "As always."

"But this time I mean it. You have come from Marules, yes? He has asked for this, correct?"

"Yes." Diaz looked surprised. "Call him if you like."

"I had a message from him already, but I was having my lunch. And then you called me."

"Yes, yes," Diaz assured him, "Marules sent us. He called to speed things along, Pirí. So let's get to it."

"The party came through customs on . . ." Pirí referred to a file, giving us the date. "She was detained for looking excessively nervous, and her baggage was searched. No contraband was found, although it was noted that there was very little in her luggage, just clothing and what appeared to be photographs of a family in Cuba. An Instamatic picture was taken at that time." He slid his fingernail under something apparently glued or taped to the file. "You may look, Diaz, but not take. Clear?"

"You must let me copy the photo, Pirí. It's useless to me if I can't show it to anyone."

"What do you want from me, Diaz?" His voice and his color rose. "You want me to dance through the main room to the copy machine? Under the eyes of everyone? Are you crazy?"

"Photographs must fall out of files all the time," Diaz protested. "Just let me have it."

"And what if someday someone besides you is interested in the file? What then?"

"Who will know you took the file? Put it back. No one will ever look at it, but even if they do, so what? The picture fell out. It got lost. None of your concern."

I was getting nervous. What if Diaz's theory needed to be verified at some point? What if this photo could, down the road, be used as proof of a passport scheme? I hoped I wouldn't regret watching evidence disappear into Agosto Diaz's pocket.

The customs agent was shaking his head.

Diaz slipped something into his hand. The agent glanced at it, eyebrows raised. He said, "This woman is very important to you, eh?" With an avuncular sigh, he added, "I never could deny you anything, Diaz. You and Marules are like family to me."

He closed the file, letting the square color snapshot flutter to the ground. He turned his back on us, pretending to look through some papers.

Diaz quickly plucked the photo from the worn, superwaxed linoleum. It was in his pocket before Pirí turned back around.

As we walked back through the airport, Diaz whispered to me, "Two *mordidas*—he is a vulture, a bloodsucker! It won't be easy to pad my expense account sufficiently to hide this, believe me. The accountants are not as practical as Marules."

When we were back inside the car, Diaz took the snapshot from his pocket. He almost dropped it, he was so excited.

"I couldn't risk this disappearing, which it definitely would if certain people knew about it. *Caramba!* It was worth the extra pesos."

"You recognize her?"

He laughed deep in his throat. "Oh yes. I'm not surprised the illiterate vampires in customs did not. But, oh yes, a great many Mexicans would recognize this face."

I stared at the big-eyed, hollow-cheeked, middle-aged Cuban woman in the photograph. "Who is it?"

"You do not recognize Cuba's most famous poet? Or perhaps she has not been translated into English?"

"You don't mean—"

"Yes, yes. This is Lidia Gomez."

"But . . . I saw Lidia Gomez. In Cuba. She was under house arrest. Her face was bandaged."

"Bandaged? Like *The Man in the Iron Mask?* The real Gomez escapes to Mexico while her double remains sequestered?"

"I guess so." No wonder there were no guards at the back window. Gomez was long gone. "Why would someone pretend to be her? Why would the Cubans want that?" A sense of unreality settled over me. The last few days seemed almost imaginary. "It makes no sense."

Diaz frowned. "They do not want anyone to know she has managed to leave. Nor even that she would wish to leave, perhaps. Or . . ." A smile lit his face. "Perhaps they believe she is the real Lidia Gomez."

"If Gomez made it out of the country, why didn't she speak up? Why didn't she go public, discuss

Cuban politics, try to build pressure to get Myra Wilson out of prison?"

"Mexico does not share your government's attitude about Cuba. It would very likely extradite Gomez. The question is, why did she not go to your country? Did she lack confidence that you would take her in? One thinks she could have traveled north to make her denunciations."

"We've taken in every Cuban who's ever floated into Miami," I pointed out. "And we especially love dissident writers."

"We wondered why Cuba announced repeatedly that Myra Wilson was convicted of smuggling. Not that they could have kept it secret, but frequently they prefer to let these matters leak out as they will."

"You think they were trying to smoke Gomez out of hiding?"

"If they believed she was here in Mexico, yes. Because in that case she would certainly be returned to them." He started up the Volkswagen and backed it out of its parking place. "Whereas if she crossed the border to your country, she would become a poster child for anti-Cuban propagandists in Miami."

The Beetle engine was so loud he was practically shouting. He pulled onto the freeway, where at least a tenth of the other cars were Beetles. No wonder the air was a brown-tinged gray. Diaz drove at rattling speed, making me hope we had somewhere in particular to go.

"But why would Myra Wilson play along all this time?" I asked him. "If you're right."

"Because she is in custody. Because, perhaps, she is protecting Lidia Gomez. The sentence would be no shorter for passport fraud than for drug smuggling. And it may be that in exchange for her lies, they have promised her better treatment. Or promised not to search for Gomez."

"Using the women against each other?" Were the Cubans using Wilson as a hostage to keep Gomez quiet? With Wilson playing along to keep the Cubans from coming after Gomez?

He glanced at me, his brows raised. "It is a happier alternative than Gomez observing the silence of the dead."

But the theory must not have inspired much optimism. Our next stop was the city morgue.

There, Diaz left me on a wooden bench in a vast corridor that looked as if it had been built for titans in a grander past. He went inside to try to match his expensive Instamatic photo to those clipped to Jane Doe files. A friend who worked in the morgue had to be bribed first, of course. But the sum for medical examiners was small, Diaz observed. Not like the *mordida* for judges and politicians.

He came back out into the corridor an hour or so later, looking tired. He shook his head.

"So far so good. But she could have died anywhere." He stuck his hands into the pockets of his tennis slacks. "Equally, she could be living anywhere. If she is maintaining her silence in order to protect Myra Wilson . . . Well, I don't know how we could find her. We certainly can't show her photograph to the entire population of Mexico City."

"Is there anyone at the university, maybe in the

literature department, she had close ties to? Someone she could have gone to for help?"

He rubbed his chin. "A good thought. Let's check with Marules. He knows all the literary people. He is their groupie—he adores them."

I looked forward to talking to Marules. I'd been sitting in a corridor for (it seemed) half the afternoon, marveling at what Diaz had discovered. Lidia Gomez had slipped out of Cuba using Myra Wilson's passport. She might still be here somewhere, keeping silent to protect the woman who'd made her flight possible. I was still boggled by the news. I wanted to watch someone else gasp over it.

"But why Myra Wilson?" Diaz said, when we were back inside the cramped hell of his car. "Why this woman? We have of course researched her life when she was arrested—the only American woman in a Cuban prison. My impression was of an uneducated woman of the working classes, nothing special. So why has she done this for Gomez? We will have to rethink our story, undertake our research from an entirely new angle. Perhaps . . ." He cast a glance at me. "Perhaps we should go to the hometown of Myra Wilson."

"Jersey City?"

"Jersey . . . ? But no, I am sure that she was from San Diego, California. I recall that Martin sent someone from one of our small news bureaus, one close to the border, into San Diego to interview her family."

"But she told me she was from Jersey City."

He shrugged. "Perhaps this was her way of trying to protect her people in case you were not simply a tourist but a reporter. Although, if you were a good reporter, you would have known it wasn't true."

Dennis and Cindy hadn't corrected me when I'd told them. Had they known? "Maybe that was the point? To see if I contradicted her?"

"Or perhaps under the circumstances, it simply did not matter to her what you believed about her origins." He glanced at me. "If she has people still in San Diego, perhaps it is worth a trip?"

I wanted to burst into tears. I was so tired already. I just wanted to be home.

But I also wanted to know what the hell had become of my mother. And having run out of other options for finding her, I guessed I'd go just about anywhere.

15

$\mathcal{M}$artin Marules looked a half-shade away from apoplexy. "But no! No! Lidia Gomez here—I can hardly take it in."

He was seated behind a desk so heavy and grand, he should have been wearing purple robes with gold threads. Everything about his office was ornate, especially the high ceiling and the Rivera-style murals of nineteen-thirties reporters typing on old manuals or rushing around with notebooks and fedoras.

Marules, with his heavy frame and thick hair, his ageless suit and Mexican good looks, might have stepped straight out of a mural panel. Only his computer, his television with VCR, and a tiny microwave created a sense of contrast. Modern journalism, his office seemed to say, was a matter of Internet research, videography, and quickly heated takeout.

"Willa here"—I was surprised to hear Diaz speak my name—"she has suggested we go to the university, see if perhaps the famous poet found refuge with someone in the literature department."

"Ah," Marules said. "Leave that to me."

"Ask them if they've seen Lidia Gomez since she got here in March," Diaz put in.

Marules raised a hand as if to say, *I know my business!*

"March?" Something about this set off an inner alarm. What had happened in March?

I hadn't moved to Santa Cruz yet, but I'd started work on a pro bono case there. Mother, I recalled, had been scrounging computers for a caravan to Cuba. The idea had been to drive a convoy of trucks across the Mexican border, then air-ship the parcels from there. But the convoy was stopped at the Mexican border by U.S. Customs and State Department officials. The computers were off-loaded in the rain, ruining them. Then they'd been confiscated.

It was the kind of political high drama Mother claimed to find heartbreaking but actually adored. If nothing else, it had cemented her resolve to go to Cuba herself.

Now I wondered about the timing of this particular call to arms. Had the convoy been organized in response to a particular event? A call for help from Cuba's writers union, perhaps?

"When did the union expel Gomez?"

Diaz shrugged. "A matter of some days before. I believe the announcements were almost simultaneous: the troubles for Gomez, and the capture of an American woman drug dealer."

Marules nodded. "Yes. We ran the stories together on the same page, along with a companion piece written by Dennis on the general state of affairs in Cuba."

"The tunnels?"

"That was part of the story, yes."

Diaz crossed to the computer, and with a quick, "*Permiso?*" began typing in commands.

Within minutes, he had the information. "The Gomez story broke too late for previous day's edition. We ran it March the nineteenth. St. Michael's day." He crossed himself.

Marules hunched behind him, reading over his shoulder.

March nineteenth. I would have to check my phone records to be sure, but I thought Mother had phoned around the end of March to say the computer convoy had been turned back. As a (former) star in the Cuban writers union, perhaps Gomez had helped organize the convoy—and perhaps she'd gone to the border to meet it. As "Myra Wilson," she could hitch a ride "home" to San Diego on one of the convoy trucks. Who would look for an escaped Cuban in trucks full of Americans regarding Fidel as the personification of the Sermon on the Mount?

And if her passport were checked, so much the better. She was Myra Wilson, a U.S. citizen returning home from a frustrated goodwill trip. She was just one more Southern Californian who spoke only Spanish.

But if Mother had met this "Myra Wilson" on a convoy truck, what must she have thought when she toured a Cuban prison and was introduced to yet another woman with that name? My mother was a pathological blurter—she would surely have mentioned it, and that might have made someone very nervous.

Agosto Diaz was saying, "We want to go to San Diego and talk to Wilson's people. What do you say, Martin?"

Marules sat back, obviously surprised. "You are a fact-checker, Agosto." He looked at me. "He thinks he is Clark Kent, this one."

"Yes, I am a fact-checker. Fact number one: Dennis and Cindy are somewhere in Cuba without passports. Fact number two: You know as well as I do that they are there for some purpose, on some errand, secret to us. Unless you sent them?" He watched Marules carefully. "No, I didn't think so. They could be in grave danger, Martin." His voice dropped about an octave. "I won't let you leave them there like that."

I wondered if they were as attached to their UPI and Reuters people. "They work for Associated Press, right? Not for your paper?"

Martin cast Diaz an annoyed glance.

"Yes, but they are our friends. They have become part of the family." Martin's voice was husky, but, I thought, not quite sincere.

Maybe Cuba had burned out my trust-strangers circuitry.

"If you don't send me, I will go anyway," Diaz declared. "Cindy and Dennis would do it for me."

Martin didn't look convinced. But, with a sigh, he said, "If you must go, then go." He began typing something into his computer. "But I warn you, *chico*, your expense account will get more scrutiny than the bikinis at Cabo."

16

$\mathscr{S}$an Diego was what Cuba might be if it had the cash. It was sunny and breezy and bright, full of tropical plants and thin palms waving along the skyline. Broad boulevards traced white sand beaches, and this part of the city looked like those housing developments built around golf courses. The houses were big, the sea was blue, everything glowed with fresh paint. There was some variation in architecture, but not much. A few lawns were less green than others, but only a little. Probably anyone from Havana would have felt blessed to be here. But to a San Franciscan (now Santa Cruzan), it looked like a vast Republican cloning project, a place you might encounter Gerald and Betty Ford on any corner.

Agosto Diaz could hardly contain his enthusiasm for the town. "The air is very clean, is it not?"

"Today." San Diego could also sit under a humid beige cloud like Mexico City on a good day.

"And it is very elegant."

"Right here." The older sections, with the Spanish-speaking population crowded into small bungalows, looked more like hilly versions of Compton or East L.A.

He turned in the passenger seat to look out the side window. I though he might hang his head out like a happy dog.

I drove the rental car, hating every minute of it. I'd spent most of my life on streetcars and buses. Some things, I think, are learned young or not at all. Changing lanes, parallel parking, merging onto and off freeways—they don't come easily after thirty.

But I was in a bad mood anyway. I'd finally reached my father and had my faint remaining hope dashed. My mother hadn't come home. She hadn't been in touch. My father started crying on the phone. And I hadn't been able to offer any news, much less any cheer.

I'd asked him to fax me Mother's phone bill for March. Other than that, the call accomplished nothing except to further depress us both.

Agosto tore his attention from the scenery long enough to consult the map. "Soon you must turn to the right." He held the map up so I could cast a quick glance. "Then we are only a few blocks away."

Unless the neighborhood was about to undergo a huge change, Myra Wilson had lived in a pleasant enough suburb. The ocean wasn't in sight, but you could smell it in the wind. The houses here weren't huge, but they were on ample lots. The front yards sloped up to boxy bungalows that predated the ranch-style sprawl of newer, but now tackier, neighborhoods.

Agosto observed, "I have lived in apartments my entire life."

I didn't think it would take him long to miss the splendor of Mexico City, the palaces made of Aztec stones, the thirty-foot statues, the cobblestone plazas, the pillared buildings with marble eagles on their eaves.

I recognized the name of Wilson's street, and turned onto it, slowing to check addresses. We were still several blocks shy.

The neighborhood grew a little less pricey, a little more working class, with kiddie pools in front yards, half-dismantled cars in driveways, and the chatter of televisions through open doors.

A block short of the address, I slowed, murmuring, "No way."

Agosto was leaning forward, his forehead close to the windshield. I heard him whistle.

Up ahead, two police cars blocked the street, lights swirling. An unmarked cruiser had a cherry light on its roof. An ambulance pulled away from the curb, probably empty, since it was taking its time, its lights and sirens off. A big white truck—a coroner's van?—was backing into a driveway.

I continued on, hoping the congregation just so happened to be visiting Wilson's neighbor. When we reached the unmarked car, a plainclothes cop motioned us to drive past in the parking lane.

Instead, I stopped. To Agosto, I said, "Let me have the snapshot." I rolled down my window.

The cop, a well-tanned man with sun-bleached hair and a light summer suit, bent closer. "Drive on, please."

"We're here to see a woman we think lives there."
I pointed to the house, definitely Myra Wilson's
address.

Through the open door, I could see men milling
around. It didn't look like good news. But that didn't
mean Lidia Gomez was inside. For all we knew, she'd
never left Mexico City.

But if this crime scene had nothing to do with our
booking tickets to Wilson's hometown, it was a hell
of a coincidence.

Agosto handed me the Instamatic of Gomez, and I
showed it to the cop. "We've never met her, but we
have mutual friends. One of them suggested we stop by.
Was there a break-in or something?" But I could see the
coroner's logo on the truck. Someone inside was dead.

The cop squinted at the photograph, chewing the
inside of his cheek. "Can I see some identification?"

I dug my driver's license out of my bag, motioning
for Agosto to hand me his.

The cop's brows rose when he saw the Mexican ID.

"He's here for the weekend," I told him. "His
English isn't great. We flew in together this morning.
On Monday, he's going home and I'm going back up
to Santa Cruz."

I was overexplaining, and the cop seemed aware
of it. "Do you have your plane tickets?"

I pulled mine out of my handbag, translating for
Agosto. He removed his from the glove compart-
ment. The cop looked them over, comparing the
names to those on our IDs.

"Who's the person you're wanting to visit?" he
asked.

"Her name is Lidia Gomez." I didn't want to lie about her identity—if she was dead, we'd need to reveal a great deal more. But for now, I felt safe in assuming the cop wasn't a poetry buff, that the name wouldn't mean anything to him. "We've never met her. Like I said, a friend suggested we look her up."

I translated for Agosto, who nodded.

The cop suddenly switched to heavily accented, unidiomatic Spanish. "She was expecting you?"

"No, no," Agosto assured him. "I have never before met her. She does not know me at all."

"Is she okay? Is all this"—I waved my arm at the police cars and coroner's van—"is it about her?"

The cop squinted at the snapshot. The skin around his eyes was cross-hatched with sunbaked crow's feet. He asked Agosto, again in bad Spanish, "This is a picture of her?"

"Yes. She was traveling then—perhaps she does not always look so tired."

She looked more than just tired. She looked scared and haunted, like a Cuban with an altered passport about to have her baggage searched.

The cop motioned to a woman in a police sergeant's uniform. She trotted over, heavy and pigeon-toed, looking flustered. He handed her our IDs and plane tickets. "Check these out. Make sure they were on this flight."

As she returned to her cruiser, he scowled at her hips as if they were an affront to him.

Then he bent closer to the car window. "I'm afraid your friend's dead."

Agosto sighed, his olive skin going suddenly pale. He shook his head slightly.

"Dead how?" I asked.

"We really can't talk about it, not at this point." He glanced over his shoulder at two uniformed officers stringing crime scene tape. Neighbors stood on their lawns watching. Some took the opportunity to water their grass.

"It's definitely the woman in this picture?"

"Well, she looks older now."

"This was taken in March." How much older could she look?

"Must be a good picture," he suggested. But instant photos are rarely flattering. "Although, from what we can see, she doesn't live here, she works here. Housekeeping. So I'm not saying this is for sure."

Lidia Gomez worked in Myra Wilson's house? I translated for Agosto.

He shook his head. "A maid? For—Can it be?"

"Tell you what," the cop said. "Take the picture with you to the police station at this address." He pulled a business card from his jacket pocket. "You'll need to give a statement, anyway. And take the plane tickets, too."

Gomez must have been killed while we were en route. Otherwise, we'd have been detained here. Or, at the very least, escorted to the station.

Inside the police cruiser, the uniformed cop was making a phone call.

I took the proffered business card. "So she only worked here? Whose house is it?"

He raised his brows. Wouldn't I like to know?

"You won't tell us how she died?" I persisted. "Did it happen very recently?"

"Just wait here," he advised. He walked over to the cruiser, talking to the uniformed woman.

A few minutes later, she returned with our IDs and plane tickets.

"I gather it was pretty bloody," I said.

She made a sound that told me that was an understatement.

"Was it quick, at least? Did she suffer much?"

"No, don't worry." She had doe eyes and a high-pitched voice, Shari Lewis in uniform. "When the carotid's sliced, they pass out quick."

Agosto understood enough to turn away.

Lidia Gomez was dead, her throat slit. And, barring a wild coincidence, it must have happened because we'd booked a flight here to see her.

"The owner of the house," I continued. "Wilson?"

"No, Doctor—" She stopped herself.

"He's away on that trip," I guessed.

"Scuba diving. I do it myself when I can." She was looking past me at Agosto.

He was staring down at Gomez's picture.

"That's not her," the cop said. "You're not thinking that's the woman in the house?"

I could only gawk.

"Oh God, you did think—! No, unh-uh, it's a different woman."

"Are you sure? The other officer said . . ." I fumbled for the snapshot, handing it to her.

She held it close to her face. "There's a similarity, they're both Hispanic. But this woman's younger, thinner." She glanced at the house, looking a little cranky. "He really thought this was her?" She looked again at the photograph. "I'll go talk to him. Let me take this with me. But I can tell you right now—No, let me talk to him first."

Her gait was quick and determined. She shook her head as if planning what she meant to say.

I looked over to find Agosto with his jaw dropped and his eyes wide. He raised his hands in a shrug that said, What could possibly be going on?

I shrugged back.

A few minutes later, the woman loped back to our car.

"Sorry for the scare," she said. "The good news is, it's not your friend."

And the bad news was, the killer hadn't known the difference.

17

My worst job ever was, ironically, also my best-paying. I'd spent a year with the megafirm of Wailes, Roth, Fotheringham & Beck. I started out in its San Francisco office, earning about four times what I'd made as a frustrated labor lawyer, but working virtually around the clock for it. A particularly vile circumstance then forced me to move to the Los Angeles office. I'd barely lasted a year there before overdosing on chat about *the* new glass artist or what to look for in a BMW. I knew I was in trouble when I started longing for the conversation of my parents' friends.

From my present perspective, however, there was one very good thing about Wailes, Roth, Fotheringham & Beck. It had a satellite office here in San Diego. And right now I needed a computer with good snooping software. I needed to access property tax records so I could learn the name of the doctor who now owned Myra Wilson's house.

Even so, I hesitated. I knew it would mean a series

of those what-are-you-doing-now conversations. And there was little status in being a sole practitioner in a funky little beach town. Nor were my clothes cute enough to deflect the pity my former associates would make sure I heard in their voices.

Nevertheless, I went and I endured. I was quickly updated on who'd joined which county commission (hard to make partner without proof of "social involvement"), how many languages their toddlers spoke, which Yuppie Adventures had become de rigueur—cross-country skiing, it seemed, was giving way to parasailing, though kayaking was still important to the corporate Eskimo. Agosto remained by my side, my hint of multicultural bad-girlism. Judging from the looks I got, younger men were quite the fashion accessory this year.

Finally, I borrowed a computer and pulled up county property tax records. I found the name of the doctor who'd purchased Wilson's house. Maybe I should have guessed. It was (I'm not kidding) Ernest B. Hemingway. He bought the place on April 27, paying cash. I had no idea who signed the deed or who banked the money for Wilson.

And all I knew about Hemingway was that Myra Wilson had cooked for him. And that he was, according to the policewoman at his house this morning, off on a scuba diving excursion.

I spent over an hour in Wailes, Roth's conference room, going methodically through Yellow Pages listings of scuba shops, asking if they knew of any in-progress scuba trips. Every shop knew of at least one. I was beginning to think most of the county's citizens were currently underwater. But

Hemingway's name had the advantage of being memorable, and the clerks were sure they hadn't signed him on.

One of Wailes, Roth's partners wandered into the conference room to ask me some pointed questions about Agosto. She noticed the Yellow Pages ads.

"Are you looking to rent some gear?"

"I'm trying to reach a friend who's on a scuba trip."

"Maybe he popped up to Santa Barbara, do some boat diving off the Channel Islands. That's where I always go." She looked pretty smug about it.

Hoping Wailes, Roth wouldn't begrudge me a few long-distance calls, I phoned Santa Barbara information for the numbers of dive shops there.

One of them had indeed signed Ernest Hemingway onto an excursion. The boat would return to Santa Barbara tonight. I checked my wristwatch. With rush-hour traffic through L.A.—and there was no other kind—it would take us about four hours to get there. We'd barely make it, if we were lucky.

I extricated my handsome Mexican friend from two female associates and a gay male partner, and, with a minimum of thanking and yanking, hustled us back out to the car. I pointed us toward Los Angeles, and prepared to do some aerobic steering wheel gripping. For me, a drive through L.A. was always followed by a day of aching biceps.

As if the drive weren't grim enough—bumper to bumper in eye-stinging smog—Agosto kept exclaiming over the murdered maid, harping on the likeliest possibility: The poor woman must have been murdered because someone thought we'd pointed the way to Lidia Gomez.

Agosto worried that Pirí, the customs official, had sold us out ("And yet I offered the precise *mordida!*"), telling a higher bidder we'd requested Myra Wilson's file. And I worried—though I kept my mouth shut—that it might have been someone closer. That it might have been Agosto's friend and mentor, also linked to the Cuban Yum King. Given the circumstances, it was hard not to suspect the only person in whom we'd confided, the person who'd booked our flights, Martin Marules.

He knew Lidia Gomez had managed to get out of Cuba, and that she might be living in Myra Wilson's house. He'd tried to discourage Agosto from pursuing the passport angle, then tried to contact Pirí before him. He'd been reluctant to send Agosto here, relenting only when Agosto vowed to come on his own. With just a phone call, he could have arranged to make sure Gomez wouldn't talk to us.

Except that she wasn't in the house. A Hispanic maid was there instead.

I worried and drove for four rotten hours, but we made it to Santa Barbara's harbor before the dive boat pulled in. We stood in the chilly wind, looking over an ocean that would have been lovely but for a row of oil derricks spoiling the shoreline.

"There it is—*Scuba Do.*" A motorboat was coming in slowly, a row of people at the front rail watching the dock. With such a corny name, that had to be it.

We watched it get closer. I could see that some passengers wore Polarfleece while others still wore wet suits. I could almost make out their facial expressions.

All of a sudden, a passenger in a wet suit turned, hurrying toward the back of the boat. Whatever he did there caused a big commotion. Other passengers ran back. The boat honked its horn. I could hear shouting.

When it finally docked, passengers were gesturing and shaking their heads, taking their time getting off.

We all but pounced on the first couple off the boat. "What happened?" I asked.

"One of the people in the group dived into the harbor."

"Fell overboard?"

"No." The woman looked confused. "Tumbled off like he was going for a regular dive."

The man added, "He strapped on a B.C. and a tank, all that, before he went over." He looked angry. "What a dummy! This is no place to dive—all these boats. Jeez. He seemed like a smart enough guy before this. I don't know what the hell he's thinking."

"Was it Dr. Hemingway?"

They nodded. "How did you know?"

"I recognized him," I lied. I'd had a fleeting impression of a man with brown hair.

"Why would he do such a thing?" she demanded. "It's ridiculous."

"Believe me," I said, "I have no idea."

Unless he knew me or Agosto by sight. Unless it was very important to him that we not see him and identify him.

Other passengers came off the boat. Many were

talking about Hemingway, and the consensus seemed to be that he was a crazy fool. More than one person commented that it didn't seem like him.

"He flashed the okay sign after he hit the water," a woman reassured us. "So there was no reason to cut the engine and go in after him—he wasn't drunk or anything like that. And it would have been too hard to turn the boat around. It was his choice, and stupid as it was, he was competent to make it."

"But you have no idea why he did it?"

"We heard he made a call from the boat's phone a while ago. And he's been pointing his binoculars at the dock ever since."

As if he were watching for us. As if he'd recognized us. Or one of us.

"What did he look like? I thought I saw someone get out of the water."

"Dark hair, brown eyes, Cuban," the woman said. "He told us he came over on the Mariel boatlift back in nineteen eighty, when he was a college student. A nice man."

"An idiot," her partner contradicted her.

More to the point, a *gusano*.

18

*W*e'd booked a room (with two beds) in Agosto's name so that he could expense-account my portion to help offset the bribes he'd paid. Unfortunately, we'd booked the room right off the bat, and were now constrained to drive back to San Diego. Besides, my father's faxed phone record should be waiting there.

While I picked up the fax, Agosto went up to the room. I followed a few minutes later, a mass of aches and fatigue from all the driving. I got off the hotel elevator, surprised to see him still standing in the open doorway of the room. I approached with some trepidation. He was just standing there, arms dangling, head tilted.

When he heard me coming, he turned. He looked weary, a little cynical, maybe sad. I didn't know what to make of the expression.

He said, "Our baggage is gone."

I stood beside him. It was a typical hotel room, too much beige, ugly bedspreads, every inch of the place visible from the door. My bag had been near the closet. I'd opened it to change my T-shirt, leaving it gaping and rummaged. Agosto's bag had been on his bed, a few toiletries removed and scattered.

Now, without our bit of clutter, the room looked pristine.

I sat on my bed, sighing. I was too tired to go downstairs in search of a still-open shop selling toothbrushes and sleepwear. "What's the point?" I wondered. "Why take our stuff? Why not just look through it?"

Agosto remained in the doorway. "Perhaps he was sent after our things. A hireling. Such a person would not know what to look for."

I dropped my handbag. "This is what they should have gone for. My purse is where I've got my passport and credit cards and plane ticket."

"Perhaps they are not looking for credit cards and passports." He closed the door. "To have taken everything . . . it must be something subtle. Something which they believe you have taken from Cuba, perhaps? Something from Cindy and Dennis?" He rubbed his forehead. "It makes my head ache. We have accomplished so little and yet, I think, caused so much damage."

"Yes." I assumed he referred to the murdered housemaid.

I reached for the phone, and called the desk, asking them to send security up.

It took almost half an hour to explain the situation, fill out the paperwork, and receive the assurances and apologies to which the management felt we were entitled. But the gist of the conversation was that they would not be held accountable for items not placed in the hotel's safe.

I insisted that we be moved to a different room, and asked that the registration records disguise it. This seemed to confuse the manager, but he agreed anyway. He gave us "a significant upgrade," which meant the new room had a love seat, a couple of ugly end chairs, and a faux-marble table.

Housekeeping sent up toiletry kits including toothbrushes and hair combs.

When everybody finally left, I dropped onto one of the two king-sized beds. I was still holding the hotel envelope with the fax of my mother's phone bill. I opened it, unfolding the sheets of paper it contained.

I looked at the long list of calls, almost two hundred dollars' worth. She'd made calls all over the country, no doubt organizing the Cuba convoy and other protest actions. The words "San Diego" leaped off the page.

There were three calls to the same local number. All were about five minutes in length. They took place on March 16 and 17, the two days before her convoy set out for the Mexican border with its load of computers. I reached for the phone and dialed the number.

A musically accented Latina voice said, "You have reached the answering machine of Dr. Hemingway's residence. In case of an emergency, please call . . ." A phone number followed, then the usual instruction to leave a message after the tone.

I hung up. "It's Hemingway's answering machine. At his house. Which is odd, because back then, it was still Myra Wilson's house."

"He has kept the same phone number, perhaps, when he has moved to Wilson's house."

"Unless he lived there before. He must be Wilson's boyfriend. She said she'd cooked for him."

Agosto sat on the edge of the other bed. "And so when she is arrested, he buys her house and banks the money so that she can . . . what? Why would she need money? She is after all in a Cuban prison."

"Lidia Gomez isn't. Maybe Wilson had to bribe some officials. Who knows what else she might have done with a bundle of money?" I was struck by a sudden worry. "We keep assuming Wilson helped smuggle Gomez out, that that's why she's in prison. But maybe it's because she was bringing cash in. The Cubans would have to be afraid of what a person could do with thousands of dollars, how much they could buy and who they could buy."

Agosto nodded. "Myra Wilson's boyfriend hates the Cuban government, which we can assume if he came to this country on the Mariel boats. Castro did not often allow *gusanos* to flee. And with Mariel, people threw stones and garbage at them as they boarded the boats. They were so desperate to leave they gave up everything and everyone and left with only their shirts, knowing they would never be allowed back." He lay down, crossing his arms beneath his head. "So Hemingway—can this be his real name?"

"Maybe his mother lived near the Hemingway house. Maybe it's more of a place name than a family name."

"In any case, this Dr. Hemingway cannot return to Cuba, so his girlfriend, Myra Wilson, goes instead. But she does not go simply as a tourist."

"She either smuggled money in or smuggled Gomez out, or both."

"So it is only reasonable to believe that Hemingway has conspired also to help Gomez."

"And it's reasonable to believe someone thought Hemingway's maid was Gomez."

"Unless the maid was herself a person of interest or distinction. A Cuban?"

I nodded. "Could be. We'll have to see if we can get some information about her."

"This will be difficult, will it not? The police will not wish to share information with strangers?"

"I might have a friend . . ." Oh, Willa, don't even think it. "A homicide lieutenant in San Francisco, he might be able to get some information for me. As a favor."

Agosto rolled onto his side, facing me. "Ah," he said knowingly.

I gave him a sharp glance. What had he heard in my voice?

He was smiling. "A love affair?"

"No. Believe me."

"You have a lover now?"

I hesitated, but not because I didn't know the answer. The imp of lawyerliness prompted me to respond, "Why do you ask?"

"Because you are unhappy over the San Francisco policeman."

"No. I was unhappy, years ago."

"And in the meantime, you have had many lovers?"

In the meantime, I'd had many jobs. I had many hassles. I'd had many cases. And I'd had exactly one more sexual encounter than Mother Teresa. But I didn't really want to say so.

"And yet you are very lovely." Agosto smiled. "When you know me better, perhaps . . . ?"

I felt myself flush. Was he suggesting that, when I knew him better, I'd want him for a lover?

I looked at the handsome, intelligent young Mexican. No perhaps about it.

19

$\mathcal{M}$y first order of business the next morning was a trip to the store. I bought some shorts, a pair of jeans, some underwear, T-shirts, a sweatshirt. I wondered if Ernesto in Cuba would find them as "fine" as the ones they replaced.

I stopped in the hotel lobby to make a couple of phone calls. I told myself I might as well let Agosto sleep in, enjoy some time alone. But I was the one who needed the privacy.

With a here-goes sigh, I punched my credit card number into a pay phone and dialed San Francisco Homicide. It took me over five minutes of being transferred and remaining on hold before I heard his voice. Luckily there was a little settee next to the phone.

Judging from the rapidity of my heartbeats, my viscera hadn't quite gotten the message that I was over Homicide Lieutenant Don Surgelato. After an affair consisting of a couple of near-kisses and his returning to his ex-wife, I was long since back on my feet. (Getting onto my back had been the problem.)

"Surgelato here."

Hearing his voice reminded me of being a law student, then a newbie lawyer. It reminded me of a lot of things that were even less fun to recall.

"It's Willa Jansson." I let it hang there like the bad news he probably considered it.

"Willa? Where are you?" His tone of voice implied I'd run away to join some cult.

"Right now, I'm in San Diego. I was hoping you could do me a favor."

"Go on." His voice promised nothing. In fact, that about summed up our relationship.

"A woman here was murdered yesterday, probably in the early morning, before noon for sure. I need to find out her name and nationality—anything about her. But I'm sure the police won't want to tell me."

"Is this for a case you're working on?" His tone was guarded. He wasn't going to feed the civil litigation machine, not if he could help it. "What firm are you with now?"

"It's not for a case. And I'm in solo practice now. Down in Santa Cruz."

"I heard about your UFO case."

"Yeah, well, you know how the news distorts things," I said lamely. "Anyway, this has nothing to do with work."

"I think you'd better tell me what it does have to do with. You know I can't be passing information to civilians."

"It gets a little complicated. It involves my mother."

He snorted. My mother had picketed the building

he worked in, leading an entourage whose signs demanded his immediate resignation. She'd gone after him for killing, in the line of duty, someone she'd known rather well. For a lot of reasons, most of them that she's a big blabbermouth, I'd never told her the whole story behind that shooting. Only Surgelato and I really knew what happened. And because of it, he'd been suspended, investigated, and nearly fired. And then, when he'd finally been cleared of wrongdoing, my mother had staked out the sidewalk beneath his window.

"Oh yeah," he said, "anything for your mother."

"I know, but this is . . ." I took a few deep breaths. "It's very important. I won't use the information in any way. I'll just know, okay? I won't tell anyone. And no one will know you told me. But it's life and death, it really is."

"Life and death?"

"Yes." To the maid, maybe to my mother.

"Then you better fill me in."

Oh, right. Like we were so close. "I can't. But I . . . Look, I'm afraid this woman was killed because someone knew I was here to ask her some questions. About my mother, about where my mother is." I touched my cheek. It felt hot. He always did that to me. "I'm looking for my mother, okay? I'm afraid she could be in a lot of trouble. And I came here to ask—"

"Looking for her where? What kind of trouble?"

"I can't say."

"Something illegal, I gather?"

"Nothing immoral, nothing you wouldn't expect from a bleeding heart who's trying to do the right thing." He'd seen only her implacable opposition to him, her harsh manner, her on-a-roll ranting. He'd never looked deeper to see the altruistic sweetheart, the naive plunger-ahead, that she really was.

I started crying, thinking of her. Poor Mother, I hoped she was okay.

"Willa?"

I pulled myself together. "Yes?"

"Tell me."

"I can't."

"It'll stop here. You know my word is good."

I did know that. I also knew that if I waited a couple of days, long enough for the San Diego police to notify next of kin, I would learn the identity of the slain maid without him.

A couple of days. Would it make a difference? Would something bad happen to Mother in the interim?

Waffling, I looked up to find a man in a hotel security blazer standing in front of me.

"Just a second," I said to Surgelato. I covered the mouthpiece. "Yes?"

"You're in Room 412?"

I was startled. No one was supposed to know we'd changed rooms.

He looked over his shoulder to a man behind the desk. The man nodded to him.

He said, "Room 412? Ms. Jansson? Is that right?"

"Yes."

He took a deep breath. "I'm afraid I need to have a few words with you. It's rather urgent. Can I accompany you to the office, please?"

My hand dropped from the mouthpiece. I was too

scared to care what Surgelato overheard. "What's wrong?" I asked the man.

"I think it's better if we go into the office."

Through the glass lobby doors, I saw two police cruisers pull up. I could hear an ambulance close by and coming closer.

"Just tell me what's happened," I pleaded.

When the officers walked into the lobby, the desk clerk pointed at me.

"Am I being arrested?" I asked him. But I could see the ambulance pulling up. "Agosto! Is he okay?"

I stood, hanging up the phone.

The police flanked me, while the security guard said, "The office is right through here."

I watched two more officers meet a man in a gray suit and walk to a key-operated elevator with him.

"What happened to Agosto?" I asked the cop beside me. He was a baby-faced man with a sunburn.

As I was hustled into an office, I saw medics walking hurriedly to the desk.

We were in a room filled with television sets showing surveillance camera images of various parts of the lobby, parking garage, and hallways.

"What happened? What's going on?"

The security guard hung back, standing near the door. The sunburned cop said, "It appears there's a problem in your room. I think we should wait a few minutes until we have verified data." He patted my arm. "Please try to relax for a few minutes."

I looked at the other cop, hoping he might be more forthcoming. But he was mumbling to the security officer. A few seconds later he left the room.

The sunburned cop said, "I'm sorry to make this kind of request, but . . . we'd like to have a look in your purse."

"My . . . ?" I handed it over. I didn't want to ask. I was afraid to.

Police, an ambulance, now they were searching my bag. Something terrible had happened to Agosto, and they were making sure I hadn't done it. They were searching for a weapon.

The security guard returned a moment later holding the clothing bags I'd left beside the pay phone.

The policeman tilted his head toward them and said, "Do you mind?"

"No."

I watched him paw through my new clothes. He looked carefully at the receipts. "You used a credit card?"

"Yes."

He nodded. The receipts were computer stamped with the time of purchase. The credit-slip signatures would show I'd done the purchasing. "We may have to keep these," he said.

"Just tell me what—"

The other cop returned. He saw the receipts in his partner's hand.

Sunburn said, "Four purchases within the half hour from nine-thirty to ten."

That seemed to settle something for the other cop. He looked at me, and sighed. "I'm afraid we have some bad news."

No kidding, and here I thought I'd finally been cornered by the fashion police.

He waited. But I couldn't make myself ask. I sat

back, wishing I never ever had to hear it, never had to find out.

"The man you were with," *were,* "I'm afraid he's dead."

I felt like I'd been kicked. I couldn't speak.

"He tried to call nine-one-one, apparently. The hotel has a record of an attempt to get an outside line just before ten o'clock." He looked sympathetic. "You have to dial nine here to get an outside line, so it went through as an aborted long-distance call. You know, nine for an outside line, then one for long distance. The phone was left off the hook."

I continued staring at him, watching him grow blurry as tears filled my eyes. My face was so hot I thought my skin would curl off. There were rocks in my chest. I heard myself say, "Please don't. Please don't say . . ."

The sunburned cop squatted beside me, offering me a tissue.

"Housekeeping found him. It looks like a homicide," the other policeman said. "And I'm afraid, from what the medics tell me, that it's too late to help him." He watched me sit there, just sit there. "We understand you and your friend filed a report with security here regarding a theft last night," he continued. "So when you're up to it, the sooner the better, why don't you tell us about it?"

"How did he . . . ? You said it was a homicide?"

"We'd better wait a little bit, until we have more details, before we discuss it. Beyond telling you he's dead, we don't want to misinform you."

It was already too late to help him, and it had happened between nine-thirty and ten, if the receipts were exculpating me. So it had to have been violent. It had to have been a gun or a knife.

Maybe a knife across the throat. Just like Hemingway's maid.

Poor Agosto. What had I gotten him into? What had my mother gotten us all into?

20

I didn't know what to do. I didn't know whether to continue with the half-truth I'd told the police at Hemingway's house or tell them everything in hopes it helped them find Agosto's killer. For a while, the point was moot. I was too upset to be coherent.

That didn't last long. The San Diego police weren't going to let me impede their investigation of what might be a double homicide. Dr. Hemingway's maid and Agosto Diaz must have been killed for related reasons, if not by the same person. Why else had Agosto and I shown up at Hemingway's house the day before? Why else had he been murdered the same way, with an immobilizing blow to the head followed by the severing of the carotid artery in his neck?

I gave up on trying to protect myself and my mother. At least two people were dead because of something I couldn't figure out. It was time to tell all.

I told homicide investigators the whole long,

strange story. Then I told two FBI agents who'd driven down from L.A., and three officials from the U.S. State Department, who'd flown in from Washington. It would certainly bulk up the package when I filed a Freedom of Information Act request to see my government files. But no one mentioned pressing charges. And, as small a loophole as it might be, I continued claiming I'd spent only Mexican pesos in Cuba.

Given the larger stakes—three Americans unaccounted for in Havana, a famous poet sneaking out with a now-jailed American's passport—my transgression didn't seem to strike them as especially heinous. I hadn't gone to Cuba to cut cane and sing songs about the glorious revolution, I'd gone to find my mother. Maybe they'd make trouble for me later. Right now, they had other matters to attend to.

My father flew down almost immediately, looking shockingly changed. The murders had made him pessimistic about Mother's fate. He appeared ashen and bent, and he was so distracted he could hardly carry on the simplest conversation.

For a few days, men in suits came and went, interviewing me and sometimes my father in a hotel conference room. (My father and I remained at the hotel—not in room 412, of course—without charge, thanks to a freaked-out hotel management.)

Martin Marules flew to San Diego, too. He seemed to have aged fifteen years overnight. He wept so much and so openly—so Latinly—that I thought I'd go crazy watching him.

Sarah Swann, one of Mother's companions from the Women's International League for Peace and

Freedom, showed up, too. She was closeted for hours with the State Department officials, talking about the group's trip to Cuba. Afterward, her eyes glittered and her jaw was clenched—she looked like the Amazon Queen after a fierce and bloody battle. I presumed she'd made it clear what she thought of their Cuba policy.

Sarah and my father held hands and had anguished conversations. Sometimes they tried to console Martin Marules, who kept repeating that he'd lost a son.

I took long walks just to get away, just to keep them from magnifying my already unbearable grief. I felt untethered in a crazy world, adrift in tragedy and dread. I clung to memories of Agosto. I suppose I'd forgotten the warmth of a friendship deepening into romance—it had been so long since I'd had one.

Sometimes I tried to puzzle things through, but the police remained tight-lipped about Dr. Hemingway and his maid. And they'd made it very clear I'd be in big trouble if I tried again to contact him. Not that I cared much about pleasing them—it seemed irrelevant. I had already cooperated to the point where Mother and I could be charged with a federal offense. Agosto had died in a room we'd shared. So I couldn't work up much distress about displeasing the San Diego police.

As often as I could, I escaped the hotel and everyone in it, hoofing for hours through Spanish stucco business districts and bland suburban streets and palm-lined beach-front boulevards.

And as often as not, I would end up at Dr. Hemingway's house. I would stand out front and stare as if the place could tell me something. I'd walk around back, peeking into windows and through French doors. I saw rooms full of plain, serviceable furniture with color-coordinated drapes and carpets. But I never caught a glimpse of anyone inside. And if the house was being watched, no one ever came and rousted me off the property.

Sometimes I'd find a pay phone and dial Hemingway's number just to hear the voice on his answering machine, the voice of his dead maid. I memorized her beautifully musical accent and wondered if my coming here had killed her.

Once, I called the "in case of an emergency" number on the tape. I reached a doctors' consortium answering service. Dr. Hemingway was not available, I was told.

I dialed Dr. Hemingway's office several times, but got only a machine saying the doctor's office would be closed through next week, and to call the emergency number for the on-call doctor.

As much time as I spent in phone booths, it never occurred to me to call my house and check my own machine. Those messages, that life, might as well have belonged to someone else. Someone who wasn't avoiding a grief-stricken father, a teary-eyed WILPF organizer, a sobbing Mexican journalist, and five government agents with ever-growing lists of questions to which I had no answers.

So I just walked. Walked anywhere and everywhere. Oddly, the longer I walked, the more stares and smiles I got. I guess I looked like a sunkissed tourist instead of a woman mourning a would-be lover and, perhaps, a mother.

It was after one of these walks, returning to the hotel lobby with my face composed to pretend I didn't notice the stares of valets and bellmen and desk clerks, that I saw Don Surgelato.

I stopped halfway across the lobby, feeling my jaw drop. From the moment I'd hung up on him, I hadn't thought of him again. Eventually, I suppose I'd have called back and explained. I saw him rise from a lobby couch, and I guessed he'd gotten tired of waiting.

He hadn't changed much, and yet he couldn't have looked more different. In my mind's eye, I saw him in terms of my connection to him, my gratitude toward him, my mixed-up longings, my inappropriate feelings, my out-of-bounds actions. I saw him in glimpses tinged with my own embarrassment and angst. I saw him in tableaux where I was the cringing star, where the hot lights beat on me and my discomfiture, and left him in shadow, a short, powerfully built man obviously of Italian extraction.

Now, in the bright afternoon light through the lobby's plate glass, he came into unaccustomed focus—ruggedly compact with short black curls and clothes that, though casual, bespoke a fortune inherited from Italian entrepreneurs who'd set up one of San Francisco's first banks.

Maybe I seemed different, too. He looked at me as if I did.

The last few days had nearly inured me to serious-looking men coming to see me. I crossed to him and stuck out my hand. He looked slightly taken aback, but he shook it.

I said, "I forgot to phone you back. I'm sorry."

"Don't worry about it. I know you've had your hands full."

"Why did you come down here?"

In the past, the few times I'd urgently needed his help, he'd sent a crusty Homicide inspector named Krisbaum. So it was strange to see him here, unbidden.

He smiled as if my question were a little too complicated to answer. Maybe I should have followed up with, Did you bring your wife?

"You want to go somewhere and talk?" he suggested.

"Sure." I looked around the lobby as if a place would appear for us by magic. My reasoning skills were somewhat impaired by circumstance and too much sun.

"You want to come up to my room?" he asked. "It's private."

I tried not to smile. Ironic to hear this now and in this context. God knew, I'd tried to elicit these words many times in the past. "Sure," I said again.

He put a light fingertip on my elbow as we walked to the elevator. Weird to feel electricity there still.

The elevator was slow and crowded. We didn't try to talk. But I noticed in the mirrored panels that he kept glancing at me, his low brows knit. With his prominent nose, dark brows, full lips, and cleft chin, he looked like a hit man or a deli waiter or a football player. He looked physical and sensual and not all that smart. But if that were true, I'd probably have gotten him into bed years ago.

We got off at (presumably) his floor. He pulled out his room key as we walked down the quiet corridor. A room-service waiter stared at me as he passed. I was the big celeb around here, the black widow herself.

Surgelato noticed the waiter's look and scowled at him. He still scowled well, with macho authority and a cop's scariness.

We reached his room, and he unlocked the door, swinging it open for me to precede him in. It was a small, drab room. My comped suite was at least twice as big, and the furniture was real wood instead of particleboard. They really treat you right when your traveling companion is slaughtered in one of their beds.

Surgelato closed the door, offering me the room's only chair. He sat on the bed, facing me.

"Aren't you always supposed to position the suspect so the light's in her face?" I asked him. I had my back to the window. He was the well-lighted one.

He smiled. "I'm off duty."

"Why are you here?"

"See what's up with you."

"I would have called you back eventually. Or you could have called me."

"I did call you."

"Oh." I hadn't really checked my room messages. Everyone I needed to talk to was down here already.

"So tell me about it." I must have made a face, because he added, "I'm not just indulging idle curiosity, Willa. You know that."

I nodded. You didn't get to be The Man in San Francisco's Homicide Division unless you had something to offer. "It's just that I've been talking about it for days. San Diego police, FBI, State Department, U.S. Customs, and that's not even . . . Agosto Diaz worked for Martin Marules—he's down here now. He hasn't stopped crying. And my father's here. One of my mother's friends came down. I'm just so sick of it." I felt myself flush. "That must sound pretty cold."

He raised his brows. "No. Of course not." He started to reach toward my knee as if to pat it. But he stopped, dropping his hand awkwardly. "I know a little less than the cops down here know. But I've been on the phone to them plenty."

"You have?" I pushed my hair off my face. "Didn't they think that was a little strange?"

He shrugged, obviously not caring. "I vouched for you. They told me what they knew. We didn't get into the whys and wherefores."

"They're very close-mouthed about the maid." I leaned forward, hoping he wouldn't be. "What's her story?"

"Alicia Mendoza," he said. "She was originally Cuban, but her family moved to Guatemala when she was a teenager. Her father had something to do with importing clothing from there into Cuba. He took his family on a trip to Los Angeles and then refused to go back to Guatemala, saying they'd make him go back to Cuba. He died after running through the family savings getting all the paperwork and green cards and all that. So Alicia's been a maid for quite a while. She worked part-time for six different local families, about seventy hours a week."

I raised and lowered my shoulders, trying to unknot them. I'd been so tense lately I kept imagining I was having a heart attack. But it was just the strain of keeping my shoulders up around my ears.

"Did you already know this?" Don wondered.

I shook my head. I would dwell on Alicia Mendoza's circumstances later, in the privacy of my own room.

He said, "You didn't kill her, you know." I guess my lack of affect didn't fool him. "Or Agosto Diaz."

I jerked at the sound of Agosto's name. Every time I heard it, it was like a Taser zap on a raw wound.

"One possibility the police are considering," he continued, "is that someone stole your bags so you'd have to go shopping. Basically assuming you'd split up to do it. Which would imply that he was the target all along, that whoever did this wanted to separate you from him."

I was sitting as still as I could, trying to control how much I let in, how much I let myself understand. Because I didn't want to cry. I'd been doing so much of it. And everyone around me had been out of control. I wanted to keep it together at least until this conversation was over.

"Under that theory," Don continued, "he must have known something or been close to something. Whoever did it wasn't worried about what you knew, or that you were a threat. But somehow Diaz was." He sat forward, his elbows on his knees and his fingers laced. "It's tricky, huh? Something Diaz hadn't told you, but that he already knew. Can you think of any possibilities?"

"Jeez, virtually everything. I only knew Agosto a couple of days. I knew almost nothing about him."

"But it would have to be about this situation. Think—Cuba, Dr. Hemingway, the Associated Press reporters, the Cuban poet . . ." The SDPD certainly had filled him in. "Any inkling? Anything Diaz might have been getting ready to talk about?"

"No. I don't know." I rubbed the spot between my brows. I'd just taken a long, exhausting walk and my head was aching.

Don got up and poured me a glass of water. "You look hot."

I took a long drink, then pressed the glass to my forehead. "If I had to take a wild guess, I'd maybe say Dennis and Cindy, the reporters. If he knew something in particular he hadn't brought up, it would probably be about them. He'd known them for two years. Martin Marules, his boss, said they were good friends. Dennis and Cindy had his number programmed into their autodialer." I shrugged. "But we didn't really talk much about them. We talked about Lidia Gomez and Hemingway and all of that. Because it was right in front of us." I set the water glass down. "And because he was worried about them like I'm worried about Mother. He didn't talk about his friends and I didn't talk about my mother. It would have made everything too hard."

Don nodded. "So tell me, what do you know about the reporters? Tell me what you know for sure, first hand, then what you think they wanted you to believe, and then what you've been told about them." I must have looked boggled, because he said, "I know it sounds laborious. But go with me. Let's try to do some work."

I wanted to say, no, I don't work for you. I'm too tired, too sad, too close to falling apart.

But he was a pro. And if it helped us figure out who'd killed Agosto, we might be closer to knowing what had become of my mother.

"Okay," I said. "In no particular order . . ." I blithered about the time I'd spent with Cindy and

Dennis in Cuba—the car rides, the dinners, the hike to Lidia Gomez's house, the drive to the women's prison, their appearance in the plaza when the white-coated man accused them of being CIA agents.

"You told all this to the FBI and State Department people, I gather?"

"Oh yes. Many times."

"And they didn't comment." It wasn't a question. "Okay, go on. What did you learn about them in Mexico City?"

I described their apartment. "Marules and Agosto didn't talk much about them. You know, like you don't about someone you both know."

"But you didn't know them. They didn't say anything to you like, 'It would be just like them to . . .' or 'How odd of them not to . . .' Nothing like that?"

"If so, it's not coming back to me. I'll think about it."

"Fair enough. What about when you came up here with Diaz? Did he talk about them at all?"

"No. I don't think so."

"And you attributed it to worry. Same reason you didn't talk to him about your mother."

"That's right."

"I'm really sorry about your mother. I hope you know that. I hope I wasn't, you know, on the phone."

I made a hand motion—copacetic. I couldn't really talk, not with the lump in my throat.

I gave it a minute, then said, "Tell the truth. Do you think there's a chance . . . ? Do you think she could be in Cuba somewhere? Alive?"

We stared at each other. He looked as though he was struggling for the right words.

Finally he said, "The Cuban government would have every incentive to find her and send her home. And she'd be so damn conspicuous there, easy to spot, easy to find. So . . ." He squinted as if it pained him to say so, "I guess, no, I really don't think she could be missing in Cuba. I don't believe she wouldn't find a way to get word to you. She'd find a helpful Cuban or one would find her. And you'd know if she was there."

"If she was alive." My voice sounded flat.

He didn't say anything.

I sighed, sitting back in the chair. I could feel tears spill down my cheeks. "That's what I think, too," I said. "My father, too. And the State Department people, you can tell they think she'd have turned up by now." I swallowed, wiping my cheeks with my hands.

Surgelato slid off the bed onto one knee. He took me in his arms and I put my forehead on his beef flank of a shoulder. He stroked my hair.

I hadn't spoken to him for two years before this week. But it didn't matter. We'd done something years before that cemented a connection. In the interim, he'd remarried his ex-wife and I'd moved away. But something was still there. At least, I felt it.

I put my arms around his neck and clung to him as if he were the tether I'd been wishing for.

I don't know why he clung to me.

$\mathcal{W}$e went home with nothing resolved. I stayed with my father until he got over the worst of it, until he stopped rattling around the big Haight Street flat like a moth in a lantern. Then I went back to Santa Cruz, to my new place near the yacht harbor, a place I'd hoped to love, but could now only live in.

I listened to news broadcasts and C-SPAN speeches, but if foreign policy toward Cuba was affected, it was impossible to tell. We still shook our fists at them and kept our citizens from spending dollars there. We kept out computers and clothes and food and medicine, as usual and as best we could. But that had nothing to do with my mother, or with Cindy and Dennis, or with Myra Wilson and Lidia Gomez. It was the same course we'd been steering for almost forty years.

The San Diego police hadn't closed the file of Alicia Mendoza or Agosto Diaz, but if they'd had any new leads, they sure hadn't called me.

I never thought it would end this way, with my

mother lost. I never envisioned giving up before I'd found her. But what more could I do? I couldn't return to Cuba. Even if the State Department didn't find a way to stop me, the Cubans had thrown me out. They certainly wouldn't let me back in.

And I didn't know where else to look for Mother or for Dennis and Cindy.

I had, at one point, driven back down to San Diego out of sheer frustration, hoping to thrust myself upon the elusive, scuba-diving Ernest B. Hemingway, M.D. I had already learned that he'd been Myra Wilson's boyfriend, as Agosto and I had supposed. She'd gone to Cuba to see for herself the conditions her partner had fled. When she didn't return, Hemingway purchased the house so Wilson wouldn't lose it to a mortgage company in her absence. At the time, he'd begged the State Department to raise a fuss and get her out, but they wouldn't, saying they couldn't interfere with a drug bust. Later, when he'd learned about the computers-to-Cuba caravan, he'd resorted to asking WILPF to go to the prison and see Wilson, make sure she was okay. My mother and Sarah Swann, her WILPF buddy, had both spoken to him about this. Though they considered him a *gusano,* they'd agreed.

They were certain, Sarah explained to me, that they'd find Wilson thriving in a perfect penal environment. And the scary thing was, Sarah thought they had. She and my mother had been favorably impressed with the "airy, homey" women's prison.

And as for Dr. Hemingway, he claimed to know nothing more about my mother or the San Diego murders.

So why had he jumped off the dive boat? He'd called home on the boat's phone and learned his maid had been killed. He saw me and Agosto waiting on the pier and assumed we were reporters wanting to discuss the murder—and wanting to dredge up painful stories about Wilson's arrest.

His explanation held together well enough to pass muster with the police. It may have even been true, though I doubted that was all there was to it.

When I pulled up in front of his house after a long bummer of a drive, ten hours from Santa Cruz, I knew right away something was different. I knocked at the door, and found a play group of toddlers being minded by a harried-looking woman. She'd purchased the place from a Dr. Hemingway, yes. She believed he'd moved out of town. He'd closed his practice, she knew that. But she didn't know where he'd gone.

I got his office address from the phone book, and I drove there. A different doctor's name was on the door. The receptionist told me that Dr. Hemingway was in Iowa now. Or was it Indiana?

I ended up driving back up the coast, keeping a firm grip on the wheel in case my evil twin tried to wrench the car off the cliffs into the sea.

I drove straight up to San Francisco, and spent the next day with my father. He seemed so old without the impish humor, the quick flash of dimples, the goofy wit that rarely found expression anymore. The place was quiet without my mother and her constant phone calls, her infinite outrage over little things, her sudden volcanic enthusiasms.

My father had been spending more and more time

with his computer guru, Brother Mike. Mother had loathed Brother Mike because he was apolitical, a New Age cybernetics wizard with a quantum physics vocabulary. Without her carping, my father was growing more and more cerebral, living in cyberspace and working on the guru's quasispiritual computer projects. Because Mother would have hated it so much, that was almost the hardest thing to bear.

And as for my new practice, well, I made sure I did enough work to pay for my little house and my little office. But I preferred, above all else, to sleep. I put a hammock in my back yard, and most afternoons by four o'clock, when the pain was unbearable, I would go home and lie in the hammock and rock in the sun until it set. The hammock, I sometimes thought, was the only thing keeping me together.

I had two friends in town, Fred and Edward Hershey. They stopped by fairly often despite the fact that I was lousy company. Edward, a private eye, kept going down to San Diego, trying to get new information. He never mentioned it to me, but I knew. For one thing, he was fond of my mother. And Fred, a psychiatrist, kept trying, as tactfully as possible, to draw me out and help me work through my feelings. Neither of them had any success.

And so it went for months, five and a half very long months. Autumn blew through with cold, fragrant winds that whipped leaves off the liquidambars. Winter brought cold mists and high tides. Now wildflowers were coming up everywhere, so colorfully and plentifully it would have seemed like heaven if I'd been happy.

Then one day that seemed just like the days

before it, my home phone rang, and it was Don Surgelato.

His voice was tight and deep with excitement. "I may have a lead," he said.

I hadn't even presumed to think he was still working on it. I leaned against a wall to steady myself. Hope can knock you off your feet.

"What do you mean, a lead?"

"San Diego Homicide's been sending me copies of what it gets in, you know, professional courtesy, all that."

He'd spent two days in meetings with various cops and government officials, months ago in San Diego. They'd respected his rank enough to include him in the nitty-gritty of the investigation despite his having no real business there. They must have thought it was odd, or maybe they assumed that we were lovers or former partners. But if they hassled him about it, he never let on.

When he returned to San Francisco, he kept in touch for a while. My father said he'd stopped by the flat a couple of times to see how he was doing. But I hadn't spoken to him in at least three months. I didn't realize he was still keeping involved.

"What did they send you?"

"You know the State Department interviewed Jamieson and Travolta?"

"Yes." The Cubans believed "Mr. Jamieson" and "Mrs. Travolta" were CIA agents, and assumed these were the real names of Dennis and Cindy. But according to Martin Marules, they were merely Cindy and Dennis's landlords. "I was told they'd been interviewed in Belgium, but that they had nothing to contribute to the investigation. Or words to that effect."

"Well, they got back to Mexico City last week. Moved back into the apartment. It's been sitting empty all this time." He paused. "Are you okay?"

"Yes." It was just hard to think of Cindy and Dennis vanished, their things packed up and shipped off to family members somewhere, their apartment reclaimed by its previous occupants. It was as if they'd been erased.

For a while, their fellow AP reporters, as well as friends at UPI and Reuters, had made something of a mission of going to Cuba to try to track them down. But the months had passed, and there was so much news to cover all around the world.

Don continued, "I got word they were back. But nobody had the manpower . . . and it was just a hunch." He cleared his throat. "I was just hoping to fill in some of the gaps."

I couldn't figure out what he was trying to say. I waited.

"I hired a couple of detectives to go down there and watch them for a while."

"You did?"

"Look, I didn't want to tell you because probably nothing would come of it. And, well, you know, I've got the money, it was no big deal."

Yes, he had the money. But it certainly was a big deal. "Are you saying the detectives found out something?"

"Don't get your hopes up, but maybe. Do you have a fax there at home?"

"No."

"Okay, then I'll fax a photograph to your office. Can you go there and take a look?"

"Who's it a picture of?" Don't get my hopes up? It was as if someone had taken a defibrillator to them.

"Remember I had you do a session with our police artist?"

"Yes." Surgelato had gotten hold of photographs of Cindy and Dennis; Myra Wilson; Lidia Gomez; Agosto; Dr. Hemingway; his maid, Alicia; and a few other players. But he'd wanted artist's sketches of the rest, the ones in Cuba—Señor Emilio the Yum King, the supposed Radio Havana man in the white jacket, Ernesto, the Chinese guard I'd yanked into the tunnel and fallen on top of. "Of course I remember."

"Okay, today Jamieson and Travolta picked up someone from a Cubana de Aviación flight. I'm not sure if he's one of your Cubans. My guy got a picture of him. I want you to go take a look at it."

I stood with eyes closed. Oh, please, let it be. Let there be something more that I can do.

"Don, thank you. Either way."

"No, don't even . . . Just call me back."

I raced to my office, a little suite in a building with two small law firms and an accountant. It was right downtown, and my upstairs room had a view of leafy, light-strung trees and Starbucks's patio. I shared a receptionist and a conference room downstairs. Parking was impossible, but I liked being a staircase away from bookstores, outdoor cafés, and weird little galleries.

I entered as the other lawyers were leaving. Only I closed up shop at four o'clock. Only I needed hammock therapy then, though I suspected a couple of my suitemates popped Prozac. I skipped the small talk and ran upstairs to my corner room. My fax already had a sheet in the tray. I pulled it out, my hand trembling and my breath held.

I stared at it, shaking my head.

I stepped backward, toward my office chair. I was just sinking into it when the phone rang. I hit the speaker button. The receptionist, cranky to have been delayed on her way out, said, "A Mr. Surgeelo?"

"Put him on."

A few seconds later, Don's voice crackled out of the speaker. "You got it?"

"Yes." I stared at the young face, with its wide eyes and excited smile. "It's Ernesto. From the sea wall."

A brief silence. "The boy you ran away from that last night?"

"Yes."

I listened to him breathe. Finally he said, "You want to leave this to the police?"

"The San Diego police? Isn't it way outside their jurisdiction? Would they even care? Ernesto certainly didn't have anything to do with the murders up there."

"They'll take this photo and file it. I know they won't cross the border to question a Cuban national with an alibi."

"And the Mexican police have never been involved."

"The FBI might go down there. The State Department." He sounded a little angry. "But then again, they might not. And this kid could be on the move. He could be gone tomorrow."

"I want to go down there. I want to talk to him. I can't stand to think of him slipping away."

"Then let's do it."

I stared at the phone's speaker as if that would explain what I'd heard. "You're offering to come?"

"Yes. Let's do it, let's go. Maybe nothing's going to come of it. But I agree with you. We can't let the kid slip away."

This was scary enough without hearing him use the word "we."

He continued, "I'll book tickets out of San Francisco. I'll call you back with flight information. You can meet me at the terminal. How long a drive is it for you?"

"An hour and three-quarters."

"Okay. I'll try to get us on something as soon after that as possible. Preferably tonight. Sit tight. I'll phone right back."

"No, call me at home. I'll go throw some things in a bag. Don?" I didn't know how to say this.

He seemed to know what was coming. "Naw," he said.

Then he hung up.

22

$\mathcal{M}$exico City is about as far from San Francisco as Chicago is, so it was a long flight. I kept glancing at Don. He still wore the suit he'd worked in, dark gray wool with a white broadcloth shirt now unbuttoned at the throat. I could see dark chest hair on his olive skin. I could smell his toiletries. Whenever he caught my eye, there was a short intense flash of something, sympathy maybe. Or determination. At one point, he took my hand, holding it until I pulled myself together.

In San Diego, he'd worn a wedding ring. Tonight, he didn't. Not that it made a difference. But I noticed it within seconds of spotting him in the airline terminal.

The flight seemed endless. I tried to talk myself into being realistic: Probably nothing would come of this, probably it was just a waste of time. I shouldn't count on anything. After all these months, any leads were likely to be cold and any news was likely to be bad.

On the other hand, Ernesto had presented himself to me as an impoverished young Cuban who dreamed of floating to Miami on a homemade raft. Now he was among the palaces and plazas of Mexico City, a guest of the couple whose tenants he claimed to have seen the evening after they disappeared.

Ernesto was no poor Cuban boy, that much was certain. He knew something about Cindy and Dennis, and maybe about my mother. I just prayed he didn't slip away from Don's detectives. He was all I had.

At Don's urging, I managed a few brief naps. I would be glad of it later. It took hours to get through customs and into a rental car. It was almost dawn before we reached the apartment of Mr. Jamieson and Mrs. Travolta.

The first thing Don did was to drive around the neighborhood, scowling out the windshield as if memorizing every turn and landmark.

Then he pulled up behind a black Volkswagen Beetle. I was surprised when he flashed his headlights. I hadn't noticed a man slumped behind the wheel as if dozing. But when the light hit his rearview, he sat up, grabbed something from the passenger seat, and slid out of the car.

He was a portly, dark-haired man with a bristling mustache and mussed hair. He climbed into our back seat.

"Good to see you, sport," he said to Don. His accent was Southern Californian. I guessed he was a PI out of San Diego, not a local.

Don shook his hand, introducing him to me as Conner. Without giving me a chance to say hello, he said, "What do you have? Any activity the last twelve hours?"

"Plenty." Conner handed him a stack of papers. They were handwritten sheets, some with Polaroid pictures paper-clipped to them. "There were folks coming and going all evening, till midnight or so. The last one never came out."

I looked up at the balcony doors of the second-story apartment. Beige curtains were drawn across the plate glass.

Surgelato scooted closer to me, clicking on a penlight. "I don't want to turn on the interior light. Can you see okay?"

"Yes."

I aimed the thin beam at a very bad snapshot of three people entering the building. One was Ernesto. The others were familiar only because the San Diego police (or perhaps the FBI) had shown me copies of their passport photos.

Garrett Jamieson was a small, slender man with pinched lips and a long, flaring nose. Angela Travolta looked several years older, with a puffy face and overratted hair.

"They started getting visitors around eight o'clock," Conner continued.

With Don leaning close, I looked at the other pictures, each clipped to a sheet showing arrival and departure times.

They were taken from too great a distance to show facial detail. They were of a well-dressed woman and a short, bowlegged man. They could have been any of thousands of Mexicans in this city.

Then I reached a photo of someone I recognized. The quality was poor, so I had to squint at it for a minute. But standing beneath the porch light, looking rather nervous, was the receptionist of Martin Marules's newspaper, the woman to whom I'd handed my note to Marules.

I told Don. He nodded. "Good. Keep going."

The next picture on the stack made me gasp. "It's Pirí, the customs agent, the one who was so friendly to Agosto. The one who gave him the Instamatic photo of Lidia Gomez."

Don stared down at it. "This is the guy who's still up there?"

"Right," Conner confirmed.

"What did you tell the FBI and State about this character?" Don wanted to know.

"I described what happened. I described him. I gave the name I heard Agosto call him. Apparently it's a nickname, though. There's no one there with that last name."

"I wonder, did they even follow up?" Don shifted to face Conner. "Find out for us tomorrow."

"Okay. Let me get a few hours' sleep. I'll try to be back on it by noon. You want me to leave this stuff with you?"

"Yeah. Thanks."

"Should I finish out this shift? Or you guys taking it from here?"

I was relieved to hear Don say, "No, I want you to go in with me as soon as your relief shows up. I want Price out here as backup. You get that gun for me?"

"Yeah. Hold on."

He returned to the Beetle.

"You're going in armed?" I asked him.

"Don't worry about it." A twinge crossed his face.

He'd taken a gun to a rendezvous on my account once before, and it hadn't turned out very well.

Conner returned with a bundle, handing it to Don through the car window. Then he trotted back to the Beetle and slumped in the seat so you could hardly tell he was there.

I watched Don unwrap the gun—square and chrome and not much bigger than his hand—and check it. He stuck it into his waistband just behind his hip. He slid what must have been an extra clip of bullets into his pants pocket.

"Nice and comfy," he murmured. "All we need is the obligatory Merlot and we're ready to go pay a call." Then, "I'm sorry, I shouldn't joke."

Shouldn't joke. Jesus, he'd flown us a couple of thousand miles on his dime to try to find my mother, whom he didn't even like. As far as I was concerned, he could do any damn thing he pleased.

"You're okay?" he asked.

I nodded. "I'm going in with you, right?"

"You're up for it?"

"Unless you speak Spanish."

"Just enough to order food. But, yeah, it's better if you come in. You find out what they've got to say, and I'll knock heads if I have to. Conner will back us up, and Price will be out here if we need him." He bent closer. "But if you're nervous about this . . ."

"I'm not a wimp." Well, technically, I might be. But if it helped find my mother, I'd go in, nervous or not.

He spoke what seemed to be a nonsense syllable under his breath, then he put his arms around me and kissed me. We'd kissed once before, years ago, and it had messed me up for a long time. Now I remembered why.

He murmured something in my ear. "Don't stop till they're past." Another kiss.

Through his caressing fingers, I could see a couple walking by the car. I could hear the woman's hard-soled shoes click on the pavement.

I felt myself stiffen with embarrassment. I hadn't seen the couple, hadn't known this was a ruse. For me, it had been real.

I backed up just enough to look at Don's face, expecting to find his eyes on them. But he was looking at me, his lips still parted. He put a finger under my chin and leaned in again.

Then he shifted in his seat, looking up at the balcony window. "Did you see them go in?"

I swallowed. "No."

"I'm pretty sure they did. That makes six people up there now. You didn't recognize them?"

"No. But I didn't get a good look."

"They weren't anyone I've seen pictures of." He squinted up at the window. A minute later, he said, "Did you see those flashes?"

"No."

He frowned. "Passport pictures? Couple goes up there, gets photographed, your customs official Pirí is there. If I'm right, the three of them will be back down here before long."

"That'll leave Jamieson, Travolta, and Ernesto. Just three of them."

"Better odds," he agreed. "I hope I've got time—"

He opened the door, and moved quickly to the car ahead. He murmured something to Conner. Then he returned, getting in and shutting the door just seconds before the couple emerged from the building, followed by Pirí.

Don slid me down so he was half on top of me, his arms circling me. He was so wide and muscular—and God help me, I love heft. I could hear the woman's shoes on the pavement. I didn't know how long this kiss might last or if it would ever happen again, so I went with it. Hardly the action of a wimp.

We didn't unclench until the threesome was surely out of sight.

When we sat up, I saw that the Beetle was gone.

"I told him to follow them," Don explained. "I don't want any evidence walking away." He checked his wristwatch, a thin sliver of silver. "Backup's late." He looked at me intently. "We should wait for Price."

"What if more people come? Or they take off—if they scatter now, we could lose Ernesto." I was doing my best to sound *macha*. "Let's just go." Unless you're scared, *gringo*.

He hesitated.

"I know cops believe in having backup and not putting civilians at risk," I said. "But it's my mother."

"I wish I didn't have to— But you're right, we've got them together." He shook his head. "Hopefully Price will get here."

"Will he know we're inside?"

"He'll know something's up when he doesn't find Conner out front. It's just a matter of getting his attention. Anything goes wrong, go to the window and wave like crazy."

We got out of the rental car and walked to the row of doorbells. He rang the one labeled "Jamieson."

There was no reply. He pressed it again, leaving his finger on the buzzer.

Finally, a man's voice said, "We hear you! Who is it?"

Don turned away and said, "Piri." His accent was Italian, not Spanish.

Apparently, through the tinny speaker, it was close enough. The buzzer sounded, and we pushed the door open.

Don went up the carpeted stairs at a run, two steps at a time. I jogged after him.

When the door began to open, he hurled himself against it like the football star he'd once been. He was barking out orders by the time I reached him. I stepped through the door a few seconds later, closing it behind me.

Don had bullied Jamieson over to the couch, where Mrs. Travolta was bent over some kind of scrapbook, reader's half-glasses on her nose. He was waving his badge as if it meant something here.

But my attention was focused on Ernesto, standing near the balcony doors in pressed linen pants and a tasteful blue shirt. His eyes widened at the sight of me.

I wanted to walk up to him and hit him. Slap him for the long, scary bike ride whose purpose must have been to lose me or lead me into harm. I wanted to slap him for the lies he'd told me. For trying to lure me away with the promise of taking me to Cindy and Dennis.

Don was saying, "We've identified this Cuban as a

key player in a passport scam. We can prove he killed three Americans there."

I probably flinched. Ernesto didn't.

"Pirí," Don continued, "is being followed right now, along with his new friends—they'll be in custody soon. They'll be asked to give information against you in exchange for leniency." He leaned in close to Jamieson. "You don't know it yet, but I'm a friend of yours. I'm here to help you. I'm going to let you tell us about it, nice and friendly. And if you tell me the truth, I'll walk out of here, and I'll give you time to do the same. The alternative is, the men outside will come in and baby-sit you till you explain the whole thing to the Mexican police, the FBI, the U.S. State Department, and the San Diego Homicide Division." He pointed a finger at Ernesto. "Tell them I'm not kidding. Tell them who this woman is."

I would have translated, but Ernesto's sneer told me he understood. He just stood there, arms folded.

I approached him with the fascination of a visitor at a zoo. In Cuba, looking undernourished and scruffy, his face had seemed angelic with its high cheekbones and wide smile, its look of wonderment and longing. Now, with his curls gelled and his fine clothes, he looked like any young man who doted on himself. He looked like a real American.

Jamieson said, "May we examine your identification?" He spoke a drawling Yale English. "For more than a—"

I turned to see that Don had drawn his gun. "Don't threaten me." His voice was cold and his face looked like a stone carving.

Mrs. Travolta, her voice more cultivated than her

bad dye job would have led me to guess, said, "We have no idea what you're talking about. This young man is our guest. His visa is in perfect order."

"So when we pull him in for murder and passport fraud, we won't be able to get him for visa problems? Gee, that's disappointing." Don's voice was low and humorless. "Or do you mean we should just take him away, and not bother you about it? You're pretty sure, I guess, that he'll keep zipped about what you've been doing. And Pirí, too, he's a loyal guy. He'll protect you at any cost to himself."

Jamieson put his hand on the couch cushion between himself and Travolta. She slipped a wrinkled hand over his. But they looked stoic, not scared. I turned back to Ernesto.

"Where's my mother?" I asked him. "Where are Dennis and Cindy? If you tell us . . ." I looked over my shoulder at Don. He'd taken on both the good-cop and bad-cop roles. I wasn't sure what that made me. Sidekick? Designated wimp? "We'll leave you alone."

Ernesto's eyes showed a flash of feeling, but he said nothing.

"Dennis and Cindy?" Jamieson sounded surprised. "Is that who you're looking for? We've never actually met them, you know. We just sublet our apartment to them."

Don made an exasperated sound. "And it's just a hell of a coincidence that your friend here ran into them in Cuba."

Jamieson's lips pursed as if he were considering the nature of coincidences.

Don leaned in closer. "Let me be as clear as I can.

I've gone to a lot of trouble to photograph everyone who's been in and out of this apartment, and to document what's been going on here. We've got police artist sketches of this Cuban dated months ago, with full transcripts of statements about what he was up to in Havana. Just me alone, I've got documentation enough to make sure you end up in a Mexican prison. And the FBI and the State Department, they've got a hell of a lot more. So if you do bribe your way out of jail some year, you can talk to them, too. I'm not just a jerk with a gun, believe me."

Jamieson said, "Whether I believe you or not, the gun is understandably my concern at the moment."

"Well, that's why I brought it," Don said. "It makes people more willing to listen to me. I just want you to know that it's not my real weapon. My big guns, so to speak, are tailing Pirí and his friends. My big guns are stacked in police and FBI filing cabinets."

I continued watching Ernesto. If there was something we could say to scare information out of him, he hadn't heard it yet.

"While I'm in a confessional mood, let me add one more thing," Don continued. "If I were to shoot you and drop this gun, it would never be traced back to me because it's not mine."

"Well, bully for you," Jamieson said crossly. "But you won't find who you're looking for, will you?"

"I was thinking I'd shoot you just to get Ernesto's attention." He glanced at the young man. "If that's your name."

"Ernest Hemingway," the boy said in English. His accent owed as much to London as to Havana. "And you?".

"F. Scott Fitzgerald," Surgelato said.

"Oh, bother," Mrs. Travolta said. "If we give you a phone number, will you please dial it?"

Don motioned me to the telephone. I punched in a series of numbers, eleven or twelve of them, as Travolta recited them. I watched Ernesto as the number rang through. How could he look so calm? I could feel everyone else in the room watching me.

"Yes?" came the reply.

"Tell him you're with us," Travolta said.

Don nodded. His face had clouded. Some realization had come to him, and he didn't much like it.

I cleared my throat. "I'm with Mr. Jamieson, Mrs. Travolta, and Ernesto from Cuba," I said.

"What would they like me to do for you?" The voice was nasal and East Coast.

Mrs. Travolta said, "Ask him his location. That should do it."

"Tell me where you are."

He rattled off an address in Arlington, Virginia. "We'll be expecting a callback soon." He hung up.

Jamieson was staring at Don. "If you don't know the address . . ." He shrugged. "If you do, please put the gun down."

"Shit," Don said. He lowered the gun.

"What are you doing?" I demanded.

"CIA," he said. "Your white-jacket guy in Cuba was right. These assholes work for the CIA."

I gawked at Ernesto. "You, too?"

He nodded.

"And you didn't hurt Cindy and Dennis?"

"No."

"Did they really rent bicycles from you?"

"No. I wanted time with you, and you seemed anxious to avoid me. But you needn't have run away. I was only taking you to a friend's house. We would have waited there and chatted until you got tired of it. That's all."

"Why did you lose me on the bike ride?"

"I wanted you to find the tunnel so you'd tell people—journalists in particular—that you'd seen it. But I didn't want to be with you when you found it."

"Why?" I was close to slugging him. "I could have been caught. Arrested."

"You'd have been sent home, that's all. I didn't want my cover blown."

For all I knew, I'd killed a man down in the tunnels. The Cubans would have done a hell of a lot more than slap my hand. It made me sick to think how much more.

"So where's my mother?"

He shook his head.

"Cindy and Dennis?"

"Either in *combinado del este*"—the prison he'd called "throw away the key"—"or in the AIDS colony. Two places no one gets into on tour and no one gets out of, period."

Mrs. Travolta rose with a sigh. "Or China. The Cubans may be exporting prison labor in exchange for goods. We've heard rumors, though we can't prove it."

"No." I didn't want to believe it. "Why would Cubans disappear foreign journalists? Of all people?"

"Isn't it obvious?" I couldn't get used to Ernesto speaking English, especially with a hint of a British accent. "The powers that be—the powers that have been for a very long time—don't believe Dennis and Cindy were robbed of their passports. They believe they sold them or gave them away."

"Gave away their passports? Leaving themselves with no way to get home?" It was ridiculous. Did he expect me to believe it?

"You have to think like a Cuban. Not like an average Cuban, but like a ministry official, a faithful Fidelista. Would a Cuban harm a tourist—the country's lifeblood—in order to steal a passport and flee like a *gusano?* No, foreign enemies of the revolution must be supplying passports to embarrass El Comandante." Ernesto shrugged. "It's deluded and paranoid, of course. Every government action there is."

"You can hardly blame them for being paranoid about the CIA—you especially," I pointed out. "And how would you know what it's like to be a real Cuban?"

"Ah, but I am a Cuban! I was born there. I escaped on Mariel when I was eleven years old. I was adopted by an East Indian family in Miami and taken to London. Later, I returned to the U.S. to go to Yale. I was recruited there. Yes," he smiled, "I am a young-looking fellow. But I'm pushing thirty, you know. I've done more than one stint in Cuba. And when I'm there, I'm as Cuban as anybody could be—everything I told you about the place is true. Except my purpose, which is to find out what American tourists are up to. Especially the ones who sneak in through Mexico, like you did."

I thought back on our encounter at the sea wall. He'd seemed to be gushing on about his life and dreams, but he'd learned very quickly why I was there.

"That's where Pirí comes in," Jamieson said. "He looks through the paperwork and gives a shout, as it were. He tells us when Americans enter Cuba through Mexico. He's not attached to us, you understand. Just contract work, simple commerce."

"Did he tell you Agosto Diaz went to see him?" I could feel tears sting my eyes. "Did you kill Agosto?"

"Of course not."

"Then who did?"

"Señor Marules, I presume." He pointed to the phone. "If we don't call back soon—"

"Marules? You're lying."

"Just a guess. Do you mind?" Jamieson reached for the phone. "Really, all hell will break loose if we don't call back."

Don said, "Give him the phone."

As Jamieson dialed, he continued, "Who else knew you were going to San Diego? Who but Marules knew where you were staying?" He stopped as if listening.

"You're lying," I repeated. I crossed to Don, grabbing his arm. "They're lying."

Jamieson spoke into the mouthpiece. "A slight wrinkle," he said. "We have San Francisco Homicide Lieutenant Donald Surgelato and Santa Cruz attorney Willa Jansson here. Our options, unfortunately, were limited. To minimize outside involvement, we had them make the call." He listened, watching us as he did. Then he nodded and hung up.

"Luckily," he said, "these are kinder, gentler times. Just as you offered to let us go . . . rather than shoot us," he smiled, "I am authorized to reciprocate."

"It's not too late to shoot him," I said to Don.

Ernesto (or whatever his name was) laughed.

Don slid the gun into his pocket.

Jamieson waved his hand as if to say, Think nothing of it. "The important thing is that this goes no farther. We've pulled Ernesto out of Cuba, as you can see. And we'll be moving on, as well. That's why your knowledge is not . . . a problem for us. But it could become a problem if you choose to share it. We have ears in many places."

He did look a little like Mr. Potato Head.

"Tell us where June Jansson is," Don said. "That's all we want to know. You tell us that, and you've got our cooperation."

"We haven't a clue," Ernesto replied. "I'm sorry to have to say that—it doesn't really speak well of our efforts. But believe me, I've done my share of asking around. I can tell you one thing: if she left Cuba, she didn't use her passport." He raised his brows. "There's certainly a growing criminal underclass there. Perhaps she was attacked."

"If I were you," Mrs. Travolta said, "I would ask Señor Marules."

I walked to where she stood. I looked at the scrapbook she'd left on the couch. It seemed to be filled with clippings about cats and cat shows.

I asked her, "Why would I believe you over Martin Marules?"

"Because I didn't know you were on your way to Myra Wilson's house, did I?" She glanced at the scrapbook.

"Pirí could have seen our names on the departure list. And what else would we be doing in San Diego?"

I ran my fingers through my hair. "Or he could have told you we'd looked through Wilson's customs file. That he gave us the photograph."

"Ah, the famous photograph. I don't doubt it was a photograph of Lidia Gomez. But are you sure it was taken in Mexico City?" She took off her half-glasses. "Perhaps it was just a way to keep you busy."

The photo background showed the customs office wall. Pirí had sold Agosto genuine information, I was sure of it.

And my mother's phone bill proved she'd talked to someone at Wilson's house. No one had faked that.

What were these people up to? What else were they lying about? My mother? Cindy and Dennis? Everything?

I glanced at Don. His face was composed, his eyelids partly lowered. He said, "I've been a police investigator since I was twenty-four years old. And in all these years, I don't know if I've ever heard a better blend of half-truths, expedience, and outright bullshit. You think we can't touch you. You think you can make life a lot harder for us than we can for you." He sighed. "Fine."

He walked over to me. He put his arm around me. Jamieson and Travolta exchanged glances.

"Here's the deal," Don continued, "you can tell us the truth about June Jansson or we can make a big mess finding out on our own."

Jamieson raised his palms as if to say, Do what you must.

Don, arm still around me, began backing us

toward the door. I noticed the gun was out of his pocket again.

When we reached the door, he groped for the knob and opened it. He said to me, "Go!"

I hesitated.

"Go!" he insisted.

I ran down the stairs, turning to see if he followed. The car keys landed at my feet.

I grabbed them, then ran out to the car. I fumbled maddeningly getting the driver's door open, then I started the engine and made a hasty U-turn, pulling the car as close to the building as I could. I honked the horn.

Seconds later, Don came out, walking backward. I reached across the passenger seat and flung the door open. When he climbed in, I stepped on the gas.

After rounding the corner, I looked over at him. The gun was still in his hand, but he wasn't looking out the back window. He was frowning straight ahead.

He said, "Where the hell is Price?"

I was still reeling from the encounter with Ernesto, from the news and lies and information, from the frustration of knowing more without knowing the one thing I'd hoped to find out. "Price?"

"Our backup. Why didn't he show up?"

Since it hadn't made a difference, I found it hard to care.

"Pull over," he said. "We've got a problem."

That much I knew. I pulled over.

He climbed out of the car, coming around to the driver's side. I slid over to give him the wheel. Nice of him to ask.

He doubled through a back alley. The time he'd spent exploring the neighborhood before we parked was paying off. He skirted the building we'd just left, zipping down every side street around it.

I didn't want to say it, but it sure looked like we'd been out tough-guyed. "They were lying."

"No shit."

"Are they definitely CIA? They weren't lying about that part?" I wanted to believe it was all false, every bit, because none of it was good news. I wanted to go back and threaten them again.

"Yes. The call you made, that address—I recognized it. Never known anyone to mention it, but we know about it."

"We?"

"Upper management law enforcement."

"Then why did you leave there holding a gun?"

"You expect me to trust the CIA?" He shot me a look. "And you an old hippie."

"Were they lying about my mother?"

"I couldn't tell. They're pretty seamless, aren't they? It's hard to guess where the crap ends. Except when they get flagrant."

"About Cindy and Dennis?"

"Yeah. The AIDS colony, the prison—pretty convenient for them to say there are places so mysterious and impenetrable no one can take roll. That's a hell of a big rug to sweep your mistakes under."

I couldn't stand to ask what he meant by "mistakes." Did he think Mother had been killed doing something the CIA wanted kept secret?

"Chinese labor camps, Jesus." He shook his head. "What next, shark attacks? Ebola outbreaks?" He looked at me, his eyes glinting. "I'm sorry they put you through that. Don't believe them."

"Cuba does have an AIDS colony." I'd researched it. "They segregate Cubans who test positive for HIV. They're in barracks surrounded by barbed wire. They're fed well, so a few people have contracted HIV on purpose to go there. No one's allowed to leave even for a visit. They're there till they die."

"I guess they don't want to be another Haiti, half their population infected. But there's no possible reason to throw an American tourist in there. Not even one as—" He stopped himself. One as annoying as my mother?

I hoped he was right.

"Whatever happened to your mother and those two reporters, the CIA doesn't want anyone to know about it—that's my impression. But I don't have a clue what it means."

"If the CIA wants to hush it up?" My chest was tightening. "That's a good sign, right? They'd want anything negative about Cuba brought to light."

"True—the cold war's not over, not where Cuba's concerned. But in this case, whatever's going on, it seems to be embarrassing the hell out of both sides." He took another ride around the block. "And it's also made one of the best PIs in San Diego a no-show."

23

$\mathcal{W}$e walked across the Zócalo. The washed stones of the Palacio National, pillaged from Aztec pyramids, glinted in the morning sun. The cathedral and the courts opened their carved doors. Soldiers marched away from bright flags they'd just raised above the square. Smartly dressed Mexicans hurried to work. Restaurants spread pink cloths over outdoor tables.

In spite of everything, it was a beautiful morning in a fairy-tale city.

We soon reached the side street where the newspaper office was located. Don ushered me inside, murmuring, "That's her?"

I looked at the receptionist, a heavy woman whose makeup ill concealed the puffiness around her eyes. "Yes."

Don stepped up to her desk. "Do you speak English?"

"Yes." She looked up at him with a smile apparently reserved for handsome men. I certainly hadn't gotten one when I'd approached her months ago. Nor did she offer me one this morning.

"Good." Don pulled the Polaroid of her out of his pocket, holding it close enough for her to see.

She made a sound as if she'd been hit.

Don put the picture back into his pocket, then unfolded his badge ID, giving her a good look. "As you can see, this apartment is under surveillance. What were you doing there?"

She shook her head, then shrugged slightly, then raised and lowered her brows. She seemed to be silently rehearsing different answers.

"I have no jurisdiction here," Don continued, "so I'm under no obligation to discuss this with your police or your customs officials. But I'd have to have a reason not to."

She opened a desk drawer and began groping for something, her eyes still on Don.

He said, "That's not what I mean."

I saw that she'd extracted a wallet.

"I don't want a bribe. I just want the truth. What was your business with these people?"

She chewed the lipstick off her lower lip.

"It won't go any farther. Unless you lie to me."

She began rocking in her steno chair. I felt like we were pulling wings off a fly.

Don leaned closer. "Is it Marules you're afraid of? Are you worried I'll get you fired?"

Her eyes welled with tears. "This is a very excellent job, Señor."

"Then don't make me tell him."

She glanced nervously over her shoulder. "I have

collected certain information at the request of the man who lives in this apartment."

"He paid you for it?"

"Yes." Her plump cheeks glistened with perspiration. "Occasionally I have taken information from the computer. Not often. This is the first time I have been to visit him in a very long time, I swear to you."

"What did you drop off this morning?"

"Please?" She looked pained. "You will say nothing?" Another glance over her shoulder.

"If you tell me the truth."

"Mr. Marules has a database—that is the right word? A list which he keeps on his computer—this is called a database?"

"Yes."

"I have received a phone call before I close the office door. I stay late, and with a password which I am supplied by Mr. Jamieson, I am able to copy this database to a computer disk." Her eyes were wet. She certainly seemed remorseful about having been caught. "He does not wish to come here, and so I have usually taken it to him, although once a woman with bad hair came to me at the Zócalo, and took it from me."

"What's in the database?" Don's tone was friendly. She was warming to her confession, adding details. He was keeping her comfortable.

She grimaced with full Latin emphasis—she didn't know or couldn't tell. "It is a jumble, *señor.* Code." She leaned forward. "He has put it in code perhaps for such an occasion, and it may be they do not even understand it. So it is not so bad what I am doing."

"Can you get us a copy of what you gave to Mr. Jamieson last night?"

She recoiled, her eyes widening.

"You said yourself," his voice was gentle, "that it's in code."

She nodded uncertainly.

"Do this, and that'll be the end of it," he promised. "I won't tell Mr. Marules or Mr. Jamieson." He paused, his voice losing its warmth. "Or the police."

When he spoke the word, she jumped as if he'd jabbed her with a pin. "Please, *señor*, I am the only support of my two children."

"Then it works out fine for everybody," he said.

She didn't look so sure about that. "I can meet you, perhaps at seven o'clock?"

"We'll be in the Zócalo," he agreed.

She gasped when someone else pushed the door open. She shot the newcomer, a young woman holding a sheaf of paper, a look that cried, *Save me!*

The young woman didn't seem to notice. She queued up behind Don.

Don said, in a more impersonal voice, "Is Mr. Marules in?"

The receptionist's mouth gaped.

I stepped up beside Don, assuring her, "Not about this. About something else."

Don nodded.

"I don't think— I don't know—"

"He'll definitely want to see us," Don insisted. "Tell him Willa Jansson is waiting."

That got her attention. She stared as frankly and ghoulishly as if I were Lizzie Borden. She'd clearly heard that Agosto Diaz was murdered in my room.

I had to turn away.

I heard her speak into a telephone. "Tell Señor Marules Willa Jansson wishes to see him."

For a long minute, there was silence. Then she hung up, saying, "He will send his secretary to show you the way." She glanced at the young woman behind us as if willing her to disappear.

A moment later, a thin woman in a tight blue suit and a tall chignon came out to greet us. "Allow me to take you to Mr. Marules," she said, in nearly unaccented English.

We followed her along a high-ceilinged corridor with marble panels inset between carved strips of heavy wainscot. The floor was well-worn alabaster. Don looked around, a half-smile playing on his lips. It was a hell of a lot nicer than the *San Francisco Chronicle* office.

When we reached Marules's door, the secretary knocked, waited a few seconds, then opened it, standing aside for us to enter.

Marules was already on his feet to greet us. He looked thinner and older, not as well integrated into the murals behind him.

"My friends!" He stepped to our side of his desk and shook our hands, clasping them in both of his. His eyes filled with tears. "It is good to see you again. You are well?"

It was a little hard for me to talk.

"You know." Don shrugged.

"Ah." Marules gave my shoulder a quick squeeze. "So there has been no word about your mother? I feared so. But I have been . . . I'm sorry, I should have called. ne becomes reluctant to hear more bad news."

I nodded.

He motioned us into heavy wood chairs that matched his desk. "May I offer you coffee? Ah yes, you look eager for it." He motioned his secretary, still standing in the doorway, to go fetch. When she closed the door, he asked, "What brings you here? A holiday?"

Don shifted closer, straightening the tie he'd put back on for the occasion. "We found out that Jamieson and Travolta were in town. We came to talk to them."

Marules's dark brows went up. With his smooth olive skin and slightly bulbous nose, he looked like a child's sketch, all easy, rounded lines. "Has this been useful? I believe they had been in Belgium?"

Don just sat there, not quite frowning.

Marules looked at me. "You have been to see them already?"

I nodded. We hadn't discussed what we would say or do when we got here. I didn't want to make the wrong decision off the cuff—I like to put a little thought into my misjudgments.

Marules looked from me to Don, then back to me. Our silence brought creases to his forehead.

There was a tap at the door, and his secretary came in with a tray containing three china cups with a matching coffee set. She left the tray on the desk and walked out.

Fixing the coffee took a few moments. I tried to catch Don's eye, but he seemed absorbed in thought, inaccessible even at arm's length.

When I sipped the strong brew, Marules said again, "So you have been to see Jamieson and Travolta?"

"Have you met them?" I hedged.

"Yes. I met them . . . at a party? Perhaps a meeting of some type? It was some years ago."

"What's your impression of them?" Don asked him.

"Well . . . she is certainly not a chic woman. Too loud in her manner and her dress for my taste. But not a foolish person, certainly. Her conversation, I recall, was good. Her companion seemed by comparison without color. Perhaps he has lived in her shadow so long he has grown pale. It is not good to live with a loud woman unless you are yourself even more loud." He smiled. "But I have no basis to criticize, you understand, having spent so little time with them. Did you find them . . . pleasant?"

I almost choked on my coffee.

Don said, "They didn't make us feel especially welcome. But then, we didn't call ahead."

Marules's head was tilted. He was watching carefully now, waiting for more.

Don set his coffee cup back on the tray. "We asked if they'd found anything missing from the apartment, if they'd had any unusual visitors or calls. Anything suspicious."

"And?" Marules prompted.

"And they pointed right at you." Don just left it hanging there.

I could hear a clock ticking somewhere in the room.

"Me?" Marules said, finally. His face suffused with color. "But why would they—? They do not even know me. No more than I know them. Perhaps you ᵌve misunderstood?"

"No. They brought up the fact that you knew Willa and Diaz had gone to San Diego. That you knew where they were staying."

Marules shook his head. "No." His voice was quiet. "That is not the case—I did not know where they were staying." He swallowed, crimping his lips. "Not until the police phoned me. I wish I had never learned. I wish I had never had occasion to learn the name of that hotel!"

"I don't know if they've made these comments to anyone else," Don said. "I thought you should know about them."

Marules looked at me. "You did not . . . ?" Believe them? He seemed to realize it would be an odd question. "I'm sorry for the pain they must have caused you," he said. "I had not considered . . . I suppose that there must be"—he took a few deep breaths—"speculation about the hotel room."

I flushed, knowing he meant our taking one room instead of two.

"Can you get us back into Cuba, Marules?" Don asked him.

For a moment, I thought I'd misheard him. As much as I wanted to find my mother, I didn't see how this would be possible. I'd be thrown out again, or worse, not be allowed to leave. I might be called to account for the things I'd done there—sneaking through a tunnel, tussling with a Chinese soldier. And even if they were just bogies invented by "Ernesto," I was terrified of *bota la llave* and the AIDS colony from which no one ever emerged. I dreaded returning to Cuba, not because America had demonized it for forty years, but because of th scarcity and sadness hanging over it, swallowing up residents and tourists alike.

Marules, too, looked taken aback. He sat flaccidly in his chair, his mouth open. "Go back? But how can you go back? Willa was escorted from the country—this is no minor matter. They will not have forgotten her so soon." He looked at me. "And surely your State Department does not wish it? The matter is far more delicate now that your government is involved. They cannot want you there like a, like a . . ."

"Loose cannon?" I offered.

He nodded vigorously.

Don stated the obvious: "As far as we know, June Jansson never left Cuba." And, boy, was she a loose cannon. "We're never going to find her by sitting around Mexico City, are we?"

"You, Lieutenant, perhaps you alone," Marules suggested, "you could go there. You have not been barred from doing so. Well, except to the extent that American law bars tourism. But Willa . . ."

"My Spanish isn't good enough," Don said.

"I could perhaps arrange for you to hire a translator?" He kept glancing at me as if checking for signs of mesmerization or codependency.

"Here's another alternative." Don sat forward, gripping the edge of Marules's desk. "You have a friend in the Interior Ministry, a high-ranking official. Clear it with him. Tell him if he lets us in and leaves us alone, we'll find her. We'll take her home, and that'll be it. None of the crap he'd get from the State Department."

"But, my friend," Marules objected, "your State

Department would learn of it upon your return, if not before. The problems for Cuba—and indeed, for you—would arise later if not sooner."

"Let me be blunt," Don said. "Just so your friend in the ministry understands. I can get in there and find her, alive or—" He glanced at me. "I can do it quickly. If it's bad news, your friend finds out first, then we come home and keep our mouths shut. If she's okay, we'll hustle her out of there, and we'll tell the State Department anything he wants us to. He gets first crack on the spin, okay? He can give us a script—we'll say anything he wants us to." Another glance at me. "That's okay with you, isn't it?"

I nodded. If I could get my mother back, I'd vote Republican if I had to. "Anything," I said.

Marules turned his palms upward. "I admire your determination, your bravery in wishing to flout your own authorities. But, please, I am only an acquaintance of *compañero* Emilio. I have met him on his trips to Mexico City and acted as . . . oh, how to explain it? . . . a chaperone, a host, one who makes the introductions at important parties. But it is not as if he owes me anything. Simply put, I do not think I can accomplish this for you."

"Try." Don's tone was cold. "We're offering to clear this up for him. It's got to be a pain in the neck having the U.S. government inquiring about it. Tell him I guarantee if he lets us in on his authority, I'll make this go away, one way or another."

"But how?" Marules wondered. "Cuba is not San Francisco. You have no connections, no authority there."

"Just give him the message. Can you?"

He certainly didn't seem anxious to. "I will do this, yes. Of course."

"Can you do it as if you mean it? Put our interests above your reservations?"

Marules started to say something, but then stopped, looking over at me. "I will try."

Don was squinting at me as if hoping for something from me.

Against my better judgment, I said, "Please, Martin. Please act like you're a hundred percent sure we can find her. If you don't"—I couldn't speak for a moment—"if you don't, it's over. I've lost her."

Marules sank deeper into his chair. He seemed to be looking through me, nursing his own grief. "I will be as adamant as you are, Lieutenant. I will do all I can to persuade Juan Emilio he would be a fool not to let you solve this problem."

Don took a deep breath and sat back. "It's true. He's a fool if he doesn't let me try."

"You are a very confident man, Lieutenant."

"People don't usually put it so politely."

I felt a chill of fear. No one had ever accused me of being a confident person.

I tried to get a grip: If I continued as I had been, I'd only go on trudging through the days, clinging to my hammock, watching my father disconnect from reality and crawl deeper into cyberspace to hide from his grief.

But when I thought of returning to Cuba, I kept seeing Myra Wilson's dazed, blank face as she handed fabric to an involuntary seamstress in the women's prison.

"When can we call you for news?" Don asked him.

"To telephone Cuba is not an easy matter. Let us say by early afternoon. Let us hope the telephone lines are working with us." To me, he said, "You have the strength to go there?"

"Yes."

I would stick with Don, whether or not his scheme was crazy. No one else was offering to help. And he'd gotten me out of an impossible situation once before. As much as I could trust anyone, I trusted him.

He looked relieved. I wondered how he'd look when he saw the inside of a Cubana airplane.

24

$\mathscr{S}$itting in the Zócalo almost ten hours later, I felt numb. We'd spent the rest of the morning at a hotel trying to catch up on sleep. As much as I tossed and turned and worried, I suspected I'd gotten more of a nap than Don. He hadn't looked at all rested when we met for a late lunch. He'd been on the phone with Conner, he said, going over some things.

Conner reported that Pirí and the couple had made a stop at another apartment, and then had gone to the airport. Pirí had started work, and the couple had boarded a plane to Belgium. Mostly, Don and Conner had talked about Price, the no-show detective. Conner recommended a local guy he knew to fill in, and another to help track down Price. Recounting this, Don seemed tense, almost grim.

And I knew I was no picture of cheer. Martin Marules had been successful. We were flying to Cuba tonight. It would require a "special facilitator" both ends, but strings had been pulled and red tape cut. Our bags were already in the trunk of the rental car. As soon as Marules's receptionist delivered the computer disk she'd promised us, we were leaving.

From our sidewalk café table, I watched helium balloons jostling above carts of ersatz Aztec whistles. Blankets near the cathedral were spread with Guatemalan weaves and home-sewn kites and corny statuary. Children ran across the square, their sandals flapping and their curls bobbing. Spotlights shone in bas-relief crannies of colonial buildings as the sun set. Porticoes glowed with yellow lamplight. The sound of Peruvian flutes floated over cobblestones.

Our waiter kept refilling our glasses and bringing more bread. The restaurant buzzed with talk and laughter. It smelled of sauces and grilled meats. Knowing we were flying into a city with little light and rationed food took some of the pleasure out of this bright plenty.

My musings were interrupted by the sight of a short, plump woman in a business suit. She was walking a slow circle as if looking for someone. "There she is," I said.

Don stood, dropping his napkin onto the tabletop. He swung over the metal patio rail, and walked across the Zócalo toward her. When he reached her, he put his arm around her and walked her into a crowd. I could sometimes see them and sometimes not.

Several minutes later, Don returned through the restaurant's patio door. He sat back down, nodding.

"Do we have time to find a computer and read the disk?"

"No. If the database is in code, it probabl

wouldn't mean anything to us anyway." He ran his hand over his hair. "I arranged an airport drop-off—Conner will pick it up and deal with it." He shrugged. "If nothing else, maybe it'll tell us something about the receptionist. She might be a more accomplished liar than she seems."

I nodded. It wouldn't be difficult to take a file—any old file—and encrypt it. She could be trying to divert us with a diskette full of junk.

He smiled.

"What?" I asked.

"I just . . ." He shrugged. "I never would have imagined us going to Cuba together."

"I always hoped to radicalize you." I immediately regretted the joke. Why bring up the past? Too many bad memories, including the difficult favor he'd done me, including my showing up at his house when his wife was there.

He stared down at the tablecloth. He looked as if he was going to get serious.

For better or worse, the waiter came with the check. It was time to leave for the airport.

By the time I sat in a Cubana de Aviación seat with no armrest, watching the overhead light panel spark, I was sick with dread, almost enough so to brave the stench of the airplane restroom. Only shame kept me outwardly stoic. Valium would have been a handy backup.

Don scowled out the window. We'd been sitting on the tarmac for hours, so he'd had lots of time to examine the still-uncleared wreckage of a charred Cubana plane. When the stewardess came down the isle with a plate of hard candies, Don recoiled. My mouth was so dry I'd have taken one if I hadn't noticed ants in the bowl.

With the delay and the time difference, we landed in the early morning. We were greeted at the gate by a trim woman in high-heeled mules, a tight blue skirt, and a shirt in a matching shade. She wore a thick necklace that looked like a cloth-covered PVC pipe. I had seen a hotel desk clerk wearing a similar ornament. If it didn't contain a microphone, Cuban women had weird taste in jewelry.

"I am Teresa, your facilitator. You speak Spanish, yes? Please follow me. We have arranged a special customs passage."

I think that's what she said. It would take me a while to hear the n's and s's the Cubans routinely dropped.

We followed her through a big room with few amenities and lots of tired-looking travelers dragging bags through long lines. She ushered us into a small room with an unwashed linoleum floor, a wooden table and chairs, a one-way mirror, and nothing else.

"Please give me your tickets and your passports. We will bring your luggage to you shortly."

We handed her the tickets and passports. She left, closing the door behind us. Sitting alone in a tiny room with Don brought back memories of being interrogated by him. How romantic.

We sat for over an hour, making occasional desultory comments. When the facilitator opened the door, I caught a flash of People's Republic uniforms behind her. She said, "Everything is in order. Your baggage is now aboard the bus."

She led us out to a tour bus that had seen better decades. It was full of squirming people, steaming in the muggy heat of what would certainly become a scorching morning. Judging from their exclamations of "Finally!" and "At last," the bus had been waiting for us.

We rattled slowly toward Havana, the facilitator standing next to the bus driver, chatting to him about a college class they had apparently taken together.

Don stared out the window at overgrown fields dotted with banana plants and palms. Now and then, a mule-drawn cart bounced by, the drivers waving and smiling. Boys on dented bicycles sometimes rode beside us like dolphins accompanying a ferry. Don looked troubled. Unless he really had a plan, he should be.

The bus pulled up to a hotel not far from the one I'd stayed in last time. The facilitator motioned us to get off first, then led us inside.

"The driver will bring your baggage," she explained. "I will take you to your room now. Soon, a car will arrive to collect you for your appointment."

The hotel lobby was papered in a yellowed fleur-de-lis pattern, with high ceilings and potted palms in curtained alcoves. The furniture must have been fabulous once, with carved claw feet and rosette backs. With fresh paper and a few hundred yards of reupholstery fabric, it would be a vision of prewar splendor.

Teresa walked us up two flights of cement stairs (bad news when locals won't ride the elevators) and down a corridor that reeked of mildew. She nlocked a door, holding it open for us.

"Your luggage will be brought to you shortly. If you will please meet me in the lobby in one half hour?" She simultaneously frowned and smiled.

It hadn't occurred to us to tell anyone we'd need two rooms—we'd assumed we'd take care of it when we registered.

I stepped inside. A breeze stirred sheer curtains in open windows, bringing in the smell of flowering vines. The room was small and drab, with one barely double-sized bed.

When I turned around, I found Don inside, too. He was looking at the door, his lips parted as if he'd been about to say something when she closed it. I watched him do a quick survey. There was no couch here, and probably not enough room to sleep on the floor.

There were any number of nonchalant ways to deal with the situation, I'm sure. But when he looked at me, I blushed deeply.

Suddenly on the spot, I said, "What are you thinking?"

"Honestly?" He smiled, glancing at the bed. "Thank you, Fidel."

A knock at the door startled a gasp out of me.

A grinning man with few teeth handed in our bags. While he did, I fled into the bathroom. It looked as if it had been built before the First World War. I took my time washing up. When I was through, I took some deep breaths, and decided to wash up again.

When I emerged, Don was standing at one of the windows, looking outside. He turned. "It's beautiful, isn't it?"

"It would be," I agreed, "if they had paint."

He walked over to me. "I don't think I've ever spent an ordinary minute with you, you know that? You're a pretty exotic date."

He kissed me without the least pretense of having to do so to fool passersby. For the first time, there was no sense I'd led him into something impulsive and foolish and wrong.

So of course there was a knock at the door.

Our minder (as Cindy and Dennis had called these people) was standing there. "The car is early. Please come."

I guess one didn't keep Señor Emilio waiting.

Teresa led us to a Russian car. The passenger side had been scraped, maybe keyed, leaving thin troughs that were invisible until you got close. Plastic did have its advantages.

The Moskvich driver was a dark-skinned Cuban with clothes you might see on an American golf course. Here, they were probably the equivalent of an Armani suit.

He glanced at us in the rearview mirror fairly often. And he certainly had the time. We took a ridiculously long route to the building where Cindy, Dennis, and I had previously spoken to the Yum King. I supposed the driver had instructions to avoid the neighborhoods. Instead we drove along the Malecón, the long sea wall bordering Havana.

We passed a huge billboard with a cartoon of a foot-stomping Cuban shouting across the water to a cartoonish Uncle Sam, "Mr. Imperialist, we are not at all afraid of you!" Fake graffiti on apartment building walls read, "Socialism or Death!" Perched above the sea wall, the black stones of an eighteenth century fortress pointed antique cannons seaward.

In twenty minutes of driving, I don't think we passed half a dozen moving cars, only perfectly waxed specimens from the forties and fifties, lined up like museum pieces beside the road. When we finally reached the building, parking was not a problem.

Our minder clicked along ahead of us, hurrying through a courtyard of gargantuan plants I'd only seen in gallon pots before coming here. They were clearly enjoying the sticky heat a lot more than I was.

We entered the building that resembled a suburban junior high school, minus fresh paint or anything electrical. Through partially open doors, we glimpsed people working on manual typewriters.

Finally, the minder knocked at a closed door. As she did so, she straightened her spine and shook out her hair. When she heard, "*Entra!*" she put on a wide smile.

"Señor Emilio," she said, her voice all honey, "may I present—"

He cut her off with the barest flick of the fingers. She motioned us to enter, but didn't follow us in.

Señor Emilio's curls fell softly over his ears and his collar to his shoulder blades. His dark brows met in a cranky frown, and he looked as if he were sucking in his cheeks. He wore a purple polo shirt. His jeans looked stone-washed. His sneakers looked new. He rose from his chair, every inch the young urban Marxist.

He looked down at Don, who was perhaps five-ten to his six-three. He took in the details of Don's attire—

gray twill slacks, a blue cotton polo shirt that strained at the biceps, black leather shoes—with apparent envy. He spared me only the briefest glance.

To Don he said, in a rapid Cuban mumble, "You are a lieutenant of the San Francisco police, I am told. An important and respected man with many men working for you. And now you have insisted upon coming here. As if you believe that your gadgetry and technology make you a detective superior to our own, capable of solving problems which have eluded our primitive abilities."

"*Señor,*" I tried to interrupt.

He waved for me to be quiet—waved as if I were a gnat buzzing at his elbow. The revolution's New Man.

"So what is it you can do for us here? What marvels of modern detection do you bring us? What miracles will you work for your monkey neighbors?"

"He doesn't speak Spanish," I said, with gnatlike satisfaction.

He made a disgusted sound. "And he has come to Cuba to solve his problem?" He turned away, shaking his head.

As he returned to his chair behind a huge desk, Don murmured to me, "I gather he didn't say, 'Good to meet you'?"

I quickly conveyed the gist of Señor Emilio's statement: "You're not so smart, nyah nyah."

Don looked around the room, then grabbed two folding chairs to position near the desk. We sat in them, though Señor Emilio might behead us for it.

Don said, "Translate as I go, can you?"

"We'll find out."

Pausing often so I could mangle his meaning, Don told him, "I gather you don't think highly of me. That's fair. You don't know me. But I hope you're going to give me a fair chance because we've both got a problem here, not just me. I know I can find June Jansson if you cooperate, if you don't hamstring me." (Like I would really know the Spanish word for "hamstring.")

"And how do you suggest that I cooperate? Shall I drive you and your translator to the tourist stores? Shall I take you to the beaches where the old lady tourists go wading?" He slapped his hand on the desktop. "Where can you go that we Cubans have not been? What will you ask that we have not already asked?"

I boiled it down: "What are you going to do that he hasn't?"

Don slapped the desktop, too. "Who do you think you're talking to? A politician like yourself? An amateur? I've been heading up the Homicide Division in one of the biggest cities in America since you've been out of diapers! You think I can't help you? Bullshit!"

I translated faithfully, though I considered substituting, *Mine is bigger.*

"Do you think we have no police here?" But at least Emilio wasn't shouting now.

Don countered with, "How big is this city? How much crime do your policemen see? Your people aren't used to this. I am."

"It is true our crime rate is very low. But you do not know that a crime has taken place, Mr. Police."

"Of course there's been a crime. Americans don't

go native in Cuba. Something happened to June Jansson."

I translated, then added, "She's my mother. You've met me before."

He frowned and tucked his head back, looking affronted that I'd spoken. Sexism, the universal language.

I continued, "I came here with two reporters. They asked you about Lidia Gomez. Now they're missing, too."

His nostrils flared. He turned to Don and said, "With whom am I conducting business, Mr. Police? With you or with your woman?"

To me, Don said, "I gather he's immune to your charms."

"He won't talk to me."

"Let it go," Don said. "This is too important. No ego."

Yeah, sure, the tao of dickhood.

He turned to Señor Emilio. "I'll need maps, and I'll need some police officers. I prefer creative people, problem-solvers."

I translated like a good geisha.

"And with these people you will then do what?"

"I want to search your tunnels. I want to run a motorboat around the coast. And I want to go out to your villages, the smaller the better."

"And what will this accomplish?"

"We call it a dragnet. It's a standard approach. It gets results."

As I translated, Emilio's scowl relaxed slightly.

"How many people would you presume to require?"

"You tell me," was Don's response. "Or better yet, let me work with a police official who can tell us both."

"Now that," Emilio said, "is the best thought that I have heard from you. Yes, I will let you speak with your equivalent here in Havana. He can tell me what he thinks of your plans and what will be appropriate."

Don didn't seem satisfied. "I can find June Jansson. Don't let anybody convince you I can't."

If nothing else, Señor Emilio seemed impressed to find a man with an ego as grand as his own. (He'd obviously never been bar-hopping.)

For now, we had no choice but to leave it at that.

25

$\mathcal{W}$e were ushered into a small office in a building in central Havana. It was probably built in the fifties, when the whole world was in love with high-rises. Now, with electricity in short supply, the design must have been a nightmare. Keeping an elevator running probably sucked up enough power to keep a neighborhood lit for a week.

A man in green military fatigues stood to greet us. He looked to be in his early sixties, slim, mixed race, with sunken cheeks, sharp eyes, tight gray curls, and a long beard. His office reeked of cigar smoke. His walls were covered with maps, well-drawn originals, nothing mass-produced. His desk was stacked with papers—a rare sight here.

He extended his hand. We were surprised to hear him speak English.

"Hello. Hello. I am General Miguel. Please take a chair. I have spoken to *compañero* Emilio. Please sit down. Do you like coffee . . . ?" He smiled at our surprise. "I have been to college many many years ago in Massachusetts. I have even played professional baseball for you. Ha!" He had a bark of a laugh.

We sat facing the general.

"You are here to find this lady's mother." He smiled at me, showing nicotine-stained teeth. "This will be now the fourth attempt that we make." He ticked them off on his fingers. "When she did not leave with the American ladies, we looked for her. When this lady"—he nodded at me—"came to seek her, again we undertook to search. When we are asked by your government to do so, we forgave the insolence of the request." He leaned toward me. "Because we know your government does not speak for your people. We have met too many Americans to confuse the actions of your Mafia and your senators with the feelings of the real people. For the sake of a woman, your mother, who has come to Cuba to admire our struggle, we ignore our anger. And now"—a broad shrug—"now we will try again another time. It is better to try one time too many than one time short of success."

"I couldn't agree more," Don told him. "I'd like to do a dragnet that includes your tunnels. Someone would have spotted her in a neighborhood, even a tourist area. So she's either in the tunnels, or she's someplace so remote nobody's run into her, I mean, nobody your investigators talked to."

"You are correct, I believe," the general commented, "to say that if the lady was in the city of Havana we would know this already." He nodded. "But you refer to tunnels?"

"The tunnels beneath Havana." Don stated it as if it were common knowledge.

"Why do you say so?"

Don didn't glance at me. Nor did I think it would be a good idea to bring up my foray beneath the city.

"I've read it in Associated Press accounts," Don said blandly. "And I've been told so by members of the U.S. government."

"Really? Which branch?"

Don went for it: "The CIA."

"Ah, you have spoken to someone in your CIA?" He pronounced it as a two-syllable word, *seeya*.

"Yes, we have," Don confirmed.

"Your CIA, I'm afraid, is not reliable. You are a student of history, I hope?"

"To some extent."

"Then you know this is the case."

"But in this instance, I talked to someone who was born in Havana and knows it well. He spent the last two years here. Are you denying you have tunnels?"

"Of course." He nodded vigorously. "It is ridiculous. You have been misinformed."

The men looked at each other as if trying to guess their respective suit sizes.

Finally Don said, "If you won't let me search the tunnels, I'll have to hope you've done it yourself. That you've done it thoroughly. That you can absolutely rule it out."

The general didn't reply.

Don sighed. "Then let's talk about outlying areas. Is it possible to hide out in the mountains?"

"For some people, yes. For an American lady, no." He smiled wolfishly. "I have stayed hidden myself, from Batista's men. But in those days, it was easy.

No one worried for the fate of shoeless men subsisting on land that could not produce money for the *gringos*. If the land could not be planted with tobacco or cane for sugar and rum, it mattered to no one. That is my point." He leaned back, putting his big black military boots onto his desk. No more shoelessness for him. "Now we care for everyone." He pulled a cigar out of his pocket. "My father worked like a slave for the American cigar companies." He held the cigar aloft. The end was cinched like a candy wrapper. "He could not afford to smoke the fine products he created. He was permitted to roll for himself only a cheap blend, this one, with the end left rough as you see here. A Havana Twist, it is called. Now Cuba owns the factories, and the workers earn the same as doctors or professors. They can smoke what they please. But I prefer the Havana Twist in respect for my father and the generation which did not live to see the revolution. To remind myself how far we have come."

Don nodded. "My father emigrated from Italy with next to nothing." He left it at that, apparently finding it counterproductive to mention that the family parlayed it into a banking fortune. No Italia Twists for Don. "Let me tell you what I have in mind," he continued. "And you tell me if you'll let me have the manpower."

Don outlined what was, in essence, an island-wide dragnet.

The general listened, showing no surprise. Then he stood, saying, "I will consider the matter." He waved his cigar to forestall Don's next comment. "I will send a car when I am ready with an answer."

I don't know how our minder knew the interview had ended, but she was at the door within seconds.

Don tried to reinitiate conversation, but she got between him and the general, all but pushing him out the door. As she did so, she effusively thanked the general, assuring him he need only phone when he was ready.

I glanced back at him. His expression was sly and cynical, and his eyes were cold. He'd seen a great deal since his days as a mountain guerrilla and had plenty of reason to hate America. But his face told me he'd lied about not blaming U.S. citizens for their government's policy.

26

*W*e sat together on the bed in our hotel room. Don's lips brushed my ears. I could feel his breath. But his words were difficult to make out even at a few millimeters' distance. There was no help for it—the microphone in the overhead fixture might be powerful. There might be others closer to the bed. A satellite mike might be pointed through the windows.

And so while my viscera danced at his touch, my brain strove to fill in missing words.

"I'm not sure what their agenda is, letting us come here. But I don't think they're going to let us look around. I think they're going to keep us busy, divert us."

"They might go for your dragnet idea," I whispered.

"No, I was just blowing smoke. I need them to think I have a plan—they'd never trust a man without a plan. But it's just show, and it wouldn't work. They'd be crazy to go along. I wouldn't, not if some yahoo came to San Francisco and tried to deploy my men."

Just show? I'd believed him. Worse, I'd let myself take comfort in his plan, invest some hope in it.

"I was just looking for a way to get us here." For a moment, he let his lips rest on my ear. "Now we've got to get away from all these ears and eyes. Do you think you could find the building where the tunnel came up?"

"Yes. I mean, I don't know what it is, but I remember what it's near, and what it looks like."

"Then that's what we'll do—leave the hotel, and start there." He was clearly not hung up on achieving a consensus.

"I don't suppose you'd like my opinion?" I whispered.

He grinned. "That's what Krisbaum always says. But I don't see any alternative. They've for sure got people watching the lobby. But they've given us a window out back, through the bathroom."

I must have shown my alarm.

"Don't worry, there are vines covering the walls. They'll hold us."

Considering he was built like a minotaur, this seemed a little optimistic. "If we get caught?"

"We're not under hotel arrest. No one told us to stay inside."

"Then let's just go out the front door. If they follow us, they follow us."

"We've got more options if we're on our own," he persisted. "And it's no use getting ushered from one tough guy's office to another. If we can get hold of something, anything, with wheels . . . I'd go alone if I could."

"I'd let you," I agreed.

With a sigh, he stood up. He yanked me to my feet

and led me into the bathroom. A small window opened to the viney wall of an air shaft.

There was no one below. Presumably, the Cubans didn't think we were stupid enough to try to human-fly our way down the ivy. And they were right about one of us.

I was relieved when I heard a knock at the door.

Don preceded me out of the bathroom. "Who is it?" he asked.

"Teresa. You are awake?"

Considering it wasn't yet dinnertime, that was a safe bet.

When I emerged from the bathroom, she was standing in the room fingering her microphone cum necklace.

"Señor Emilio has asked that you be taken to the Women's Prison West."

I backed up. "As a visitor." I didn't dare express it as a question.

"Yes, yes, but it is not a short drive," she fretted. "We must leave without delay."

The prisoners wouldn't be there if we tarried? "Why are we going?"

"The warden wishes to speak with you. She says that she has met you before." Teresa seemed astonished this could be so. "You have been to Women's Prison West?"

As if I might have met the warden elsewhere, at a little barbecue I'd had last week. "Yes."

"Then you know it is some distance. Let us please hurry." She was clearly nervous. Would the Yum King have her guillotined for tardiness?

We followed her out to the Moskvich, and

climbed into the back seat. Our natty driver again traced the Malecón—apparently the state-sanctioned route to anyplace.

We passed big houses with fresh paint and obviously operational cars—the diplomatic district. I half listened as Teresa pointed out various embassies and residences. A glance at Don told me he was paying enough attention for both of us.

I stared at garden walls showing tops of huge exotic blooms. Evening was falling, bringing the relief of cooler air.

Could Mother be hiding in a foreign embassy?

I sighed. Why would they take her in? Why wouldn't they notify the United States? And what the hell would she be doing there anyway?

What could an American woman do in Cuba for almost six months?

No, not any American woman. My mother was Superlefty. She was indefatigable and passionate if her heart was touched and her outrage roused. She'd suffered seventeen arrests, fourteen trials, eleven sentencings, and scattered months of jail time because of it. Mother wasn't capable of seeing distress without wanting to fix it, to organize or picket or walkathon it away.

But what could she do—what could anyone do?—to help Cuba? Something embarrassing to both Cuba and the United States, Don had guessed. Something neither country wanted brought to light.

It grew dark out, but still I couldn't think of anything. If Mother had attempted some elaborate errand of mercy, I couldn't imagine what it might have been. And I hoped this trip to the women's prison wasn't going to give me an unwelcome answer.

Don scooted closer, putting his arm around me.

I felt the cooling air on my face and the tension of muscle in Don's arm. I tried to focus on that.

A hormone rush made it surprisingly easy.

27

*W*e sat in the warden's office sipping syrupy coffee (which I'd missed). She looked nervous, to say the least. She kept squirming in her light brown military uniform, glancing at the smiling woman who'd accompanied her last time. Again, I had the impression that the smiling woman, despite her pains to remain in the background, was pulling the strings.

"So . . . Señor Emilio has asked me to be of service to you," the warden explained in rapid mumbling Cuban.

"In what way?" I asked her.

"As may suit you?" She seemed to be asking her smiling companion, seated beside and just behind us, for direction.

"May we interview Myra Wilson?" What else could the Yum King have had in mind, sending us here? "I'm told her family asked my mother to check on her. Do you remember my mother's group at all? Members of the Women's International League for Peace and Freedom?"

"No, I am sorry. We have very many groups coming to study our methods of rehabilitation and retraining." She looked nervous. "But we are glad to bring Myra here. Then you may question her directly."

While they did, I brought Don up to speed. He looked puzzled. Why did Señor Emilio want this aspect of our inquiry speedily concluded?

Myra Wilson was led into the room by a woman in fatigues. Wilson wore a dress resembling a wraparound hospital gown, cinched in front with frayed ties. The bleached part of her hair had been snipped off. Though the cut was short and unattractive, she looked better without two tones. Her eyes were red and puffy, but she showed no outward signs of abuse.

She seemed surprised to find the room full of people.

The warden said, "Myra, come and sit here." She indicated a chair beside her desk. "These Americans have asked to interview you briefly. They are looking for someone. This has nothing to do with your crime, and you should not be afraid. They are asking only for your help." To us, she said, "Is that not correct?"

I shifted into English so that Don could follow. I was certain the smiling woman understood it well.

"My mother came here with a tour group almost six months ago. She didn't come back." I watched Wilson. She just sat there, her expression glazed. "In the course of searching for her, I went over her phone bills. Before she left for Cuba, she called your house—the house you used to live in. She phoned the doctor who bought the house from you."

Wilson's voice was tiny and girlish. "Ernie? To ask him questions about Cuba? Is that right?" Her words were slow. She looked at the warden as if for approval.

"My mother is a radical socialist," I explained. "It wouldn't be like her to seek out someone . . . whose views of Cuba were negative, who considered himself an exile."

"Ernie's not an exile." Wilson looked confused. "He didn't have any family left here, that's all. He left to find his aunts and uncles. They were over there." It sounded like something she'd memorized, maybe even learned to believe. In this environment, it must be hard to be a *gusano*'s girlfriend.

"I assumed because he came over on Mariel . . . Anyway, his maid was murdered when I went to San Diego to talk to him."

"His maid?"

"Alicia Mendoza. Did you know her?"

She shook her head. Her posture was so bad I ached just looking at her.

She must be medicated. Nobody could hear such news, hear the name of a distant lover, with so little emotion. During my two months in the San Bruno Jail, the mere mention of the name Edward—Edward Hershey had been my boyfriend then—would bring tears to my eyes.

"The man I was traveling with"—it still hurt to think about it—"he was killed in exactly the same way as the maid."

Her face twitched and her eyes seemed to flash. It was as if something endeavored to crack through.

I glanced at Don. He'd turned his attention to the warden, studying her reaction.

"We tried to talk to Ernie," I continued. "He was on a dive boat, about to dock. He jumped overboard so he wouldn't have to see us."

She just blinked. "He likes to scuba dive."

I tried again to get through. "When I went to see him, his maid and my companion ended up with their throats cut. Don't you find that strange?"

"Yes." She sounded like she was answering a question in a pop quiz, hoping the answer was correct.

Don said, "What were you arrested for?"

"Drugs."

"Smuggling?"

She twined her fingers, looking down at them.

"How did you meet Lidia Gomez?"

She seemed to stop breathing. She looked over my shoulder at the smiling woman. I turned quickly, hoping to catch her without a smile. No such luck.

"I don't know that person," Wilson said. Her voice was a slow warble, as if we were hearing it underwater.

"Lidia Gomez used your passport to go to Mexico," Don said.

The warden stood abruptly. "What are you asking?" she demanded. "You are discussing people, I am hearing the names of people . . . Why are these names being introduced? Myra is not here to be tormented by you."

I switched to Spanish. "We're asking her questions about her passport. Is there a problem?"

"As warden, I am here to protect my charges, as well as to rehabilitate them. I cannot allow you to prod at her without limit. You must understand that?"

"Fine," I agreed. "We won't ask her anything that's not relevant."

"But look at her!" The warden's voice was tinged with outrage.

I looked. Wilson sat there in bovine confusion, plaiting and unplaiting her fingers.

"She's too sedated to care what we ask," I pointed out.

"No, no," the warden assured me, "she is not sedated."

In English, I asked Wilson, "How often do you take pills?"

The warden flashed her a look. She said to the woman who'd brought her in, "Please take poor Myra back to her cell. We won't have her confused and distressed in this way. It is not humane."

Myra didn't seem surprised to find herself shuffled out of the room.

The warden dropped back into her chair, glancing behind me.

What the hell: I turned to the ever smiling woman. "Who are you?"

She offered a name.

"No, I mean, why do you give the orders here? What's your rank, what's your position?"

"I am only the prisoners' advocate, trained as a nurse. When there is to be contact with them, I am here as a helper. For humanitarian reasons."

The warden interrupted. "If there is nothing else I can do for you, I have another appointment."

At this time of night? Sure.

Our minder appeared at the door then, ready to return us to Havana.

I had no idea if we'd learned anything from the trip. Except, of course, what I already knew, that Myra Wilson was kept drugged.

In American prisons, inmates were heavily sedated if they posed a threat to the guards. If they only menaced and maimed each other, they were pretty much left alone.

Here, who knew?

More to the point, why had this trip been arranged at all? Because we were likely to request it anyway? So we wouldn't try to come on our own?

Surely, in his arrogance, Señor Emilio didn't believe we'd be assuaged by this? He couldn't think the highest-ranking detective in San Francisco wouldn't notice Myra Wilson was too drugged to offer real information?

So what was the point?

I felt like Emilio's catnip mouse, his jingle-toy, batted here and there for reasons I was in no position to fathom.

On our way back to the car, Don managed to whisper a single sentence to me.

"She's bait," he said.

28

*W*e were driven to Havana's tourist district for dinner. Teresa made it clear she'd join us while our driver waited. He cast her an envious look, but she didn't seem especially glad to be coming along. She scowled down at her plain skirt and high-heeled mules as if she were Cinderella after midnight.

And well she might—she was stopped at the door by the maître d'. She'd have been turned away had she not been with tourists. Her voice, therefore, was a little brittle when she informed us, "Here, Ernest Hemingway ate many times."

The place had a hardwood bar, small tables, and lots of palms in brass pots. It looked like a movie set.

Teresa asked for the table in the corner. When I said I'd rather sit nearer the door to catch the breeze, she ignored me. So did the maître d'.

I guessed we were getting the special table with the bugs.

The one time Teresa was forced to leave us because nature called, Don said, "We've got to go back and figure out a way to talk to Wilson again." I knew he was speaking for public consumption. "She obviously has a lot more to tell us."

"How do we do that?"

"I'd say bribery's our only option."

"The driver?"

"Let's hope," Don said.

He was making wet rings on the tabletop with his mojito glass, frowning down at the Olympic patterns.

He'd whispered to me that Myra Wilson was bait. Were we going to pretend, then, to be drawn into the mousetrap?

Though I blessed Don for helping me, as soon as we were alone, I had to let him know I didn't even want to *feign* illegal activity here. I didn't want to end up like Myra Wilson, no way.

Teresa returned, and we went back to uncomfortable socializing, all of us too leery to enjoy anything but the frequent and lengthy silences.

After dinner, we found the driver leaning against the side of the car, admiring the Old Spain square like a man in valet-parking paradise. As he held the door to let us in, Don bumped up against him as if he'd had a couple too many mojitos. The driver steadied him, almost reeling backward with him.

When Don got into the car, I could tell by the grim set to his mouth that he'd accomplished his mission. He'd slipped the driver some dollars. The fact that the driver hadn't protested told me we had a date with him later.

Don hadn't even asked me how I felt about it. I guess I'd been a little *too* macha back at Jamieson's.

I guess he'd actually believed me about not being a wimp.

I got so tense on the car ride back—the sanctioned route along the Malecón, of course—that I had to keep reminding myself to breathe.

I'd believed Don had a plan. Despite his protestations, I'd let him fill me with false hope. But my mother couldn't have hidden here for this many months. She must be dead. And because neither government would admit it, I was going to walk into a trap and spend the next several years of my life in a foreign prison.

I felt trapped already, claustrophobic, barely able to control an impulse to leap from the car and run, just run, gasping for air and flailing my arms.

When we got back to the hotel, our minder escorted us in, chatting as if she'd had a sudden second wind and simply had to finish her pointless story. I was so sick of her by the time we reached the room, I practically slammed the door in her face.

Then I collapsed onto the bed with a heartfelt "Uncle!"

Don laughed. Then he looked up at the light fixture, saying, "I've been waiting all day for this."

He closed the window shades. Then he clicked off the overhead light and sat on the bed, bouncing as if to see whether it squeaked. It didn't.

But I should have known I wasn't about to get lucky, as they say. He rose quietly, pulling me by the hand. I followed him into the bathroom.

He closed the door behind us, leaving the light off. The window was still open. There was no one visible at the bottom of the air shaft.

"I don't want to do this," I whispered. "I don't want to be accused of anything. I don't trust anyone here."

"I understand that. But they don't need the grief of arresting us. And it's no accident they gave us a room with an exit." But he looked apologetic. "Believe me, I'd rather stay in the room! But it's no use being in Cuba if we don't do everything we can."

He was being reasonable, which just made matters worse. I didn't know what to do with my anger. No use directing it at my mother. And no use blaming myself for being a big chicken—I'd be an idiot to feel comfortable doing this.

Nevertheless, I bent to peer group pressure. Don went first, perhaps to prove he could fit through the small window. For a few minutes, it seemed iffy. But he made it. And the ivy held him.

I had to follow. But I'd have rather shaved my head or nailed my ear to the wall.

Never having climbed down ivy before, I was surprised what a strong grip the vines had on the wall. It was easier than I'd assumed it would be. Most ways to get into trouble are.

Don was waiting at the bottom to help me down. A small utility door was locked from the inside. Don began prowling, looking into windows. One was half open. He stared in, then shoved it all the way up, climbing inside. I followed, much more clumsily. We were in a room full of folded sheets and napkins, bins of tiny soaps, and trays of silverware. Sign-out sheets listed the numbers of units. Apparently supervisors literally counted the spoons before workers left for the day.

Don cracked the door leading out. A sliver of light filtered in. He didn't move or make a sound for what seemed like five minutes. Then he slipped through, closing the door when I followed. We were in some kind of utility corridor. The floors were filthy and sticky. Apparently they didn't waste any soap on parts of the hotel the guests didn't see.

We were quick—and lucky—making our way outside. A side exit opened out to a dimly lighted corner. We crossed the street, walking as quickly as we could into the neighborhood.

As soon as we were far enough away to speak without whispering, I vented: "What are we doing? We stand out like, like . . . Americans in Cuba! Why are we—"

He grabbed my shoulders as if to shake me out of hysteria. "The building," he said calmly. "The one with the tunnel entrance. I want you to show me where it is. I just want to see it."

"Did you bribe Emilio's driver? Are we meeting him tonight?"

"Yes." His fingers dug deeper into my shoulders. "I know he isn't really bribed. I know it's some kind of trap. But walking into it is the only possible way to find out what it's about."

"Oh God." His words offered little comfort.

"If we just stay nice and safe in our room tonight, we end up with nothing. We don't learn what they expect from us, or why they're trying to put Myra Wilson in the middle of it."

"That's why you called her bait."

"They seem to want us to think this revolves around her and Lidia Gomez. And I'm afraid—look, I know this is going to be hard to hear—but I'm afraid that's what those two murders in San Diego were about. Neon arrows saying look this way, look at Wilson, look at Gomez, look at Hemingway the *gusano*."

"And don't look at what?"

"That's what we need to find out." He let go of my shoulders, putting his arms around me.

He was a good fit, as if I'd had him made to measure somewhere. But this wasn't my idea of a dream date.

"Successful killers succeed through luck or misdirection," he continued. "I don't see why that wouldn't apply to governments, as well."

"Theirs or ours?"

"Both. I want a look at that building. Can you point us in the right direction?"

No easy feat in a city with sporadic and dim lighting, a city I'd spent just a few days in months before. I tried to recall some detail of the boulevard where the theater was. Unfortunately, the bus I'd boarded (taking Cindy's place) hadn't traveled from the theater straight to the hotel. It had barreled out of town to a citrus grove.

We could hear voices now, a man and a woman ambling along engaging in a mild flirtation. "Paco wouldn't like to hear you saying that, I think!" he said. To which she responded, "And I suppose Maria knows what you do with your hands?"

I called out to them, trying to mumble my s's and n's like a good Cuban, "Where is the theater?"

The man called out a street name, telling me to turn left.

When I didn't say thanks, he added, "The street is behind you, but I hope you aren't planning to walk!"

Not planning to walk? It must be miles away. And in a while we had a date with self-sacrifice, my least favorite dance partner.

But within a block of turning onto the correct street, I saw the theater. The Cuban obviously had a sense of humor. "The other building must be up that way. Look for a metal grille garage door."

It took about fifteen minutes, but we found it.

Behind the closed grille, a light shone. There was a movement of shadows.

I stated the obvious. "We're not going to get past a closed metal grille and whoever's inside."

"There wouldn't be much point, anyway. We can't just follow the tunnel hoping to run into your mother." My relief must have been apparent, because he smiled. "I just want to know what the building is."

We walked around to the front. It was a square high-rise with lights burning in several windows, though the rest of the neighborhood, even adjacent buildings, were blacked out.

I read the words chiseled above the door. "It's the Interior Ministry."

"Well, that makes sense. You'd want to be able to get your politicians out fast when the bombs start dropping."

"Or the riots start happening."

"Do you think your mother might have come here with some proposal or comment?"

He'd certainly seen her at San Francisco's police headquarters often enough, picketing and leafleting, and generally making free with her advice. But if she'd come here, it had probably been to compliment the revolution and offer to cut cane for the general welfare. Or perhaps to ask if there was some way she could further violate American law and funnel dollars into Cuba's ailing economy.

"Are you thinking she might have come here and stumbled across the tunnel entrance?" Even if she had, she'd have lauded the Cubans for guarding against senseless aggression from their northern neighbor.

"I guess I'm wondering if she might have struck a deal."

"What kind of deal?"

"Work for the Cubans in some way."

"No matter what, she'd have let me and my father know she was all right. She wouldn't put us through this, even for the revolution."

He led me to a short wall separating a nearby building from the sidewalk. When we sat down, he said, "I know you don't want to go back to the women's prison. But we're not going to just run into your mother on the street. And the island's too big for a dragnet."

"But you told—"

"I'm just acting like they think I should. But we're here to be smart, not to run around. God knows Edward Hershey did enough of that when he came down—"

"Edward came to Cuba?"

"You didn't know?"

"No."

"Right after that business in San Diego. He spent

about ten days here, looking all over the island, asking around. He tried again about a month later. I guess he didn't want you to know. I guess he thought it would just take away whatever hope you had."

I was throbbing with shock. Edward had come here looking for Mother, and I'd never suspected. I felt tears spring to my eyes. I hadn't wanted to suspect, more likely. But considering how long Edward had known Mother and how fond of each other they were, it made perfect sense.

"You do seem to inspire continuing loyalty in your men."

"My . . . ?" Was he putting himself (never mind Edward) into the ranks of "my" men?

"You know I've been crazy about you from the minute I first saw you, the minute you started giving me shit when I questioned you about those murders at your law school."

Talk about clashing impulses: I wanted to object that I hadn't given him shit—on the contrary, he'd been the unpleasant one. And the married one.

Perhaps perversely, I found it difficult to make the obvious declaration. Maybe if I hadn't carried a torch so long. "Let's not do this now."

"Not your idea of a romantic evening? Here I brought you all the way to *socialismo* heaven."

"I'll pay you back," I promised. "I'll take you to the Nixon library."

"You don't have to go to the women's prison. We can stop a few miles short, have the driver drop us off and—"

"You'll go on without me."

"I just don't . . . I don't want to do nothing."

I didn't want to do nothing, either. But doing something foolhardy seemed an even less attractive alternative.

"I remember you've got a thing about jails," he continued. Years ago, I'd freaked out in front of him, complaining about a lawyer whose grandstanding landed me a seemingly endless two-month sentence. "Something about the matron making you sew curtains."

"I don't like to sew."

"I gathered."

"Okay, we'll drive *toward* the prison." I really couldn't promise to be any stupider than that.

29

*A*n hour later, Don became the antithesis of
Prince Charming. Rather than hand me into a coach
to his fairy-tale castle, he helped me into a car
bound for Women's Prison West. Since it's never
easy for me to trust someone else's judgment (any
more than it's easy for me to trust my own), I
remained unconvinced of the wisdom of our
course. And because we found the car parked right
in front of the hotel (odd behavior for a "bribed"
driver), it seemed we were to be publicly stupid.

We again drove along the Malecón, past the
embassies and diplomats' houses. The driver didn't
speak to us, and we didn't speak to each other.

Outside Havana, Don finally said to the driver, "I
know you speak English."

"A little," he admitted.

"You want to do us a favor and let us know what
to expect up there?"

"I will drive until you wish me to stop. That is my
only part in this."

"Who's going to be waiting for us?"

"I have agreed only to drive you." Not, *You have paid me to drive you.* His agreement wasn't with us.

Don didn't press it. "Stop the car when we're five minutes from the prison."

All too soon, the driver pulled over.

Don climbed out of the car. With a sigh, I did the same.

The night was close and muggy and moonless. Up ahead, a faint glow lit the horizon—the women's prison apparently had electricity. We walked toward it.

Don took my hand. "Not exactly the Emerald City," he commented.

"Too bad. We could certainly use a brain."

"They have all the labor they need," Don said. "Students work on farms for their tuition, and everyone's pressured to do quote-unquote 'volunteer' work, field work—five days' worth a month. I read that they truck as many as two hundred thousand people at a time out of Havana to cut cane."

"You're saying they have no need for prison labor?"

"They certainly don't need your mother."

"Just her money. And she has no access to that, not from here." We'd been over this a few thousand times already.

"Does she have any hidden bank accounts, property, CDs, anything like that? Anything someone could be draining with her okay, or without your knowledge?"

"God, no—if Mother hears about anyone in need, she immediately empties her pockets. She'd never be able to keep any kind of personal fund intact. She'd spend it in a hot second, as soon as she saw a homeless man or heard about a hungry Chilean." I wiped away tears, hoping I hadn't just delivered her eulogy.

"She's a good person," he commented. "There's been a lot of water under the bridge. But I've always thought so."

Under the circumstances, the testimonial could hardly be construed as empty. I wanted to thank him, but the words seemed paltry.

We walked on, listening to the chirp of insects in roadside grasses.

I added, "Mother throws her heart into things, but that doesn't make her foolish. If she wanted to funnel money into Cuba, she'd go home and do some fund-raising."

"Unless she's helping to set up some project here. She's got no particular expertise? She hasn't run a third-world health clinic or anything like that?"

"She knows as much about the U.S. prison system as anyone I've ever met. She's definitely done her homework on Cuba and Latin America." I'd once lived in a house she'd filled with Salvadorans fleeing the poverty and mayhem of guerrilla war. "She—just between us, okay?"

"Of course."

"She's run safe houses for illegal aliens, refugees from El Salvador, Chile, and Peru, mostly."

"Safe—" He stopped in the middle of the road. "She's been part of underground railroads out of Latin America and you haven't mentioned it?"

I was surprised by his exasperation. It hadn't occurred to me to mention it, any more than it had occurred to me to mention her myriad other projects, some merely radical, others downright felonious. "It's just one thing on a long list. She's almost pathologically active. She makes the Berrigans look like slackers."

"But this isn't just spiking redwood trees, this is relevant."

"How? She doesn't see Cubans as needing a safe harbor. She believes this is an impoverished version of socialist perfection, that all it needs is money. She might have some compassion for the people who leave here, but she's got no respect for them."

"The point is, she knows where to put people who come into the United States illegally and don't want to be found."

"Yes, but like I said—"

"They don't have to be *gusanos,* you know. They could be members of the Interior Ministry."

"The ministry? What would those people be doing in safe houses?"

"Being safe. Being inconspicuous. Arranging caravans. Rounding up contributions. Look how bad things are here. They've got to be trying desperate measures."

Oh God, put that way, it almost sounded like something Mother would do. "If it were true . . . she wouldn't be in Cuba, she'd be back home. Setting it up, making it work."

He put his hands on my shoulders. "Which would explain why no one's found her here."

Oh no: "And why the State Department hasn't made a fuss."

"If that's what she's doing, and they're setting her up to bust her, then yeah. It explains why they haven't turned this into an incident."

The air stirred, bringing the smell of cooling plants, a tropical tangle of them. Banana trees and palms were visible as swaying shapes, black against the deep blue of the night sky.

"But, Don . . . even if she had to stay underground to do this, she'd let me and my father know she was okay." She had put politics above family too many times to count. But she loved us too much to put us through this. I had to believe that.

"She could be working with someone who's not getting the messages to you."

"Ernesto? The Cuban boy? The CIA agent?"

"Obviously, she wouldn't work knowingly with the CIA." He sighed. "But they might know what she's doing, their people might have infiltrated. If not Ernesto, someone like him."

Except where the U.S. government was concerned, Mother was a trusting person. She might have entrusted a recent acquaintance to deliver messages about her whereabouts and welfare. If Don was right, she hadn't chosen her confidant wisely.

But then, wisdom would have brought her home with her tour group.

"If the Cubans have been sending people to the U.S. through Mexico, if Mother's been hiding them, then they don't want her traced back to the U.S.," I mused. "They wouldn't say any more than they had to about her. Just that they couldn't find her."

"They could have put her aboard a Cubana plane to Mexico anytime," he agreed.

"The Cubans keep quiet because it's their plan. And the U.S. keeps quiet because they're onto it, and they don't want to tip anyone off. They want to find all the links along the route before they move in and make arrests."

"They'd be looking for bigwigs, people in the Cuban government—that's basic police work," he agreed. "Played right, it could lay the groundwork for us to swarm Cuba, get rid of Castro like we did Noriega."

"So everybody clams up, and no one really looks for Mother. Because everyone knows exactly where she is and what she's doing, and it suits them all to have her keep doing it."

"If they nail her for this, they'll call it treason," he said.

We stood in the road, looking ahead at the glow of lights from our waiting mousetrap.

My chest ached. My head pounded. This was more trouble than I could get Mother out of. This had been my worst nightmare since I was four years old.

Don said, "What do you suppose they've got waiting up there? Not information—they could have given us that in Emilio's office, in General Miguel's office. And not an arrest. If they're trying to keep a low profile with this business, the last thing they'd want is another American . . ."

"In prison," I concluded. "An American in prison is nothing but trouble. Reporters trooping through to make sure she's okay, tour groups with nosy acquaintances of her boyfriend . . . Myra Wilson's too much trouble. Maybe they want us to break her out."

Castro had executed General Ochoa, a Hero of the Revolution, rather than appear to sanction drug smuggling. So he could hardly pardon an American who'd supposedly committed the same crime. But that didn't make it any more convenient to keep her locked up and ready for impromptu inspection.

I visualized the dull-eyed woman inside the prison. Was she sitting somewhere now like a bride-to-be awaiting elopement?

"We'd have to get her out, get to the airport, pretend to bribe a bunch of people there. If they want her out badly enough, they'll let it work." They'd let us play cat's-paw, pulling a red-hot chestnut out of prison for them.

"We could be wrong," he pointed out. "There could be news waiting up the road, news about your mother. If we turn back, we'll never know."

And if we didn't turn back, he could be walking into a setup. I didn't want him to do that, not even for Mother. "Let's just get out of here."

If our driver was surprised or disconcerted to see us return alone and so soon, he didn't express it. He dutifully turned the car around, and drove us back to Havana.

We had him drop us at the Malecón, not far from the hotel.

We strolled for a while, watching the ocean and rehashing what we'd just discussed. It was like twisting and turning a Rubik's Cube: when one part of the pattern worked, the flip side didn't.

A voice behind us said, "Do you need assistance?"

We turned to find a tourist cop motioning us toward his car.

"No, it's okay," I said in Spanish. "We're just getting some air."

"It is very late, and I fear you may be bothered if you remain out of doors." His smile was friendly, but his tone wasn't. He shone a flashlight into our faces. "Please allow me to return you to your hotel."

We weren't completely sure we had a choice.

When we climbed out of his car, he did, too. He accompanied us into the hotel like a chaperone. But he didn't expect the reception we got.

General Miguel was slumped in a chair, legs splayed, puffing on a cigar and looking very bored. The man I'd met months ago, Mr. Radio Havana, he of the white jacket and layer-cut hair, sat beside him. Rounding out the party was our driver, sitting beside our minder, Teresa.

When we entered the graceful room, Teresa jumped up, looking outraged. The general sighed deeply, straightening in his chair. Surprisingly, it was Mr. Radio Havana, in a blue sweater now, who spoke.

"We have been extremely concerned," he said in English. He walked over to meet us. Except for a desk clerk, the lobby was empty tonight. Or rather, this morning.

"Apparently," I replied.

"Please come and speak to the general."

The general stood wearily. "So you have returned. Do you always climb from the vines beneath your hotel window?"

"Only when you put us in a room that invites us to do it," Don replied.

"And did we also invite you to bribe our driver?"

Cigar smoke curled through the scraggles of his beard.

"Yes," Don nodded emphatically. "Yes, you did. But why call it a bribe? I hired him, that's all."

"He works for us."

"Then he should have turned me down."

The general sighed again. "I am not a young man. It is very late. Having invited our concern"—a brief flash of cigar-stained teeth—"can you tell us where you have been?"

"We took a walk. Then we took a drive. Then we—"

"A drive to the women's prison?" The general scowled. "For what purpose?"

"For the purpose of getting away from listening devices. Like the one in our room. Like the one in the restaurant." Don scowled. "We'd been to the prison, so we knew it was on a lonely road. We wanted to be someplace private, to talk."

"You cannot talk at the Malecón?"

"Without getting picked up by tourist police? No," I finished for him. "As you can see. We understood that we were free, within limits, to look around."

The general was grinning, looking at Teresa and Mr. Radio Havana as if to lament the bad manners of children today. "Of course you are free. This is Cuba, not one of America's little fiefdoms. Here, you are free to do as you wish." He bowed ironically. "But like a parent who has lost a great deal of sleep worrying because his little ones have climbed from the window without so much as a note, I will now say good night and return to my bed."

He strode past us. Teresa and the driver rose to follow, Teresa casting us a deeply annoyed look.

Mr. Radio Havana remained behind. "You are free to walk where you wish and do as you wish. But if you are discovered to be leaving from a back window and are gone many hours, you must expect to create much concern."

"How do you know we went out a back window?" I asked him. "How do you know we didn't walk out the front door?"

He hesitated. "That is what I have been told."

"Did someone go to our room looking for us?"

"I do not know. I was given a message."

"Well, I'm sorry to have cost you any sleep," I lied. I hoped he recalled rousting me out of bed and depositing me on a middle-of-the-night flight to Mexico. "But as you can see, we didn't get into any trouble."

He met my eye, looking a little confused. "May I ask truly what you have been doing?"

"I've been trying to give my friend a feeling for Havana. Since we're hoping to find my mother here."

"And the reporters who gave away their passports, you are hoping to find them, also?"

Was he offering me information? "Do you know any more about them? You never found them?"

"No." But a slight squint told me he knew something.

"And the Cubans who had their passports? Did they say anything?"

He shook his head. "Nothing, no. They are not required to defend themselves in our criminal proceedings, and they did not."

"You've already tried them?"

"Yes. They have been sentenced to fifteen years

in prison. But they have not spoken of how they obtained the passports." His brows pinched. "We are one of the few nations that will not coerce information from prisoners."

Amnesty International disagreed, but I let it go. "Do you think they'd talk to us? Now that their trial's over and they've been sentenced, do you think they'd tell us anything?"

Mr. Radio Havana shrugged, his eyes glinting as he considered the possibility. "Perhaps it can be arranged. I will contact *el combinado del este*"—the prison "Ernesto" called Throw Away the Key—"and I will let you know."

With fifteen-year sentences to serve, the pair would be crazy to tell us anything they wouldn't want their jailers to know. But Mother had taught me long ago that showing interest in prisoners helps protect them.

God, I missed her.

Don and I turned to go upstairs to our room.

As we climbed the cement steps, I considered that the room had only one bed. I grew more nervous than I'd been on the road to the women's prison.

30

$\mathcal{I}$ needn't have worried. Within minutes, there was a knock at the door.

Nothing will cool your ardor faster than middle-of-the-night company in a country that's previously deported you. There was no question of ignoring the knock.

Martin Marules stood in the doorway making the sign of the cross. "Thank God!" he said. He looked pale and tired, as anyone might be at three in the morning. "Thank Mary and Jesus I have reached you in time!"

Don stepped backward, letting Marules in.

"I have disturbed you." Marules made the understatement of the year. "But it is urgent, very urgent." He was dressed as if for work in a dark suit and white shirt. He carried the suit jacket, and his top shirt buttons were undone. The muggy night was having its effect. His olive cheeks glistened, his thick hair looked damp. "May I sit?"

Don motioned him onto the bed, which took up

virtually all the room's floor space. He said, "You should know the room's bugged."

"Ah." He looked around. "Are you certain?"

"No harm in assuming so," Don said. "Do you want to take a walk? Talk outside?"

Marules sat on the bed, legs splayed, shoulders rounded, hands on his knees. He looked too weary to rise. But he said, "Yes."

He reached into his jacket pocket and pulled out his wallet and passport. He held them aloft, apparently instructing us to bring ours along.

Not a good sign. I started looking for my shoes. As I slipped them on, I noticed Don scowling at Marules.

Jamieson and Travolta had accused Marules of killing Alicia Mendoza and Agosto Diaz. And by his receptionist's account, they were monitoring his computer entries. Were they lying about him? Or had he completely fooled me, only appearing to grieve the loss of Agosto as if he were a son?

Whatever Don made of it, this wasn't the place to talk. He tucked in his shirt and slipped his shoes on. And, with a sigh of profound frustration, he looked at me.

The glance was like lightning. I had forgotten this feeling.

When we left the room, I noticed that one of the doors between us and the staircase was ajar. When we passed it, a man said, "Pardon."

He wore a guayabera shirt and pants that were shiny with age. He was gaunt and dark-skinned, his hair nearly white. He said, "It is very late. If you have a problem perhaps I can help you."

We'd found our night-shift minder.

I said, "We don't need anything."

He stepped out of the room, his perturbation almost palpable. "It is not good for tourists to go out so late. Perhaps you are not aware of the hour?"

At this point, punchy from lack of sleep, I was very well aware of the hour.

"You work for the government." I stated the obvious.

"I have been asked to ensure that all goes smoothly for you," he agreed.

"We're going out briefly to have a private conversation. You don't have to follow us or notify anybody. We're coming right back." Not that I thought he'd take my word for it.

His shoulders drooped. It was clear we were making a great deal of work for him. But there was nothing he could do to stop us, short of grappling with us in the corridor.

So we went downstairs with no illusions we were sneaking off.

When we reached the lobby, the desk clerk leaped to his feet. When we passed him without stopping, he called out to us. "May I direct you—? Where are you—? Señores, señorita, please wait!"

We hurried outside, ignoring him.

A tourist cop erupted from a parked car. "Is there a problem?" he asked us.

"We're taking a walk," Marules informed him. "Please do not disturb us." The cop seemed perplexed by the Mexican accent. "Allow us to pass," Marules insisted, though he was by no means blocking our path.

The policeman slid into his car, fiddling with a radio.

We walked on. Marules had turned toward the Malecón, but I thought we'd be too conspicuous along that empty stretch of sea wall. I grabbed his arm, nodding toward the neighborhoods. We would be conspicuous there, too. And there were revolutionary watch committee headquarters every few corners. But at least there were corners to turn and shadows to hide in. If it came to that.

We walked hastily down a block of colonial manors, their stone and plaster facades noticeably pitted even in the dark. Though many windows were open or broken out, there was no noise inside the houses. At this hour, with no lights to turn on or extra candles to burn, most residents had chosen to sleep.

The air was damp and close here in the middle of the city, with the breezes blocked by buildings. The street smelled of decaying garbage overgrown by blossoming vines. If we'd been walking at night in America, a dog would have been barking. But I had yet to encounter a dog in Cuba. I supposed it was too hard to justify feeding a pet when neighbors scrambled and prayed for food.

As we passed one of the houses, I looked through the windows. A beam had collapsed into the middle of a huge room. Because of it, the house appeared to be empty, with no cloth tacked over any upstairs windows.

"Let's go in here," I suggested.

Marules, better prepared than we, clicked on a penlight as we navigated the overgrown walkway.

The thin shaft of light caught the flutter of small moths and big mosquitoes.

The house must have been magnificent, circa 1850. The steps and porch had been marble, though huge chunks were now missing, perhaps recut to patch other porches and floors. Inside, the dust from the collapsed beam had long settled. As Marules ran the light over it, I could see how splendid the wall behind had once been. The remaining wainscot was elaborately carved. Shreds of silk wallpaper hung there. A golden finial glinted on the floor.

Don pulled me over so I couldn't be seen from the door. Marules and he stood between me and the broken beam.

Don said, "Kill the light."

Marules did. After the luxury of a look around, the place seemed darker and spookier than before.

"What's this about?" Don demanded. "We've made ourselves completely conspicuous at this point. We've announced our intention to troop out here and have a private conversation. So they're good and paranoid now—not that they needed any more reason than we've given them already."

I could see Marules, taller than Don, lean closer to him. "I have learned from my friend Juan Emilio that there is dissension regarding your motives for being here. There is a belief taking hold that Willa's mother is not the true object of your search. That, in fact, she is not missing at all. That she is not in Cuba at all."

I hoped this theory was based on some information, some facts the Cubans hadn't shared with us. "Why do they think my mother's not here?"

"They believe she is in the United States. That, indeed, she preceded her tour group, leaving the night before their departure. They are quite sure she is fine." He repeated, "Fine."

Nothing concrete—I was disappointed. "She'd have gotten in touch with her family and friends." I didn't want to go into the possibility Don and I had discussed earlier, that her messages to us had gone undelivered. "And if the Cubans had any real information to support this, they wouldn't have let me back into the country to keep looking for her."

"Ah, but they did not wish for you to come! It was my assurance that your friend's police skills could prove useful that led to this rather grudging favor."

"So what's the point?" Don wondered. "You came all the way to Cuba to tell us the brass doesn't necessarily believe Willa's mother is still here?" He sounded exasperated. "Because I've got to say it's obvious that's one of the possibilities. It wasn't worth the trip, if that's all you have to say."

"No, no," Marules assured him, "I am not here to discuss this theory with you. I am here to tell you there are those who would view it as a mere pretext. Who would attempt to cast your actions in the most suspicious light."

"Are you saying we're in danger?" I asked him.

"Yes. Juan Emilio would not phone me on a mere whim. Reading between the lines, he is saying that you may be arrested. He is telling me to come for you. As a favor, he is warning me."

We stood in silence for a long moment. Except for a breeze stirring the shrubs near the glassless windows, it was silent outside.

"Are you sure?" Don said finally. "Sure it rises to that level? Maybe he'd just as soon see us gone, and he's asking you to give us a nudge."

"No." Marules sounded positive. "I believe you will be taken into custody. I believe an international incident may result, to the detriment of our hopes to reduce tensions between Cuba and your country."

"They had the opportunity to detain us tonight," I told Marules. They could rightly have said we'd bribed, rather than "hired," our driver. "But they didn't."

"What reason?" His voice was hushed with worry. "Something has happened? I have been so anxious to convey my message that I have not thought to ask you."

"No," Don said. "Nothing happened. But we've been in contact with several officials over the course of the day and the evening. They could have taken us aside any time. They didn't."

So we were keeping Marules out of the loop? Don hadn't seen him the day after Agosto's death, so he had less reason to trust his sincerity than I did. And I wasn't exactly bowled over by my faith in Marules right now.

"Why didn't Emilio just send us a message?" I wondered. "Save you the hassle of a trip?"

"But no." Marules sounded modest. "I do not begrudge a day of my time. Not for something like this. Bad enough that I have lost . . ." He didn't speak Agosto's name. But his breathing became heavy, as if he were trying to calm himself. "I was given a premonition, you know, when Agosto asked me to send him to San Diego. I had a vision of him with blood on his brow." Even in the darkness, I could see Marules crossing himself. "But it seemed a foolishness, too embarrassing to admit, something a young woman such as my wife would fear, not a journalist like myself. I have never been a religious man. But now I have vowed not to throw away the gift of fear. When I feel it—as I do now—I will respect that it has come from a force in the universe that must command my respect. Do you understand?"

"You have a feeling we're in trouble," Don said flatly. "That much, I'd go along with."

"I have made arrangements, and Juan Emilio has agreed, in order to avoid a worse situation. We may leave Cuba in a few hours' time, as if we were passengers on a plane which is landing now for additional fuel. It will leave shortly, its passengers having remained in the customs-cleared room. There is a way, with the help of Juan Emilio, that we may enter that room and then take up empty seats on the plane."

"And Emilio's going to explain this to everyone tomorrow? Tell them we left with his blessing?" Don's voice was low and calm.

"It will be clear that a high official has helped us to leave. But it must not be known that it was *compañero* Emilio."

"What else would they think?" I countered. "You come here, we leave with you, no one sees us again—and you're a friend of Emilio's. It won't take a genius to figure it out. Did he really tell you not to implicate him?"

"He has arranged an alternative explanation," Marules said.

"He's framing someone else?" Don asked him.

"No, no." Marules sounded shocked. "He is offering another scenario. I did not question him about it."

I could well believe the mighty Emilio would not be pinned down.

"What if they catch us?" I asked Marules. "What if someone comes to the airport and sees us there? Then we've broken the law for real. Then they've got a reason to arrest us."

"If Juan Emilio says he has made arrangements, I think we may have confidence." But there was an undercurrent of fear in Marules's voice.

Outside, car headlights lit the street. Don moved closer to me. None of us spoke until the car made a slow pass down the street. Tourist police searching for us?

"What I don't like about this," Don said, "is that I think I know who Emilio's after."

"After?" Marules said. "He is not after anyone. He is trying to help us."

"Do you know General Miguel?" Don persisted.

"No. Of course I know *of* him—he is a Hero of the Revolution."

"On first acquaintance, he also seems like a stand-up guy, a cop with a complicated city to watch over. I wonder if your Juan Emilio isn't trying to sweep out a few more members of the old guard. Like Castro did with General Ochoa."

"But Juan Emilio was correct to recommend Ochoa's execution." Marules defended him. "Cuba cannot tolerate the drug trade. That would be no different from a return of your Mafia. There would be dollars, yes. But also weapons, unrest, flesh sold on the street. Thirty-five years of dignity would be lost, would mean nothing."

"I'm not happy about helping to set up the general, if that's what Emilio's doing," Don complained. "I don't know what the man's politics are, so I don't know if it ends up being a good thing or a bad thing overall. Internal politics aside, I'd just as soon stick around a little longer. Let this play out, wherever it's going."

"But no," Marules protested. "Surely not if it is going toward your arrest? Toward an international incident? You cannot be serious?"

"That's quite an *if*. I don't see any support for it. Just Emilio's hints to you. And we don't know what his agenda is."

"On the other hand . . ." I was getting sick of being the voice of cowardly reason. "Things could get messed up very damn fast if Emilio needs them to."

"But how have you gotten this bad impression of Juan Emilio?" Marules fretted. "Surely he has done you no harm or disservice?"

"Let's get out of here, Don. If Emilio's right, we're already marked. And if this is a smoke screen, there's no telling what he'll do to put us in the middle of something. Either way, we're not safe." And my mother might not be here anyway, not if we had things figured right. "We're not getting the kind of cooperation and help we'd need to find Mother. So what's the point of staying?"

"It's your call." Don didn't put any warning or whining into the statement. But it was obvious he disagreed.

Standing in the dark with the two men, I wished I could feel Marules's certainty in this course, or Don's suspicion of it. I wished I could feel that my decision—either way—was right.

"Then, please, let us go now." Marules was almost begging. "I have only to make a telephone call, and Juan Emilio will send us a car. Let us find a telephone."

We left the abandoned house, Marules briefly flashing his pen light so we wouldn't stumble into a gap in the pillaged marble porch.

We barely made it to the sidewalk before a car whipped around the corner, lights catching us like deer on a highway.

Marules's knees buckled as if he might faint. Don was right behind him, grabbing his arms. Marules seemed to be murmuring a prayer in Spanish.

The car jerked to a stop in front of us. The logo on the doors was impossible to read in the backwash of the headlights. There were two people in front and one in back.

Both passenger doors were flung open. The men who emerged wore military fatigues, pant legs tucked into laced boots. One of them had a Fidel hat and a long beard.

"I am to get no rest tonight," General Miguel lamented. "You are most troublesome." He held the kind of machine gun you see in prints of Che Guevara. But he wasn't pointing it at us.

"General Miguel," Don said, "this man is ill. He's having a heart attack—he needs help."

I hoped Don was improvising, lying to get us out of a jam. Marules's knees had buckled, but I hoped it was from fear.

Whatever the truth, Marules clutched his chest, sinking to the ground as Don held him from behind.

"He's having a heart attack," Don repeated. "He runs a goddamn newspaper in Mexico City, and if he dies on the street because you're pissed that we went walking at night, you're going to look like a vulture."

Marules was making gasping noises. I stood a few paces behind the men, frozen with fear. Please let this be a ploy, I prayed. And let it be an unnecessary one.

"Ignácio," the general said to the soldier beside him, "help us get this man into the car. Go with him to the hospital."

While the soldier and Don handed Marules into the car, the general said to me, "We have little equipment and medicine, but we are still able to separate a real attack from a convenient excuse."

"Willa," Don called. "Go with him. Make sure he's—"

"No!" The general waved the car away. Don barely got clear before the soldier pulled the door shut and the car shot down the street.

"You don't need that gun," Don said. "We're not doing anything here. If you didn't have our room bugged, we'd be there right now finding out why he came to see us."

The general kept the gun pointed at the ground as if it were a natural extension of his arm. And given the life he'd led, perhaps it was. With his other hand, he pulled a Havana Twist from his shirt pocket and expertly sliced off the end.

"Tell me more about your friend," he said, patting his pants pockets.

"His name is Martin Marules. He called in some favors to get us over here."

"Ah, so that was the famous Marules?" The general clamped the cigar between his teeth and lit it. Smoke curled around him. The glowing tip showed his face looking equally cynical and interested. "You know he is a great patron of the arts in Cuba, do you not?"

"I met him two days ago, so no, I didn't know that." Don had apparently decided not to mention having met Marules in San Diego as well.

"Shall we walk back to your hotel?"

I was relieved to hear him say this. I was afraid, after Marules's warning, that we were about to be arrested.

We started toward the hotel, walking at a slow saunter. The general seemed in no hurry to part company.

"Martin Marules helps support the writers' union and also a film festival which brings many tourists to Cuba. He has donated millions—yes, you look surprised—millions for the restoration of our theaters. That is why he has in his pocket such . . . special friends here in Cuba."

We slowed almost to a stop. I was jumping out of my skin with worry, wondering whether Martin's heart attack was genuine or diversionary. But I couldn't think of any way to ask Don.

"You need not be concerned for Señor Marules— or perhaps he prefers *compañero* Marules, in the old style," the general said to me. "But these are modern times, and now the rich are well protected in Cuba. We fought ferociously to liberate and protect the poor. But in the end, as usual, it is the rich to whom we grovel. We reclaimed our land and cast out the thieves who had enslaved us to labor on it. And yet, to whom do we cater now? To the rich Spaniards of Mexico. And to the Americans, because now as then, they have dollars. It used to be the Americans took what they pleased from us. And now? Now we must sell you even that which we cannot spare. Because without your dollars, we cannot trade with other countries for the things which you deny us—food, medicine, plaster, paint, automobiles, fuel. One way or another, the dollar has long ruled Cuba." He puffed on his cigar. "Except, of course, when it was the ruble."

We loitered there, hardly moving. It was difficult not to force the pace. I was getting a major case of the creeps, wandering the streets of Havana with a general indulging in bitter reflections.

Don said, "If you're blaming Marules—"

"Oh no," said the general, "it is useless to blame the rich. Rich and poor alike, it takes two to make a bargain." He held out his cigar. "But when I think of my shoeless father, I find the bargain very bitter."

I was beginning to think the general had been making a bargain with a bottle of rum.

Standing in the middle of a blacked-out street in his fatigues and Fidel hat, his machine gun dangling, he might have resembled the posters in the CDR windows—*Viva Che!*—except that his posture bespoke weariness and defeat.

With a sigh, he said, "Do you find it difficult to enforce the law in San Francisco, Señor Lieutenant?"

"All but impossible, most of the time," Don admitted.

"In Cuba, it is not so difficult as you would expect. With poverty, there is always some theft and prostitution, even violence. But not as often as you would guess. We are lucky in our people, who have a natural benevolence. Many of our forefathers were slaves, imported from Africa to cut cane for sugar. I believe there is a genetic memory, a gratitude to have survived the great disease of slavery. And we have made it our mission to ensure one hundred percent literacy and one hundred percent integration. So we are a nation of college-educated descendants of slaves. Our very cells remember the yoke and recoil from injustice. We are the perfect socialists. Where there is crime, it is born of true desperation, it is an aberration. Whereas among your people, well . . . I will wager you cannot make this claim about them, señor."

I was surprised to hear Surgelato laugh. "Maybe not," he said. "That's why we try to keep our legal system fair."

"And your Mafia, your gangs, your ghettoes, they are fair?"

Don shrugged. "We wouldn't codify tolerance if we didn't have a lot to tolerate."

"Ha!" The general clapped him on the back. "You cannot say I have not tolerated much from you tonight. You cannot say you have been discouraged from speaking your mind."

"Then go one step farther. Tell us what's going on. Why let us come here, then watch us every minute, keep us busy doing nothing? Why keep us in the dark? Why not tell us what you know? To you, maybe it's politics. Maybe it's paranoia. I don't know, I'm no historian, I'm no scholar. But to Willa, it's her mother."

"You want the truth, *compañero* Lieutenant?" The general tucked his machine gun into a loop on his belt. "The truth is that you can search for what is lost, but you cannot find what is not here. There is nothing in Cuba for you to do except to be observed by us, to be our panda."

"Panda?" It obviously wasn't something Don was used to being called.

"Ah yes." There was a smile in the general's voice. "The Chinese have shipped to us a panda. It has been traveling to schools in our small cities as a gift from our new friends. And you, when you come to us from the bamboo forest of San Francisco, are you any less remarkable? Are you less worthy of study and admiration?"

"And we're going to get about as much out of this trip as the panda did."

The general smiled. "The panda does not appreciate the admiration of our children. It thinks only of bamboo. But you, I will bow to you tonight." He inclined his head. "And perhaps you will value the gesture."

We stood there a minute. If Don knew what to make of this speech, he was way ahead of me.

With a sigh, the general began walking again. We walked slightly ahead of him, an acknowledgment that he was armed, even if the gun was now holstered.

Before we crossed the street to the hotel, the general said, "One moment."

We turned. The hotel lights seemed bright after

an hour in the blacked-out neighborhood. Even at this distance, they lit the general's face.

After a sleepless night, there were bags under his eyes and wrinkles around them. White hairs gleamed in his beard, outnumbering the gray ones.

"A piece of advice. For the sake of friendship between us, though it is withheld from your country to mine. Juan Emilio is often absent when he should be present. No one remarks on it—and that in itself is very remarkable. I will tell you what I believe: A favor has been asked of Emilio." He made a gesture under his chin as if tracing a pointed beard. Referring to Castro? "And Emilio has carried it out, or is carrying it out. And while this is so, he is the favorite son. The old comrades in arms—*históricos,* as they call us now— we must look on in envy. We have given birth to the revolution, and we have carried it to Nicaragua, to Zaire, to Angola. But the *históricos* cannot give what we do not have. We cannot give dollars."

He made a sweeping bow, turning and walking back into the neighborhood.

I watched him, his cigar smoke catching the light after the rest of him had disappeared into shadow.

Unless I'd misinterpreted him, he'd just told us Señor Emilio could do no wrong as long as he brought Castro dollars. And that, to this end, Emilio was traveling secretly.

Was Emilio visiting the United States in search of Americans willing to donate goods and money? Was my mother setting up his lodging and appointments?

I remembered Marules. "The heart attack?" I asked Don. "Was it real?"

"No." He stared into the darkness as if the general might reemerge from it. "Marules is Emilio's ally. And it sounded to me from what Marules said that Emilio was out to get the general. So I didn't know if Marules was safe with him. I figured I'd leave it up to Marules. If he didn't feel secure, he'd go along with me, he'd pretend it was a heart attack. If I was wrong, he'd say he was fine. It was just insurance."

"Now what?"

"Now we go collect him at the hospital, and I guess"—he gave me a quizzical glance—"we get the hell out of here?"

"Yes!" The general had as much as told us my mother wasn't here. What was the point in staying?

Don stepped closer, putting his arm around me. "You're okay with leaving the panda behind?"

31

$\mathcal{F}$or once, we were glad to find the tourism cop waiting in his car outside the hotel. He seemed startled to see us. He must have expected his radio communication to result in our being picked up, as indeed one of us had.

"We need a ride," Don told him. "Our friend was taken to the hospital by your military police. We need to get over there."

The cop, light-skinned and strong-chinned, seemed nearly paralyzed with indecision. He slid back into his car to use a radio attached to the dashboard by a curly wire. A couple of minutes later, he motioned us into the car. I wasn't sure whether he'd gotten a superior's okay, or whether he'd checked the nearest hospital to see if a tourist had been admitted.

Either way, we had a lift.

The car was old, with brittle leather seats and no gadgetry except the radio. In America, it might have belonged to a working-class high school kid. Here, it was the nicest thing on the road, though the streets were lined with fine antiques for which there was no gasoline.

The hospital was close by. We got there easily enough—the trick would be leaving. Had Marules been able to reach Señor Emilio at this hour? Would a car be coming for us?

The tourism cop accompanied us into a waiting room. It was empty except for a young woman sleeping on a chair.

The receptionist bent her head over something that looked like a twenty-year-old textbook. Even in the hospital, the lights were low. She looked up. "Yes?" Her gaze wandered to the cop and lingered there.

"Did you admit a man having a heart attack about half an hour ago? His name is Marules." I hoped she wouldn't say he wasn't here. I hoped we hadn't lost Martin, too.

"Ah yes," she said. "I believe he is being prepared for surgery."

I translated for Don. His face reflected my startled horror.

He stepped forward. "Tell her we have to see him. That it's urgent."

Apparently she understood English. She replied, though still in Spanish, "I will get the doctor. But it may not be possible to see him now, señor."

"Get the doctor," I agreed.

The sleeping woman roused, sitting up and exclaiming, "Raúl? There is news?"

As the receptionist left her station, she called back, "Not yet, María. Go back to sleep."

I looked around the waiting room. It contained

nothing but scarred wooden chairs arranged in rows along the walls. The linoleum had yellowed to an unpleasant ochre.

A young man in frayed scrubs returned with the receptionist. The stethoscope around his neck looked vintage. He shook our hands.

"Your friend is fine," he told us. "But we are readying surgery for another man, and I will not have the opportunity to speak long with you. We have given your friend a bed so that we may observe him overnight. It is best if you return in the morning."

"No," I said, "we have to see him now. Can you take us to him?"

"We wish a minimum of disturbance, please." He tried again. "It is better if you come in the morning."

"Please take us to him."

He sighed, nodding. The receptionist returned to her desk. The cop stayed with us.

As the doctor led us down a dimly lighted hallway, the cop asked him about the upcoming operation. To my surprise, the doctor described a technique pioneered at this hospital. It involved grafting abdominal muscle tissue around the heart and using a pacemaker to cue the transplanted muscle to contract at proper intervals.

From what I could see inside the hospital rooms, there were no amenities there—no trays of bandages and tubes, no IVs, no computerized monitors. Just patients in beds. And, apparently, surgeons able to innovate brilliantly with very few materials.

The doctor pointed us into a room, then excused himself. As Don went in to talk to Marules, I turned to the tourist cop.

"Thank you for the ride. But we'd like some privacy now."

He squinted as if not approving of the concept. But he said, "I will be in the waiting room."

I entered to find Marules looking quite hale in his hospital gown. He sat on the edge of a bed.

"Thank God you have not been detained! I have been in such fear." He pulled Don into an embrace, clapping him on the back. "I have telephoned the assistant of Juan Emilio. A car is coming. And an inquiry into your whereabouts has commenced." He scowled. "We will ask the driver to communicate that the search for you should stop, that you are here now. It is very difficult to use the telephone. The service has been limited to hospitals and police at this hour."

Hospitals, police, and, it seemed, interior ministers.

"Emilio doesn't mind going public about helping us?" Don asked him. "If we drive off in his car, there won't be any question who got us out of the country."

Marules stood, crossing to a scarred metal closet to retrieve his clothes. He didn't say anything.

Don looked at me and shook his head. Clearly, this worried him.

But by now, I'd have risked anything, trusted anyone, to get away from here. Lack of sleep was simultaneously magnifying my paranoia and forcing me to have a little faith.

When Marules retrieved his clothes, Don and I went into the hall so he could dress.

"No one here will recognize the car," I said hopefully.

He pointed behind me. The tourist cop was leaning against the wall, still waiting for us.

The cop wouldn't let us climb into a car until he learned who'd sent it. So much for secrecy.

"He'll be told to keep quiet about it," I ventured. "Or he won't be believed." Or something, anything that meant we could hightail it to the airport.

The smell of cigar smoke wafted in from the waiting room. I could hear the clomping of boots, the rumble of men's voices. The cop went out to take a look.

Don opened the door to Marules's room. "Trouble," he said. "We've got to go now. Right now. No, leave that."

Marules, as a consequence, walked out in his bare feet, carrying his shoes and jacket. We ducked around the corner, running down a corridor toward what I hoped was a back exit.

We could hear boots in the hallway now, probably heading toward the room we'd just fled.

The back door opened into a small courtyard separated from the street by a row of overgrown trellises. We ran through a gap between them.

Headlights caught us hesitating, wondering which direction to take. As the car approached, its driver called out, "Señor, *aquí!*"

The car was in front of us before we could take a step toward it. The driver pulled away from the curb before our doors were even closed.

Two men in fatigues chased us partway down the street. The tourism police car screeched out of the front lot, following close on our heels. I turned in my seat, watching the cop pull the radio off his dashboard. In the United States, he'd have had a gun mounted there.

He spoke into the radio for a while. Then his head jerked back as if in surprise. He talked some more.

Our driver was barreling as fast as a person in a plastic Russian car can go. There was no traffic on the street to slow him.

But we didn't outrun the tourism cop—we didn't have to. I watched him slip the radio onto its hook and slow down, dropping back. His headlights stopped filling Emilio's car with light. He pulled over and made a wide U-turn, either heading back to the hospital or getting on with his shift.

Dispatch had apparently told him not to pursue. Either Señor Emilio had taken precautions or the dispatcher had a license-plate list of cars that weren't to be disturbed.

I could have wept with relief. I didn't want to look at Don. I was afraid he'd appear troubled or fearful or stubborn, that he'd bonded with General Miguel, his fellow law enforcement official, and wouldn't want to cooperate with the general's upstart rival, Emilio. That he had found some reason—perhaps an obvious and urgent one, I didn't really care—to stop this car. I was afraid he'd persuade us to return to the hotel, with its bugging devices and spies down the hall.

But whatever was on Don's mind, he didn't say anything. He just looked out the window. On my other side, Marules lay back against the seat, his eyes closed as if he were praying.

For once, we cut through neighborhoods instead of tracing the Malecón. It was a quick trip out of Havana onto the highway leading to the airport.

When the airport came into sight, we left the main road, cutting across the tarmac to a cyclone fenced area. The driver hopped out of the car, unlocking the padlock on a chain wrapped several times around the poles of a sturdy gate. He scraped it over the cement, opening it just wide enough for our sedan to pass through. He drove us inside, then got out again, reclosing the gate. Up ahead, I could see lights glowing through airport windows. Two planes stood on the runway. One was dark, showing no activity. The other had workers swarming around it, a few on foot, some on small vehicles.

I was so intent on watching the plane—presumably we would soon be boarding it, but I didn't even know what country it belonged to—that I didn't notice the headlights behind us. Not until Don muttered, "Damn," and Marules moaned.

I turned to see two jeeplike trucks racing toward the reclosed gate. Our driver stood silhouetted in the headlights, arms dangling, one hand still holding the huge padlock.

I could hear Martin Marules praying aloud. I was praying, too, praying to some vague god of irony and justice, praying that Emilio's name would be enough to turn the trucks around; that our driver would offer Emilio's patronage like a bribe to protect us from arrest.

Four men in military fatigues jumped out of the trucks, approaching our driver with their machine guns pointed. We could see the driver gesticulating, apparently offering an animated explanation. Whatever he was saying, the soldiers didn't seem to care. They motioned him to unravel the chain he'd rewound around the cyclone fence.

I reached past Don, reached for the door. I just wanted out. I wanted to run. I wanted to dash across the tarmac and vanish into a crowd, make my way back to Havana any way I could.

Don grabbed my arm.

Two of the soldiers flanked the car. One of them motioned us out with his machine gun.

Don slid out, offering his hand to help me. Instead, I cowered against Marules, reaching backward for the door handle as if, somehow, I could get past the other soldier.

The soldier pushed Don aside, reached in, and unceremoniously yanked me out, flinging me to the ground.

Don was right behind me, helping me up. By the time I was on my feet, Marules was out of the car, too.

Our driver was being prodded toward us. I could see he was a scholarly-looking young man with rimless glasses. He appeared more perturbed than worried.

The oldest of the soldiers said, "You are under arrest! You will place your hands on the tops of your heads without delay!"

I felt like I'd been hit by a truck. I couldn't breathe, much less move my arms to raise them. I grew lightheaded. I thought, for a moment, that I'd gone into shock, that my internal systems were shutting down. I thought I would faint, like some silly movie heroine.

My worst nightmare had come true. I was under arrest. In Cuba. Where our country maintained no diplomatic relations, where it had no goodwill to barter for our freedom. If it even cared about us after we'd broken the law to come here.

I watched Martin Marules put his hands atop his head. "Señor Emilio," he sputtered. "You must call him."

"You will have an opportunity in the days ahead to contact who you will," the soldier said.

The other soldier, for reasons I had missed, was hustling our driver back to his car.

Don put his hands up, too. He looked at me with the most painful apology in his eyes, as if this were his fault, as if he should have known, should have insisted on a different course, should have protected me.

When, actually, I was the one who'd brought him here. My mother had tried to get him fired years ago, but he had risked this to try to help her. I hoped he could see it in my eyes, see how sorry I was, how grateful I was. How much I loved him.

I tried to raise my arms above my head. But all I could think about was the women's prison. I thought of Myra Wilson, drugged behind a sewing machine. I thought of the months I'd spent in the San Bruno Jail, the claustrophobia that had made it the longest ordeal of my life. I recalled shivering on my bunk every night, a glaze of panic on my face, trying to ignore the bars, the locks, just long enough to sleep.

I couldn't do it again. I'd rather be shot.

Adrenaline hit me like a lightning bolt.

I turned and ran. I knew it was stupid, I knew it

was counterproductive. I knew I'd never get away from four armed soldiers and two trucks. I knew it would look inculpating, and make things worse for me. But I couldn't help it, I couldn't bear it. I was carried on a flood of fear, I was superwoman. I couldn't and wouldn't let them hold me.

I ran across the tarmac as fast as I could, hearing my heart hammer in my ears, listening hard for gun shots.

Don was shouting, "Willa! No! No!"

But still I ran.

32

$\mathscr{I}$ had almost reached the airport building, for all the good that might have done me, when a hand grabbed my shoulder. I was spun around and socked in the jaw. I went down hard, scraping my shoulder on the concrete as my head bounced.

I was too scared to feel it. I tried to scramble to my feet. I couldn't hear well or think clearly, but I could make out Don shouting, booted feet running toward me. I blinked back tears, and saw a man astride me, not a soldier but an airport worker in a greasy jumpsuit. By the time I brought him into focus, there were soldiers beside him, grinning as if I were a side show.

I scooted farther back, finding myself pinned against a wall. I hadn't covered much ground. I could see Don and Marules at a distance of perhaps forty yards, pressed against one of the trucks with soldiers' machine guns in their ribs.

I had made this harder for everyone, that was all. One of the soldiers hoisted me to my feet, then slammed me back against the wall. He and his companion pointed their machine guns at me.

Beyond them, activity around the airplane slowed. Workers stood watching, probably enjoying a few moments of drama in an otherwise ordinary work night.

I was shaking, holding my head as the blood pounded painfully behind my eyes. I could feel the swelling in my cheek where I'd been punched. A soldier pulled me away from the wall. I staggered forward a couple of yards, then he got behind me, poking the gun into my back, pushing me along with it as if herding a stray.

The soldiers took me to the second truck and tossed me up against the side. Don and Marules, I noticed fleetingly, were handcuffed now. They were trundled off into the other truck. It sped away as I was cuffed and handed into the remaining one.

Perhaps in deference to his patron, Señor Emilio's driver was left behind, sitting in the car, no doubt wondering how to explain all this.

Or so I thought until I saw him in our headlights. He was smiling. And the soldier in the seat beside me flashed him a quick thumbs-up.

Sitting sidesaddle to accommodate heavy metal cuffs fastening my hands behind me, I saw the gesture with an eerie clarity, like a blown-up snapshot with the details enhanced. Thumbs-up—thank you for your part in delivering the troublesome pandas.

Until then, I'd assumed Señor Emilio had been thwarted. Now I knew that wasn't true, that this was part of the plan. He had arranged our supposed exit, perhaps to prove his loyalty to his rich patron,

Martin Marules. Marules, no doubt, would be released soon and sent home. His dollars must have bought him that much.

And Marules wouldn't blame his friend, Señor Emilio. He would blame the military, the old guard, the *histórico* General Miguel, for sabotaging Emilio. He would contribute even more money to Emilio, perhaps, to tip the balance in Cuba. The old revolutionaries had grown too romantic and nostalgic. The young Turks like Emilio were forging the way toward a new Cuba, one that recognized the cold reality that cash was paramount. Idealism was nothing without funding.

The truck had just started down the highway when it was stopped by a sedan turning sideways to block both lanes.

One of the soldiers grabbed his machine gun and jumped out, striding toward the car. The other soldier quickly checked my handcuffs, then joined him.

I didn't know what to expect. Señor Emilio himself come to question me? His car come to take me someplace I wouldn't easily be found? The same place my mother had been taken? That Dennis and Cindy had been stashed? To some remote work farm, perhaps? To a labor camp in China?

Fear gnawed at me so ferociously I envisioned leaping out of the jeep and running down the road, though I knew I'd probably be shot for it.

I watched the car. I considered soldier-assisted suicide if a People's Republic uniform emerged from it. Or if I heard the words *bota la llave*.

But it was General Miguel who climbed out of the small sedan. "Where are the others?" he demanded.

General Miguel? Had I misjudged Emilio? Was this the general's doing after all? Had the driver of the other car belonged to the general?

"Where are they? The two men? Speak!"

The soldier took a faltering step backward, obviously frightened. "General!" he said.

I sat up straighter. The soldier sounded surprised.

"Where are the others?" The general's voice was an exasperated boom. "Leave the woman with me," he ordered. "And go after them. Bring them back here. If you fail, you will answer for it."

He strode to where I sat. He looked at my cheek, his nostrils flaring. "Handcuff keys!"

He handed me out of the truck while a soldier unlocked the cuffs.

The general repeated, "You will pay a high price if you do not return with the others."

The soldiers jumped into the truck. The general motioned for his car to back up, and the truck shot around it, barreling down the highway at hurtling speed.

The general put his arm around me. He smelled of rum and cigars, lots of cigars. "You are all right?"

"Yes." I rubbed my wrists. "You're not going to . . . we're not going to . . ."

"Prison, señorita? No. I believe you have a plane to catch, do you not?"

I didn't know what to say, what it was safe to say.

"Señor Emilio has promised you a plane ride home, unless I am very much mistaken." He began walking me toward his car. "I have wondered how he manages to get them out of the country, his workers, his fund-raisers. Only tonight, with the help of the commotion in the hospital, the call from the tourism police, the license plate number . . . only tonight has it all come clear."

He handed me into the car, a Russian model with a cheap metal body. The driver turned. It was Mr. Radio Havana. "Hello," he said. "We were very lucky to intercept you. Another few moments, and you would have been lost."

Another few moments. The moments I'd spent running away. Though my jaw might ache tomorrow, my panic hadn't been wasted after all.

The general climbed in beside me. "Emilio has brought his pet capitalist, Marules, to coax you toward something," the general mused. "Emilio is a smart man, as I have seen many times, often to my detriment. He will have dangled an irresistible lure before you. Such as . . . a plane which stops only to refuel, and therefore requires no checking of passports or visas. And so I have put together what I have seen tonight—the arrival of Marules, the reports of the soldiers I sent to the hospital to see about his heart attack, the fact that Emilio's car has abruptly taken you away. You are not being returned to your hotel, that much is clear—the tourism police are waiting for that very purpose. Rather, you are being taken out of my reach. And so, finally, I understand. And through understanding what has been planned for you, what has been offered to you, I have also grown to understand the rest. How he has moved people out of Cuba to solicit the dollars with which he dazzles us."

"You're not going to arrest me?" I didn't care about his thought process, however much of a triumph his conclusion might be. I just wanted the bottom line.

"No. A promise has been made to you, and as a courtesy to Señor Emilio, I will see to it that it is carried out."

Mr. Radio Havana gaped at him, his emotion filling the car like some huge fluttering moth. "But, General—"

"I am acting as Emilio's ally, am I not? I have seen his great patron Marules under arrest, and I have learned of *compañero* Emilio's plans for him." He patted his pockets, pulling out a cigar. "And you forget that I am still a powerful man, in my quaint fashion—there are not so many Heroes of the Revolution left. But even if my day is over, I have this last weapon that I have borrowed from the new generation. I have been schooled in it by Emilio himself." He sliced away the cigar's twisted end and lit it. "When the rest of my arsenal is gone, I have duplicity, do I not?"

I could see headlights coming up fast. Two trucks pulled to a stop beside us. Marules and Don were in one of them.

The general told me to stay put, and he got out to greet the soldiers. I heard him barking orders, as any general in any country might do.

Mr. Radio Havana turned to face me. He said, "This is a difficult time for Cuba. We are tantalized by so much, so close. And all we have ever wanted is enough. Is it any wonder that factions form and expedient methods are employed?"

I finally found my voice. I didn't know what the hell he was talking about. But I knew what I wanted to say to him. I said, "Thank you! Thank you for coming tonight."

The general climbed into the front seat, letting Don and Marules into the back. I went directly into a clinch with Don. I could hear Marules sniffing as if overcome with tears. And I didn't blame him, not a bit.

To him, the general said, "I have learned from the *compañera* that Señor Emilio has promised you passage aboard the airplane currently on the runway before us. Is that correct?"

Apparently he didn't want it getting back to Emilio that he'd figured out the scam on his own.

Indebted to him, I said, "It's true, Martin. I told him."

I felt Don stiffen warily.

"Well, I . . ." Marules seemed to be struggling with himself. He didn't want to admit Señor Emilio had plotted to sneak us out, especially since he knew the general was of a different faction. On the other hand, the general had just rescued us from arrest.

"Do not be nervous, Señor Marules," the general soothed him. "We are not allies, Señor Emilio and myself. Yet I hold him in great respect for all he has purchased—I mean, accomplished—for the Revolution. I would not for the world see him thwarted by an accident such as the inopportune arrival of soldiers." Soldiers Emilio had sent. But Marules wasn't likely to believe that. The general, it seemed, was a very foxy man. "So I have stepped in to avoid the ruin of his plan. As a token of respect for him. And so, I will deliver you to your airplane. I assume you have been given instructions for how to proceed once you are inside the gate?"

"I . . . yes," Marules admitted. "Code words, General."

"Then let us see to it you do not miss your flight." He motioned to Mr. Radio Havana.

The trucks had driven off. Our driver watched their taillights in the rearview mirror. He waited until they were out of sight, then he started back toward the airport.

A car passed us going the other way—Emilio's car and driver.

Once again, we drove across the tarmac to the waiting plane. The refueling had apparently been accomplished. The maintenance vehicles were parked farther down the field.

A thin band of orange was shimmering along the horizon. The sun was beginning to come up.

We climbed out of the car. The general motioned for a man standing at the terminal door to join us.

"You have three more passengers," he said. "They forgot to reboard. Please put the stairs back so they may rejoin the other travelers."

The man looked aghast. "But, General, according to our list—"

"No, not according to your list. According to Señor Emilio."

The man took an involuntary step backward. It was as if the general had said "Count Dracula." He looked terrified.

But this was clearly something he'd been asked to do before. His terror was unmarred by protest or questions.

Marules moved closer to him. On the runway, the plane's engine revved. It was preparing for take-off. Marules murmured a few words into the man's ear.

The latter shook his head slightly, as if fervently hoping no ill would come of it, no harm to him or his family. But apparently Emilio had made him an offer he couldn't refuse.

The man motioned to a pair of workers, then excused himself, saying he would speed things up.

The general puffed on his cigar, watching thoughtfully as stairs were wheeled back and abutted to the plane, and the door was reopened.

When the man came to fetch us, the general dropped his cigar and ground it out. He smiled at us, saying, merely, "*Socialismo o muerte.*" Socialism or death, the slogan we'd seen on dozens of billboards and revolutionary watch committee posters.

I glanced back at him as we walked toward the plane.

Socialism or death. On our bus ride to the citrus farm, Dennis had spotted yet another wall stenciled with the proclamation. There was an old joke in Havana, he'd smiled. "'Socialism or death'? Isn't that redundant?"

There weren't many Heroes of the Revolution left. It had been our nerve-racking privilege to meet one.

33

$\mathcal{T}$he minutes before the plane took off were among the most difficult of my life. The passengers gawked. The stewardesses whispered among themselves, consulted with pilots, and, in general, treated us with suspicion.

But compared to the alternative, it didn't matter. There were seats enough for us, though not together. And if the plane would just lift off, just go, with no last-minute opening of the door, no hoisting us out of our seats, no driving us off to a Cuban prison, I would be happy.

I was wedged between a plump girl in gaudy, inexpensive clothes and a gangly, dye-job redhead, neither of whom looked happy to sit beside a sweating new passenger with a flowering bruise and a dirt-streaked shirt. I kept my eyes closed, praying the plane would take off. Every time I opened them, a stewardess was watching me. So I kept quiet, kept still, and tried to keep calm.

Finally, our destination still a mystery to me, we

lifted off, flying over the western half of the island, reaching water as the sun rose behind us.

A few hours later, we landed in Mexico City. I could hardly believe our luck, though I suspected there was more at work than a fortunate coincidence. Emilio had, presumably, sneaked people out of Cuba before. Was this his usual route? For a particular reason?

Customs, predictably, proved a hassle. We presented passports showing we'd recently flown out of Mexico City. There were no exit stamps on our passport inserts from Cuba. The rest of the passengers had documents showing they'd come from Tblisi, Georgia. We were diverted out of the line.

I began to worry that I wouldn't like a Mexican prison any better than I'd have liked a Cuban prison.

But the customs agent who came to fetch us for further questioning was Agosto's old friend—and Jamieson and Travolta's business associate—Pirí. He ushered us into a small room with sickly green walls. I recognized them as the background of his file photo of Lidia Gomez using Myra Wilson's passport.

Pirí didn't seem to recognize me, though he kept eyeing me as if he knew he should. The only time we'd met, Agosto had done all the talking.

But he knew Martin Marules, all right. He didn't say so, but he addressed him exclusively.

"Señor," he said to Marules, "can you explain the discrepancy between your passports and those of the other passengers?"

Marules, looking a little better for a washup on the plane, said, "We boarded in Cuba. Obviously, as you can see from our passports, we are not returning from Georgia. Apparently, because of the tardiness of our arrival at the airport, the Cubans neglected the proper paperwork."

"Ah, was the plane scheduled, then, to pick up passengers in Cuba? Because I have been notified that you are expected to go to the Aeroflot ticket counter and pay full-price fares from Tblisi. That is, if you do not wish to be detained here by their security officers."

Last-minute airfare from Georgia—that would make a dent in my credit, all right.

Marules shrugged. "Yes, of course. Obviously, we have here a misunderstanding originating in Cuba's airport. But not of our making. And we have no wish to cheat Aeroflot."

Don sat with his arm tightly around me, his expression serious. He watched Marules as if trying to intuit an understanding of Spanish from his mannerisms and tone.

But those weren't doing the real talking. Marules had pulled out his wallet. It was in his lap, covered by his hands.

"You are a well-known personage here," Pirí shrugged. "And so I might be inclined to hurry this inquiry."

"I am pleased to hear this." Marules slid some bills out.

"A personal token for my trouble, yes." Pirí glanced at the wallet. "But also an accommodation for another party."

Marules made a face as if calculating the amount this would add to the *mordida*. Too bad Pirí couldn't just post a fee schedule.

"This party would wish a meeting with you. And a promise, which will be described to you at that time."

Marules looked surprised. "I am to promise to make a promise? How can I do this without even knowing its nature?"

Pirí shrugged again.

Marules looked disconcerted. Nevertheless, he slipped currency from his wallet. Then he rose, shaking Pirí's hand with the bills folded in his palm. However much he'd passed along, Pirí seemed satisfied.

"I shall allow you to leave without problem when the other parties arrive to fetch you, señor. Whether you will keep your promise to them, that is your concern."

He rose, smiling like a man who'd just pocketed a huge bribe. He left us in the small room.

We brought Don up to speed.

Don surprised me by saying to Marules, "I don't think it's Jamieson and Travolta coming to pick you up. There's nothing they'd want from you, nothing they could get from you. Is there?"

"Silence?" Marules suggested. "I do, after all, run a newspaper."

"Would you really print it as fact that the people at such and such an address are CIA agents?"

"Without more proof, no." He ran his hands over his hair. "But I have reporters to find proof for me, if I wish it."

"What would be the point? You don't know what they're involved in, you only know they use a certain apartment now and then. Apartments aren't that scarce.

All they have to do is move, and they're out of your purview." Don pinched the bridge of his nose as if to concentrate his thinking. "They might already be gone."

Marules looked troubled. But he didn't get a chance to say more.

Pirí stepped back in. "You two, please come with me."

Marules half rose, saying, "And I?"

"You will wait for your ride, señor. It will not be long. I will take your friends to Aeroflot to avoid the Russians filing charges against you—they have quick tempers." To me, he said, "It will simplify matters if you will pay also for Señor Marules."

"I will repay you," he put in.

I translated quickly for Don. God knew, I didn't have a high enough credit limit.

"I'll get the tickets," Don said, "I don't care about that. But I want to be here when the ride comes."

I told the customs agent.

"They do not wish it," Pirí said, with complete certainty.

"Who are they?"

"If they would like me to mention their names, you would already know. You have only to visit Señor Marules this afternoon, and ask him then." Pirí held the door open. "I am offering an easy solution to a not-so-easy problem. If you wish me instead to call the police?"

I went straight out the door. At the top of my list, as usual, was a vow to stay out of jail.

I turned to find Don looking at me, then at Marules. He didn't seem happy about following me out.

Pirí led us to a small room behind the Aeroflot counter. Don put three full-price last-minute tickets from Tblisi to Mexico City—several thousand dollars' worth—on his American Express card. Then Pirí insisted on handing us into a cab for the Zona Rosa, Mexico City's tourist district.

And that was fine with me. I wanted to go to a hotel. I wanted to take a long shower and sleep till nightfall. On this, Pirí and I were in complete accord.

But less than a mile from the airport, Don motioned the driver to pull off the highway. He found a small café in a neighborhood of drab shops, and he paid the driver to let us out there. When the cab drove off, he walked straight to a pay phone and dropped in some change.

"Conner," he said, "pick up if you're in. We're back. If you're not there already, go to the usual apartment and keep your eyes open."

Then he handed the phone to me. "Call a cab and tell them to get here as fast as they can."

With an exhausted sigh, I obeyed. When I hung up, I asked, "Where are we going?"

"Airport," he said, confirming my fears.

"It's too big and too busy. We'll never spot Marules leaving. Or Travolta and Jamieson picking him up."

"I don't think we're looking for Travolta and Jamieson," he said. He guided me into the small restaurant, which stank of rancid fat.

I didn't need any prompting to order coffee to go.

We sat on a bench outside the front door. After Cuban coffee, this brew seemed as weak as tea.

I watched midmorning pedestrians, plump

women with parcels and baskets of produce, making the rounds of markets and shops. I admired the bright colors of their clothes, the newness of the stores' plaster, wood, and paint. I enjoyed the coolness of the air here, high up the mountain.

I took pleasure in the bustle because it meant there were goods to bustle for, and because I had the freedom to sit here and watch it.

Don said, "Did I ever tell you the theory of investigation I've evolved over the years?"

Our chats, this trip aside, could be counted on one hand, so I knew the question was rhetorical.

"I tell my men to focus on what they know for sure. What you *seem* to know changes all the time, as you get more witness statements, as you weed out the lies and excuses and unintentional misrepresentations. But if you stick to what you actually know for sure, you start out with a short list, and you watch it grow until eventually it tells you something." He finished his coffee and crumpled the paper cup. "For example, Jamieson and Travolta gave us the magic phone number. We know they're CIA, the real deal."

I'd ordered a larger coffee than he had. And until I finished it, I wasn't even going to try to employ higher levels of reason. With luck, I was going to continue to sit upright, impersonating an awake person.

"Another item on the list of what we know for sure: We were separated from Marules. We were given an explanation—maybe a real reason, maybe just a pretext—and we were sent off to play tourist. But the bottom line is, we're not with him now."

A yellow Beetle taxi pulled up in front of the restaurant. I dropped my paper cup into a trash can, and we climbed in.

We rode to the airport in silence. At the best of times, I'm not much of a conversationalist in the morning.

When the cab pulled toward the arrivals gate, Don handed the driver some cash, saying to me, "Tell him we want to sit curbside and wait. If we jump out at some point, he keeps the change. And if we tell him to drive on, we pay him the difference when we get there."

The driver took the bills and grinned.

"Any idea who we're looking for?" I asked him. "Besides Marules?"

He shook his head. He was turned away from me, scanning the exits. "I just hope we didn't miss them. You don't ditch somebody unless you're going to do something you don't want them to see." He groped for my hand, still looking out the cab window. "I'd have turned the first cab around, but I thought they might have bribed the driver. If so, they think we went to breakfast."

But we'd lost twenty minutes. We could sit here all afternoon waiting to see something that had happened in our absence.

I settled into the cab seat, stretching my legs. VW taxis had no front passenger seat, presumably since the trunk wouldn't hold luggage bigger than a handbag. The back seat stank of curdled milk and body odor. But it would have taken more than that to keep me awake. I nodded off without even realizing it.

I don't know how long I slept. I was suddenly

aware of the fact that the cab was in motion. I opened my eyes to find we were out of the airport and back on the highway.

"What?" I said. "What happened?"

Don looked grim. "It's worse than we thought," he said. "It's Gomez—"

"Lidia Gomez?" I was astonished. But, perhaps because I wasn't yet fully awake, I didn't see why this was worse than we thought. Not that I'd thought much of anything.

He pointed up the highway. "We're four cars behind—luckily I know the Spanish word for 'go.' 'Hang back a few cars' was more of a challenge. They're in the Dodge minivan with California plates."

"Marules and Gomez?"

He shot me a look. "And Sarah Swann."

Mother's friend, the organizer of the WILPF caravan to Cuba, the woman who'd come to San Diego to console me and my father.

"Sarah Swann," I said flatly.

I watched the Dodge drive at a conservative speed, deeper into the smog perennially smothering the city.

Sarah Swann. Why would Mother's friend be here picking Marules up from the airport? Did Sarah really want a favor from him? Publicity for her goods-to-Cuba drives? String-pulling to find my mother?

But how would she have known to go through Pirí? Where would she have found the clout?

We knew Pirí did work for hire for the CIA. What did that mean about Sarah Swann?

She had organized my mother's trip to Cuba. If, as a consequence of that trip, Mother was running a chain of safe houses for fund-raising Cubans, could she be doing it—definitely without her knowledge!—under the aegis of the CIA?

I could hardly believe what I was thinking.

We were lucky in one regard. There were too many Beetles in Mexico for our cab to attract attention as we followed the Dodge. Likewise, there were too few minivans with California plates for our driver to lose track of Marules, Swann, and Gomez.

I sat forward, trying to catch a glimpse of them through their back windshield, as if the angle of their heads would reveal their intentions to me.

If that was the real Lidia Gomez up ahead, who had I spoken to in that apartment in Cuba? An actress put there to fool Cindy and Dennis, to show them what they expected to see? If so, why did the Cubans care what Cindy and Dennis thought?

Months ago, I'd discounted Mr. Radio Havana's assertion that Cindy and Dennis were CIA agents. But he'd risen in my estimation since rescuing me from arrest. If he was right, it would explain why they'd taken over Jamieson and Travolta's apartment. And why they'd picked me up in Havana, just as "Ernesto" had.

But more troubling, if Sarah Swann wasn't just a

nice WILPF lady with a knack for organizing computer drives and goodwill forays, who was she?

"Is Marules in danger?" I murmured to Don.

"Too early to say. It would help if we knew where they're going."

I asked the cab driver, "What are they heading toward? What part of the city?"

"Many parts," he shrugged. "Bars, offices, prison."

"Which prison?"

"Women's prison."

I shuddered, wondering what would have happened this morning if Marules hadn't bribed Pirí. What if Don hadn't had the means to pay Aeroflot for our ride? Would I be on my way to Mexico City's women's prison?

The minivan turned off the highway. None of the cars between us turned, making us more conspicuous. But the van didn't slow.

It continued down a street of auto repair shops and light industries. Then it pulled into a parking lot. It belonged, to my surprise, to the women's prison. Don and I exchanged glances. If he had a theory, his expression masked it.

The cab driver circled the far side of the lot, pulling behind a row of small yellow buses, probably designed for excursions or work-furloughs.

We watched the threesome from the minivan go inside the building.

Don paid the driver—apparently he expected to stay awhile.

We crossed to the minivan. Don walked around it, looking in the windows.

I watched the door of the unornamented box of a prison.

"Why would they come here?" I asked him. "Gomez especially." Perhaps my fear of prisons was clouding my judgment. Perhaps a person was no more likely to get arrested in a prison waiting room than in a laundromat. But it would take a hell of a lot of confidence to believe it if you were in hiding.

"Maybe they came to see someone."

I shook my head. If he was expecting a suggestion, he was out of luck.

"Your mother," he said.

I staggered back a step. "Mother? In there?"

"It would explain why General Miguel couldn't find her in Cuba."

"But why would she be here? She wouldn't . . ."

"What if she arrived in Mexico City the same way we did, tucked onto an airplane on layover? If her papers weren't in order and she didn't have the money to cover air fare . . ." Then she might indeed have ended up with several months of jail time. "You know anything about the legal system down here?" Don looked pained. "I understand there's very little leeway—unless you're willing to bribe everybody right up the line."

"Mother wouldn't bribe anyone. She's too ethical." Maybe too broke.

"Well, if you get busted in Mexico, and you don't pay the *mordidas,* you're inside till you've served your sentence. Period."

"She'd have called me or Daddy. To try to get her out. She'd have let us know."

"She'd have let you know something," he agreed. "Not necessarily that she was in jail."

"Even if she didn't want me to know she was . . ." The way I felt about jail, Mother was likely to tell me anything else, any lie. "She'd have gotten word to us that she was okay. She'd have given some excuse."

"Through a friend?"

I nodded.

"Like Sarah Swann?" He was squinting at the entrance. "Maybe she'd have Sarah tell you she was staying in Cuba a little longer to cut cane? To help at the hospitals? Something like that?"

"Yes."

"Could Sarah have told your father?"

"No. He definitely doesn't know anything—this is killing him. And he'd never keep a secret from me, not this kind of secret."

"If it is your mother in there, apparently Swann visits her."

"Why would she keep us in the dark?"

"That would depend on who Sarah is." He scowled. "One possibility, considering the little bit I know about her?"

"Yeah?"

"She organized a caravan into Mexico to drop off computers for Cuba. But the caravan was met at the border, and the computers were tossed out of the trucks and ruined."

"You think Sarah works for the CIA?" A nice WILPF lady? I couldn't wrap my mind around it.

"No, the caravan generated lots of publicity. It was a dare, in essence, and U.S. Customs took it. But in the meantime, think of all the meetings and teach-ins about Cuba. And who ended up looking bad? The Cubans, who are too poor to afford electronic equipment, or the U.S. government, which would rather ruin computers than let Cuban schoolchildren get their hands on them?"

"Making Sarah what?"

"Maybe the same thing Marules is, a very good friend of Señor Emilio."

I stared at the prison, a box of cement with wire-reinforced windows. I wanted Don to be right. I wanted to believe that my mother was alive and within reach.

I could sort out the rest later, figure out who to be angry with later. For now, I just prayed she was in there.

Don was scanning the neighborhood. "I'm going to see if they've got a phone." He pointed to a small market with bars over the windows and a dog tied to a metal rung in the sidewalk. "Why don't you go stand behind the prison vans—less conspicuous."

I didn't object. As much as I'd have liked to grab Marules and Swann and shake the truth out of them, if my mother was indeed inside, she wasn't going anywhere.

Don was gone maybe ten minutes. I assumed he was trying to reach his PI, Conner. I hoped the length of his absence meant he'd gotten through.

Just when I was thinking maybe I should walk over there and check, I saw Marules, Swann, and Gomez emerge from the building. Sarah was dabbing her eyes with a handkerchief.

It was a twist of the knife. Was Mother okay? Was she sick? Hurt?

Marules put his arm around Sarah as if consoling her. Gomez checked her wristwatch.

I hung back, staying out of sight. But my frustration level was rising fast. I wanted to dash across the street and grab Don. I wanted to do something, anything but wait here and watch them drive away.

The threesome climbed into the minivan, Gomez behind the wheel. It pulled out of the parking lot, turning as if to retrace the route back onto the highway.

I trotted across to the store. The tied dog looked up as I walked past. I entered, surprised to find it was a bar, not a grocery store. Short, dark-skinned men with gray stubble slumped at bar stools, knocking back shots. A florid woman with a white streak in her hair poured refills with apparent disapproval.

Don stood beside the bar holding a big, old-fashioned rotary phone. His shoulders were rounded and he was turned away from the bar patrons, his finger in his nonphone ear.

I didn't disturb him. Marules would be just as gone in two minutes as in ten.

When Don hung up, he seemed startled to find me behind him.

"It's going to take a while to get confirmation," he said. "If she wasn't booked under her exact name, they'll find out who Marules and Swann just visited. We'll get a name that way."

He walked me out. The woman stared at him angrily.

"You paid for the call?" I assumed.

"Oh yeah." His tone told me he'd paid a great deal more than the going rate. "My Spanish is shit. I let dead presidents do my talking for me."

"Marules, Swann, and Gomez, they left."

"I'll be interested to hear what Marules tells us later. In the meantime, Conner's on his way to pick us up."

The tied dog watched us. He looked so defeated with the rope around his neck, so sad that I nearly untied him.

"Do you think it could be true? Do you think she could be in there?"

"You'd know better than me. Would she want to hide it from you?" But he knew the answer already. He'd heard me freak out over my imprisonment years before. He'd seen what I'd done just this morning, with machine guns pointed at me at the Cuban airport. He knew how I responded to the idea of jail.

"She's been inside eleven times," I told him. "Seventeen arrests, fourteen convictions, eleven jail terms." I hugged myself, thinking of all the times I'd been shuttled to teachers' and neighbors' apartments, all the times I'd fended for myself while she'd served out her terms of conscience. All the months I'd been consumed with fear for her—and anger toward her. "She'd lie about it if she could."

"To spare you the worry."

"And spare herself my wrath." I choked on my tears, making a fine spectacle of myself.

I pulled myself together when the tied dog got up on his hind legs and tried to lick my face. You have to take stock when a chained animal tries to cheer you up.

35

$\mathcal{C}$onner picked us up in his rented black Beetle. His first comment was, "Lady, you don't look so good."

"I was socked by an airport worker," I explained.

"What, you smoked outside a designated area?"

"She tried to run from four Cuban soldiers with machine guns," Don said dryly.

Conner laughed. "In that case, you could look a whole lot worse."

"Any news about Jamieson and Travolta?" Don asked.

Conner barreled down the highway, the Beetle rattling like a Yahtzee shaker. "They walked out of their apartment and, *poof.* They started hopping in and out of taxis, walking through *mercado* crowds— they're good. They lost me pretty fast. Then I went back to their place and waited. Waited some more. Next thing I know, there's a fellow moving boxes out. Works for a storage company. Says the couple's gone. I call the landlord like I'm interested in taking the place. He says fine, but he's going to repaint first, call him next week. I followed the mover, so I know which storage place. I've been parked there for lack of anything better to do. But, like I said, *poof.*"

"And Price? He never showed up?"

"Oh, get this: He got turned back at the border."

"What?"

"Yeah. He went home to sleep between shifts—cute new girlfriend, worth the commuter flight, you know how that goes." He cast a glance at me. "When he tried to get back across the border, they made him deplane, saying he couldn't come in. He tried a couple more times, no dice. For now, he's apparently blackballed."

"How'd Jamieson and Travolta get his name?"

"He used his credit card to rent the surveillance car."

"Dumbshit," Don said crossly. "What's on Marules's diskette?"

"I had to FedEx it to my office. My guy up there's not positive, but he thinks it's letter-and-number combinations. Usually when we see that, it's flight information."

"Tell him to check the code against Aeroflot flights, especially from Georgia and other former Soviet countries. Anything with layovers in Cuba." Don turned to me. I was sprawled in the back seat. "Marules knows which flights might be carrying extra passengers from Cuba. He alerts Pirí, and if he gets a call that someone extra's on board, he pays for the ticket, pays Pirí, and arranges the next step, whatever it is."

"If my mother came in that way, why did Marules leave her dangling? Why didn't he take care of things for her?" A better question was, why did he do it for anyone? Loyalty to Señor Emilio?

"His receptionist's been handing over diskettes with this stuff on it. Maybe the CIA caught on, and tipped off the airline. Maybe Pirí's bosses were there watching."

"But Jamieson and Travolta didn't rat out Pirí?"

"No, they use him occasionally, too, to chaperone folks with phony passports through customs."

I recalled Pirí leaving Jamieson and Travolta's apartment with a couple who'd just had photos taken. Passport photos, almost certainly. Pirí worked for everyone, it seemed, for anyone who paid him. And they say Mexicans lack the Protestant work ethic.

"But wait." I sat up. "If my mother was sneaked onto Aeroflot, she'd have landed when Jamieson and Travolta were in Belgium or wherever they were."

Don nodded. "She landed when Cindy and Dennis lived in that apartment."

I sighed. Cindy and Dennis had seemed so nice. Too nice to be CIA agents. "And they went to Havana afterward to try to figure the scheme out. Try to figure out why Emilio was moving people out of Cuba. Especially an American who could have left just as easily with the rest of her tour group."

"It sure looks that way," Don agreed.

"And they used me to go places where they didn't want to be photographed. Like the women's prison."

But when they learned the Cubans knew they

were CIA agents, they decamped. I supposed a boat had picked them up, just as Mr. Radio Havana had surmised. (The desk clerk at the hotel, to her detriment, must have found their luggage and passports unattended, and seized the chance to use them.) Cindy and Dennis would be well into their next assignment by now—perhaps in Russia?

"Emilio's underground railroad—sky road— would be a perfect way to shuttle out prisoners," Don mused.

"Like Lidia Gomez?"

"Maybe she was Marules's reward, what he got in return for his millions." Don turned in his cramped seat to look at me. "Maybe this isn't just politics. Maybe it's love."

"Love?" A week ago, I might have questioned how much a person would do for love. But with my insides turning to jelly at his glance, I was more inclined to respect the concept. And Don must have been, too. Hadn't he just spent a fortune, just risked rotting in a foreign prison? "Cindy and Dennis kept asking Emilio about Gomez. They said they were friends of Marules's, and they kept mentioning Marules's wife. Like that would make Emilio more forthcoming."

"Marules isn't married to Gomez," Conner put in. "He's married to one of the richest women in Mexico. I looked it up—lots of pictures on the society pages. Rat-faced woman with a mustache."

"It's traditional among upper-class Mexican men to have a mistress, isn't it?" Don said.

Men always think it's traditional to do what suits them.

Don continued, "So Marules channels his ugly wife's millions to Cuba, to Emilio. He helps get people out when Emilio needs him to—maybe smugglers on the brink of getting caught. Emilio wants to bring in as many dollars as he can, but he doesn't want to end up executed, like General Ochoa. And in return, Marules feels like he's helping Cuba—helping get food and medicine to the little people. And, on a personal level, he gets Lidia Gomez, a brilliant literary light, probably a fascinating woman, and apparently someone he cares a great deal about."

"So why did Marules come to fetch us yesterday?" I wondered. "What was that about? He makes it possible for us to go to Cuba, then he jumps on a plane and tells us we have to hurry home."

"To lead us into a trap?" Don suggested. "That was the outcome."

"No, Marules looked so scared. If he was just there to screw us over, why did he look terrified?" I sat up, trying to clear my mind. The side of my face where I'd been punched was throbbing. Even more distracting, I had a sudden hope of seeing my mother again.

"He might have learned something about Emilio," Don conceded, "something that worried him."

One thing sprang to mind. "Like finding out his *compañero* was behind the murders of Alicia Mendoza and Agosto Diaz."

Don nodded. "Emilio's connection with Marules was burning out. General Miguel knew about it, for one thing. He knew Marules was funneling money to Emilio. And he knew Emilio was sneaking passengers aboard Aeroflot layovers—he wouldn't hav shown up at the airport otherwise. If Emilio couldn't use Marules anymore anyway, it would make sense to kill Gomez. She might go public. And if Ochoa's execution proved anything, it's that Fidel won't stand behind his people if they get caught. Not even for dollars."

"You're assuming Emilio let Gomez go as a favor to Marules."

"Yes. And that Marules was too smart to let anyone know she'd stayed in Mexico City. When Diaz went looking for her in San Diego, word must have gotten back to Emilio, maybe through Pirí. Emilio sent someone to kill Gomez—he thought it was Gomez—and Diaz, too."

"In case Marules had confided in Agosto?" I swallowed my tears. "Agosto would have figured it out sooner or later. He was a quick study."

"All the more reason to kill him." Seeing my expression, he added, "I'm sorry."

We were silent a few minutes.

"You'd think Marules would have suspected that jerk Emilio right off the bat," I fretted. "I wonder why he didn't."

"Self-interest?" Conner suggested. "Marules has been breaking all kinds of laws himself—he wouldn't want any of this coming out. Maybe he just didn't let himself think along these lines."

I considered Mother's caravan to Cuba. Marules's funding of Emilio's projects. The face-off between the practical, young urban Marxist, Emilio, and the idealistic *histórico*, General Miguel. There were certainly a great many ways to be a Cuban patriot. Whether the revolution had succeeded or not, it had inspired fervent devotion in several countries. Perhaps, as the Cuban economy neared collapse, it became more inspirational to those who didn't live there than to those who did.

"Maybe it was blind allegiance," I put in. "To Emilio, to Cuba, to the Revolution."

Cuba was an island soaked with the blood of stubborn idealists and loyal friends.

I just prayed we'd guessed right, and that none of the blood belonged to my mother.

36

We tried Marules's home, we tried the newspaper office, we tried Jamieson and Travolta's (former) apartment. But we couldn't find Marules.

Over a long-delayed meal, we talked it through again. If our theory was correct, Marules had finally learned he'd been playing with fire. Emilio had ordered the murders of Lidia Gomez and Agosto Diaz. He had tried to arrest us all.

Now Marules had been to see my mother, as if he were making apologies, as if he regretted how things had worked out: Pirí should have alerted Marules when Mother arrived. Marules should have come through with the money for Aeroflot. Mother should have been home months ago.

But for whatever reason Emilio put Mother on a plane, Marules had merely muffed things. She'd been an accidental casualty of Marules's relationship with Emilio.

There had been a far worse occurrence. If we were right, Marules would be making another apology now, one that would fall on deaf ears.

We found him kneeling in a small mausoleum, facing a drawer in a wall, one of perhaps twenty. He was rocking slightly on his knees and praying, kissing rosary beads as he did so.

Praying—not a very revolutionary thing to do. Another sign of disenchantment?

He jumped when he saw us, his arms jerking so that the beads flew from his hand and skittered across the alabaster floor.

The day was cool and overcast, and it was chilly in this small stone house. The majority of drawers bore the name Marules, with dates of death going back to the late seventeen hundreds. But he prayed to a door marked "Agosto Francisco Diaz Portillo."

Marules wore fresh clothes. He hadn't been home, so perhaps he'd stopped at an apartment he shared with Gomez. But he was, as far as we could see, alone. There was no sign of Gomez, Sarah Swann, or anyone else here. It was just Martin Marules and his ghosts.

He got to his feet, one hand clapped over his heart. His eyes were red-rimmed and puffy. He wiped his cheeks. He looked old.

"Who picked you up at the airport?" Don demanded.

He hesitated a moment. "Jamieson and Travolta," he lied.

"Why? What did they want?"

"Information. About Juan Emilio."

"How did they know you were there?"

"Piri. The customs agent. He phoned them."

I walked to the metal plaque with Agosto's name on it. So young, so much energy, so much intelligence—

there's always some cause ready to steal a life. The Cuban Revolution had claimed plenty of them.

My hand covered the date of death. I said, "My mother is in prison here. For how much longer?"

He recoiled as if I'd thrown something at him.

"How much longer?" I repeated.

"Seven weeks more." His voice was low and tremulous. "Not forever. I have done everything to make her comfortable. If there is any extra thing to be purchased for her comfort, it is immediately done."

I wanted to punch him. Judging from the look on Don's face, he was going to do it for me.

"Don't you know what you've put us through, me and my father?"

"She would not let us tell you." Tears filled his eyes. "I swear this to you. First she would not pay the *mordidas,* then she did not wish for you to know."

"She must have wanted us to know *something.* She must have tried to send us some word, let us know she was alive."

"But it would have been dangerous, do you not see? No matter what excuse she offered you, you would have gone to make sure it was the truth. You would have seen through her lie so clearly." Tears ran down his cheeks. "It was a cruelty to you. But we agreed that we could not deliver her messages. Not without your search for the truth leading you—"

"To Pirí, to the Aeroflot counter, to Emilio and his dollar-grubbing schemes?" It was all I could do to master my rage. "You didn't think I'd search for my mother if I got no message at all?"

"But your search could only be vague. You could not rule out alternatives, as you could if she had specified."

"What did she want you to say?" Don demanded. "What was her message?"

"That she was working in Cuba. In the AIDS colony. She said you would believe this."

And indeed, I would have. For a while. Then I'd have grown concerned about her. I'd have gone there to make sure it was really true, that she hadn't been arrested. Or harmed.

Marules was right. If I'd gotten her message, I'd have soon learned it was a lie. And I'd have rattled cages all over Havana, making a big mess.

I had caused quite a commotion anyway, of course. But only because Don had hired detectives. Only because he'd had the money and the savvy, and had cared enough to help me.

"Why did she leave Cuba the way she did?"

"She was discovered in the home of Lidia Gomez."

"And the house was empty because Gomez lives here with you."

He closed his eyes as if too afraid to deal with us. "Your mother was detained, and so she missed her flight. Because of where she had been, this was an embarrassment to Juan Emilio. He did not wish certain others, political enemies, to discover the blunder. And so he offered your mother a free seat on a flight to Mexico City. We had done this often, Juan Emilio and I—Pirí should have alerted me to pay for the ticket. Always before it has worked perfectly." He whispered, "I told Juan Emilio he must make the house appear occupied. He must hire someone and make it appear that Lidia remains under house arrest. Otherwise it will become known that she has escaped."

"Mother went to see her because I harped on it, I made a big deal about Gomez," I told him. "Not because she believed anything had happened to her."

"The populace has gone mad from lack of food and electricity," Marules said. "There are factions and paranoias abundant. The people attack without sense or reason. Lidia is a good revolutionary, a true patriot. Yet she was attacked by a mob. She had to be removed from there, for her own safety."

"And Emilio helped you."

"Which proves, does it not, that she is a patriot?" He blinked at us as if hoping we could agree with this, at least.

"It proves he wanted your money, your wife's money," Don said. "Gomez used Myra Wilson's passport?"

"They are *gusanos,* counterrevolutionaries, Wilson and this doctor of hers. Emilio made use of her, yes. But she chose to do this, believing stupidly that Lidia was not a patriot in a difficult time, but a worm like herself."

"You and Emilio set Wilson up to spend seven years in prison? For turning over her passport? For doing you a favor?"

"Lidia was attacked, she was not well. She was in physical danger, and might have been arrested at any moment by General Miguel. We could not wait for the usual means, the airplanes from Russia. It was urgent that she leave immediately. We did not suggest to Myra Wilson that she offer her passport. She chose to do this."

"Because she believed Gomez would come here and speak out against the oppression in Cuba!" I wanted to smack him. "She didn't do it so Gomez could come here and keep her mouth shut, living in luxury on your wife's money and blaming the Cuban people instead of its leaders. She didn't do it so you and Gomez could tryst to your hearts' content while she rotted in prison."

"No. But she is guilty of a crime, and her sentence is not unjust."

"Except that she keeps quiet about what her real crime was, assuming that Gomez is doing a lot of talking. Maybe even agitating for her release."

Don squinted at Marules. "Emilio greased the skids, letting Gomez slip out with the false passport. Then Willa's mother went to Cuba and tried to see Gomez. She found Gomez gone. Emilio detained her and she missed her flight. He told her he was sorry, the Revolution didn't mean to inconvenience her, and he put her on an Aeroflot layover. She'd think of some excuse for her family, and nobody in Cuba would be the wiser. So what happened then? What went wrong?"

"That day, Pirí swears he was watched, that supervisors and officials came especially to watch him. Perhaps it is true, perhaps it is a delusion. But so, Pirí let me down. It is the only time." He looked more than merely troubled.

"Maybe Pirí let you down, or maybe the CIA decided to mess with your smuggling scheme," Don countered. "But something else went wrong, too.

That's what's got you so spooked now. That's why you went rushing to Cuba to get us out of there. That's why you called Sarah Swann a few days ago and told her to drive down here. That's why you had Pirí phone her to pick you up from the airport this morning. That's why you went to check on Willa's mother today. You're tying up loose ends like someone who's afraid he's got the devil after him. Someone's got you running scared."

"*Es correcto,*" said a voice behind us.

I turned to find a silhouette against the white sky showing through the mausoleum door.

I was at a loss. I'd never seen this man before. And yet, here he was, pointing a gun at Marules as if it were so natural we should all applaud him.

"Ernest Hemingway, I presume," Don said.

The man inclined his head. He spoke English: "I have been listening to your interesting story. And it occurs to me that for the most part the ending is quite happy. Señor Marules is in love. Señorita Gomez lives like a princess in a fine penthouse in Mexico City." When Marules gasped, Hemingway continued, "Oh, yes, I have just come from there, Señor, looking for you. I'm afraid the attack she wished to avoid, those foolish Cubans who do not realize the loveliness of the revolution which imprisons them by the thousands, well, she cannot avoid all disgruntled Cubans forever."

Marules blanched. "You have not harmed her? Please, Doctor?"

"Oh yes, I have. Decidedly. My true love, you know, sits in a Cuban prison. Six more years before I will kiss her sweet face."

Six years. I thought about Wilson's glazed eyes, her drugged responses. Sedated, she could be trotted out and shown to visiting Americans. But how did they treat her when no one was watching?

"It has taken me many months and all my savings to learn where Lidia Gomez has gone, why she has not come to my home, to Myra's home. Why she has not spoken out." He was a light-skinned man with a great deal of gray in his black hair. Deep furrows marred his forehead. It looked like it had been a very long time since he'd stopped frowning. "You knew that I had finally discovered the truth?"

Marules shook his head. "I knew only that you had come to Mexico City, Doctor."

"Of course you knew. I made a fuss at the airport, I threatened your precious Pirí, for that very purpose. And then I watched you try to hide Señorita Gomez and run to Cuba, run to your master like a good puppet."

I was confused. If Marules went to Cuba to warn Emilio that Hemingway was looking for Gomez, why the charade about protecting us, getting us out of there?

"You meant it," I said to Marules. "Maybe you went to Cuba to talk to Emilio about Hemingway and Gomez. But then you found out he was going to arrest us."

"No," Marules said. "No. On the contrary, I learned that General Miguel had prepared the order for your arrest."

"General Miguel? But he saved us."

"He did so only because Juan Emilio had betrayed us. The general did not come to the airport to help us," Marules insisted. "He came to capture us. It is only because Emilio betrayed us, and only because the general is an enemy of Emilio, that he decided to let us go." Marules was shaking. "You see what has happened in Cuba as a result of the long starvation? They are like rats biting each other's ears. We were merely inside the cage with them."

The general would have arrested us if Emilio hadn't beaten him to it? We'd been freed just so the general could thwart his enemy?

My knees felt weak. I'd been even closer to prison than I'd thought. And, God, no wonder Marules had looked even more terrified than Don and I.

"What do you know about Cuba, rich man?" Hemingway exploded. "You make pronouncements about the revolution and the people as if you had lived there. Can you begin to understand what it is to have ears listening constantly for some word that is not sanctioned by your dictator? You who pray at this grave, do you understand the despair of praying in secret in the dark so you will not be reported to the *vigilancia,* so you will not be labeled a counter-revolutionary, so you will not be fired from your job and unable to put food on your table? When Amnesty International tells you Cuba has prisons full of poor men who did nothing but speak the wrong phrase, when they say men by the thousands are beaten and tortured there, you ignore it. You choose instead to believe rhetoric over proof. Hundreds of thousands have fled Cuba in the last twenty years, but you dismiss them as worms. Hundreds of thousands of desperate creatures give up a homeland, a heritage, to live in poverty and exile, and you discount them, refusing to hear them, refusing to believe them." He raised the gun and pointed it at Marules. "You use us for your own ends. You play upon the heart of Myra Wilson for your own purpose. You steal seven years of her life without regret."

Don lunged at him, knocking him over as he fired the gun. I screamed, seeing a flash of metal on metal beside me, feeling a hot spark burn my hand. A bullet had ricocheted off Agosto's plaque.

The mausoleum was filled with gunsmoke. It stank of saltpeter. And something else.

I fell to my knees. Don still grappled with Hemingway, but the gun was on the alabaster floor now. I would have reached for it, but Marules was on the ground, too, between me and the gun.

Funny he would be prone. Perhaps he'd reacted with panic, as well. Perhaps he'd dropped to the ground when I had, when the gun went off.

Hemingway was making wild grunting noises, a madman fighting. I had to get the gun. I had to put a stop to this before Don got hurt.

"Marules!" I cried, trying to get him to move aside. Trying to get him to grab the gun.

I started reaching over him, Hemingway's cries echoing in the mausoleum. The smell hit me again, reminding me of something I didn't want to think about. I saw the huge stain on Marules's trousers.

I scurried backward. The stink came from relaxed bowels and a voided bladder. I'd smelled it before because I'd seen a dead body before.

On the pale gray alabaster of the mausoleum floor, a red stain spread slowly beyond Marules's body.

Thanks to Don, Hemingway had missed Marules. But the bullet had ricocheted in the small chamber, hitting Marules anyway.

I looked at my hand in horror. There was a small pinpoint burn where the spark from the bullet on Agosto's plaque caught me near the thumb.

I was still staring at it when Conner ran in, having heard the shot from where he was parked, waiting.

37

$\mathcal{B}$y the time Mother was released from the women's prison in Mexico City, Dr. Hemingway had been tried and sentenced to six years. Ironically, he and Myra Wilson would be released within months of each other.

Lidia Gomez presumably recovered from Hemingway's beating—she vanished rather than face deportation. But Martin Marules didn't survive the gunshot.

I couldn't help but mourn Marules. His reasons had been complex and, in effect, cruel. But I'd lived with idealists most of my life. I knew how much they were willing to sacrifice, even when it wasn't theirs to give up.

I was more angry with Sarah Swann. She had agreed with Marules that it would be counterrevolutionary to give me and my father the numerous messages from my mother. I would see through them, Sarah was sure. I would go to Cuba, and I would learn too much. I would use it publicly to cast Cuba into a bad light. My mother wouldn't want that.

My mother had been told the family had gotten her messages—it was no use adding to her burdens, Sarah thought. It had comforted Mother to think we'd accepted her lies. She knew how much I, in particular, hated thinking of her in jail.

And Sarah Swann was right about one thing. When Mother learned why Sarah had decided not to give us the false messages, she agreed with her.

Mother agreed with her! She understood that Sarah had acted unselfishly for the benefit of the Cuban people and the revolution. She forgave Sarah almost immediately, despite the fact that I'd nearly ended up in a Cuban prison.

Mother resisted believing any portions of my story that reflected badly on Cuba. I wasn't in prison, was I? I must have been mistaken. Sarah had only done what Mother might have done under the same circumstances. She had acted in good conscience, and Mother was determined to forgive her. If anything, they were closer than ever.

Mother was much more confused about Don's motives. She was much less willing to understand his reasons for taking me to Cuba the second time. It hadn't been necessary, and to her mind, it had just stirred up animosity between Señor Emilio and General Miguel, and that couldn't be a useful thing for Cuba, could it?

Her continuing suspicion of Don, dating back to his politically incorrect shooting of a famous radical who'd killed a number of our friends (but never mind that), was particularly ironic now. Don had been instrumental in keeping the State Department from stepping in and arresting Mother for "trading with the enemy" and, in general, causing all this commotion. I didn't kid myself that they'd declined to prosecute because Mother had meant well. They'd dropped it because Don, a respected law-enforcement official, had persuaded them to.

If that didn't win him any points with Mother, it certainly cinched my feelings for him. Man, was I in love.

So the good news was that we had Mother back. And the bad news was that she hadn't changed a bit.

When Don warned me, one gorgeous evening as we lazed around his house, that I might find his old-fashioned Italian mother to be a bit of a trial—"She doesn't believe in divorce, so she's not happy about our relationship!"—I had to laugh, I really did.

Don's mother a trial.

I love my mother, but in that regard, she's got no competition at all.